JAMES PATTERSON is one of the best-known and biggest-selling writers of all time. His books have sold in excess of 385 million copies worldwide. He is the author of some of the most popular series of the past two decades – the Alex Cross, Women's Murder Club, Detective Michael Bennett and Private novels – and he has written many other number one bestsellers including romance novels and stand-alone thrillers.

James is passionate about encouraging children to read. Inspired by his own son who was a reluctant reader, he also writes a range of books for young readers including the Middle School, I Funny, Treasure Hunters, Dog Diaries and Max Einstein series. James has donated millions in grants to independent bookshops and he has been the most borrowed author of adult fiction in UK libraries for the past eleven years in a row. He lives in Florida with his wife and son.

SHAN SERAFIN is a novelist and film director whose works include the novel *Seventeen* and the films *The Forest* and *The Believer*. His most recent collaboration with James Patterson is *Come and Get Us*.

CHRISTOPHER FARNSWORTH is the author of the President's Vampire books and several other novels, most recently *Flashmob*. He worked as an investigative and business reporter before selling his first screenplay. He lives in Los Angeles with his family.

SCOTT SLAVEN is a graduate of UCLA, and both a writer and an accomplished portrait painter. He has previously collaborated with James Patterson on *Taking the Titanic*.

13 Minute Murder

JAMES PATTERSON

WITH SHAN SERAFIN, CHRISTOPHER FARNSWORTH AND SCOTT SLAVEN

arrow books

1 3 5 7 9 10 8 6 4 2

Arrow Books
20 Vauxhall Bridge Road
London SW1V 2SA

Arrow Books is part of the Penguin Random House group of companies whose addresses can be found at global.penguinrandomhouse.com

Dead Man Running first published as ebook by BookShots Digital in 2017
Kill and Tell first published as ebook by BookShots Digital in 2017
This edition published by Arrow Books in 2019

www.penguin.co.uk

A CIP catalogue record for this book is available from the British Library

ISBN 9781787462199
ISBN 9781787462205 (export)

Typeset in 11.16/14.8pt ITC Berkeley Std by Jouve (UK), Milton Keynes
Printed and bound in Great Britain by Clays Ltd, Elcograf S.p.A.

CONTENTS

13-MINUTE MURDER

JAMES PATTERSON

WITH SHAN SERAFIN

CHAPTER 1

STROLLING THROUGH THE halls of Harvard University, plotting the murder of one of its more notable students, mulling over my options—poison, piano wire, maybe a knife—I had to stop and ask myself the obvious question: How would Anna Karenina do it?

I mean, what exactly *is* the most acceptable form of murder in today's multicultural salad of etiquette? Victim under the wheels of a train? Too noticeable. Poison in a sandwich? Too risky. Sniper fire? No. Tomorrow would be windy.

"Limits," I muttered.

If you're going to kill the son of a mob boss in the middle of an Ivy League campus, you want to be decorous.

"Crosswind is too high," I added. "Second shot might nick him, but first one ends up in a bystander."

"Yeah," Milt said. "It can't be a distant hit." He described the only option we had left in two simple words. "It's gotta be arm's reach."

"Arm's reach." We were in agreement.

Milt was my partner of eleven years. Partner in crime. Partner in general skepticism. Partner who was about to split a hundred-fifty-thousand-dollar payday with me. We were now scouring the heart of the Harvard campus for its weakest ventricle, wandering the quad looking like creepy middle-aged men.

"And scrambled eggs," I added.

"No, no, no," said Milt. "Not that."

His job was analyzing the geometry: the brick walls, the brick arches, the backpacks, angles, shadows—any opportunity for our twenty-year-old victim to, let's say, accidentally fall off a ledge. My job was to study the human element. I was checking the faces of the various students passing us. The redhead. The tall Korean. The non-giggling girls on a bench. The tardy jogger. I needed to look into their eyes and see them *seeing* tomorrow's murder. I needed to see their reaction to what hadn't happened yet.

"I hate scrambled eggs," said Milt.

So did I. But we'd received no info about our target, except that he was enrolled in an economics class on Wednesdays at 11:00 a.m. in Harvard's Massachusetts Hall, the building behind us.

"We should cross the courtyard," I said. "Get measurements."

We were planning a silent hit. The type that has your target die roughly five seconds after contact. That means we theoretically had five seconds to clear the area. We would then have about six minutes to escape from the widening circle of police response.

Six minutes.

We debated the numbers all morning, betting on the reaction times of everyone around us. Trying to identify the most prototypical student, I focused on the girl on the steps reading Proust, or possibly the guy behind her sketching a quasar. We wanted a guinea pig who might be representative of the types of panicking we could expect tomorrow.

"Her," said Milt, nodding to a girl in a floral-patterned dress. "She's your test case. Go chat her up."

"Her? No."

"The body language says yes. It says yes to a tall glass of Michael Dennis Ryan."

"We're only here for the test. And no, I'm twice her age."

"Half plus seven. C'mon, man. These ladies are exactly like you. Socially dead. Sittin' around having an imaginary conversation with a book."

"I don't do that."

"Yeah, you do. Probably whisperin' to Moby Dick right this moment, while not listening to me."

I wasn't whispering. I was focused on a new development in our day. A little bit of good luck—or catastrophic luck, depending on how you saw it.

"There's the mark," I said, nodding to a particular student we hadn't expected to see yet. "And he's not alone."

We were assigned to kill Goran Šovagović Mesic tomorrow. His description: twenty years old, tall, athletic, loud. And currently walking across the courtyard.

"He's totally alone," said Milt.

"Behind him."

"Where? I don't . . . Oh." Milt saw the two thick men lagging in the distance. "Yup. Croatian Mafia. They like baiting it."

Milt meant that the kid's bodyguards followed well behind him. It meant these guys *preferred* a fight—essentially daring someone to come and start trouble. Yet it also meant we'd have access to a faster, cleaner hit.

Cleaner—as long as he behaved the way we needed him to.

Goran walked with his backpack slung over one broad shoulder, his cashmere V-neck snug. He looked exactly like what you'd expect an Eastern Bloc playboy to look like.

"A Vronsky," I murmured.

"A what?"

Vronsky, the gent who had lured Anna Karenina to the dark side. He was stately and well composed—with just the right array of anatomical features to inspire an alluring young lady of the 1800s to derail her own marriage. I didn't say all this to Milt. I summarized the essence of it. "A guy who'll always act in his own best interest."

"That's every male in Massachusetts."

"*He* happens to do it in a way that helps us. He's someone I can predict."

Milt pointed out that I'd never met him, that I knew zilch about him. That once again, I was making a big deal out of an irrelevant detail, instead of sticking to ballistics triangulation and trajectory analysis. He was right about most of it. But I was right about something, too—call it a gut feeling, or something based on years of experience: the murder of this kid wasn't going to be simple.

CHAPTER 2

"YOU CAN PREDICT him?" said Milt.

"Girl in the turtleneck," I replied.

There was a set of stairs in Goran's path where foot traffic slowed down a bit. Goran would be passing a girl in a turtleneck sweater. He'd walk by her and create a small situation. I could foresee it.

"Finger to the chest," I said to Milt. "Watch."

"Her? She's with a guy." Milt pointed to the young man on her left. "Look. She's holding hands with the kid in the flannel shirt."

"Keep watching."

My hobby is people. I see them do things before they know they even *want* to do those things. Goran passed the girl and reached out, quickly, to give her chin a brief, soft, bold, two-finger squeeze. In passing. Nothing anyone else would notice. But a grotesque violation of personal domain nonetheless. The girl hardly expected it, hardly saw who had done it, and couldn't do anything but keep walking with the crowd, in total repulsion.

"Big deal," said Milt. "Wasn't her chest."

"Not *her* chest."

I nodded, a heads-up to what was happening next. The kid in the flannel—the one holding the girl's hand, the only witness—now felt he had a duty to call it out. He let go of the girl's hand, turned around, and hurried to catch up to Goran.

But before he could finish his first sentence, Goran put his finger to the kid's chest and spoke directly in his face. Finger to the chest. I couldn't tell what the exact words were, but the message was clear: *I can have you damaged and no one will do anything about it.* Which was the first time the two bodyguards got closer. We'd nicknamed them Tweedledee and Tweedledum. Tweedledee and Tweedledum were now hovering just near enough to be "felt."

The kid saw the doom. You could *see* him seeing it. You could see the instant fear. While in Goran's face you could see the comfort. Goran would go home that night and sleep peacefully, thinking nothing of the moment, possibly forgetting it had occurred. But the flannel kid would be shaken for days. To say nothing of the girl. I'd seen it a hundred times.

Infuriating that they'd let this oily boy and his expensive gang wander the halls of such a sacred place. That's what money can buy behind closed doors.

When Goran and his thugs exited the quad, I wanted to follow him home and end his life right then. But then Milt grabbed my shoulder to remind me, "We don't get paid that way."

The job required a hit on Harvard soil. A hit tomorrow, not today.

"Floral dress," he said.

It'd be a complicated kill, but with a predictable variable in the center of the equation—the kid himself—we could make it work. We could complete the assignment and get to safety.

Just as long as we took care of the most important factor. "Need to keep it under six minutes," I said to him.

"Six? Sure. If we know our crowd well enough. Like we've been talking about. Gauging their reaction time." He loved this part. He was already fixated on the young lady he'd been fixated on. "I'm still nominating her." He pointed in her direction, packaging his suggestion in a flowery load of BS. "See how she turns to face you? That's the dead give-away, brother. How the front of the torso rotates. See? As you walk by? Rotates slowly toward the man she desires. Like a daisy in the sunlight."

"No. Not her. We need a reliable screamer."

"Who could be more reliable than a daisy?"

I'd made my choice. "The barista." She was behind the counter of the café across the street, checking her phone for likes—for whatever pic she'd just been tagged in. She was busy. She was trapped. She was perfect.

We headed over to the café. Milt was right about the behavior of his chosen muse: the floral-dress girl *had* rotated as we passed her. I'd assumed when she locked eyes with me it was out of boredom. Was he right about her all along?

Half plus seven—it's socially acceptable to date someone

who's half your age plus seven years, according to Milt. That qualified me for a twenty-eight-year-old. Not sure my wife would have enjoyed that math, but lately I'd been desperately wondering if I had *any* appeal.

We entered a room full of Harvard's finest, a café abuzz with the chatter of freshly caffeinated opinions.

I looked at Milt. He looked at me. He was clutching his chest, slightly bent over.

"You look like you're about to have a heart attack, buddy."

"What gives you that idea?"

"Books on the topic. And the fact—"

"Raaoooowwwgggggggooooddddd!" Milt screamed.

He snapped his head back and tumbled in midair to fall backward, half onto nothing, half onto a circular café table so that the table flipped up all its dishes and glassware. Milton Prescott looked like he was dying.

CHAPTER 3

MY PARTNER OF eleven years frantically grasped for his trachea, the universal gesture of zero air.

"He's choking!" yelled a brilliant mind from across the room.

Milt flailed around on the floor. He's a thick, stocky stegosaurus of a man, so he easily knocks things over. Tiny students were no match. Nobody could aid him.

Wouldn't matter, though.

As quickly as he went down, Milt got up, stood up, took a moment for dramatic emphasis, pointed directly out the front door, yelled "Marrarrrruuuuwwggh!," then ran out the opposite way, through the back exit of the café, top speed, bulldozing everyone along the way, making a spectacle.

Over before it even started.

Leaving a small but deafening moment of silence.

"Holy shit," said virtually every person in the room.

Two girls then immediately rushed to assist him—the barista and another girl, in a hat. I followed and the three of us as a team ran into the back to find an empty corridor.

"Was he stabbed more than once?" I asked the girl in the hat.

"Stabbed?" she replied.

You could see her gears turning, her pliable memory now searching for details that fit the suggestion. Stabbed?

"You saw those three guys who ran out the front, right?" I asked her.

"N-no," said the girl in the hat.

"No," said the barista confidently. Confidently...until something occurred to her. "Wait."

"Jeez, is this a shooting?" I asked, my eyes widening.

The barista looked at me. Shooting? The seed was planted. The garden of doubt—tilled. The barista was already calling 911.

I left them. I returned to the café. Thankfully, there were very few people recording video. I don't like being on camera. Especially in such drab lighting. I hustled over to the introverts in the corner. The farming had only just begun.

"Did any of you see how many times he was stabbed?" I asked the group.

A chorus of the word *stabbed* echoed throughout the herd. Child's play. Their apparent leader made the next 911 call placed. "Um, nine one one?...Okay...um...there was a man who was stabbed...I think...multiple times...definitely stabbed...at least twice. Ran out to the alley."

In this modern era, any police response to an assault call from a college campus is going to be swift and crowded. They already have patrols every thirty minutes.

The caller was doing our work for us. "We think there was an assailant who ran through the courtyard."

The beauty of a heart attack is that once the story was straightened out, hours from then, it'd stand as just a minor, weird incident while having granted me a powerful glimpse into the future. We'd tested the tissue of the local response system like a marine biologist might prod an anemone to test its reflexes: gently. Just enough of a prick to stimulate the response, but not too much that anyone would know it had happened. Harvard was the anemone. Milt was the prick.

One hour later, the cops would review whatever surveillance video the café had and realize that the guy just choked on his muffin. They'd curse the unreliable reports of witnesses, and they'd be 3 percent slower to react the next day. Most importantly, I'd have my measurement.

One hour later, Milt and I rehashed what had happened, like two janitors mopping up the stadium after a Super Bowl.

"Two minutes eight seconds," said Milt.

"I got two minutes twenty-five."

"No, no, they had the ambulance come after," said Milt. "The cops were first."

"No, I saw an SUV parked on the avenue."

"How would the avenue be clear if it was already parked?"

"You saw it clear?"

"With my own eyes."

"Not parked?" That was different. "Then we're in under six."

"In under six."

It'd be more than doable. We had eight minutes to cross out of a three-mile radius and our current estimates had us hovering just under six. That's what I'd call a professional margin of error. The kind of leeway that ensures success.

CHAPTER 4

I'M SUPPOSED TO go directly home. That was the agreement I'd made with myself. Work, then home. In that order. No other activities.

But I didn't go home.

I stopped at a place called the Alluvial Tavern, a dive bar just outside the Boston city limits. It smelled like yesterday's beer and last year's urine. The perfect environment for an outcast like me to do the one thing no normal human would do in a noisy, poorly lit environment: read a book.

I had *Le Parfum* with me, a beat-up French copy of Patrick Süskind's tale of assaults and aromas.

"Assaults?" asked the bartender. She'd asked about the pages I was turning but barely stuck around to hear my answer.

"The story of a murderer," I replied. "Grenouille. Guy's got an obsession with scents. The whole story is like this exegesis on scents, but it's got a larger meaning."

She'd left.

Which was fine by me. I really just wanted to cross the halfway point in the novel.

I ordered a trendy triple IPA, with lime quartered. I read my novel in spurts and thought in spurts, looking for the obvious idea to emerge. The book soon ended up wedged open against the bar counter, beneath my forearm. Grenouille was just about to slice open another victim. To him, the girl—his victim—smelled of both fireplace residue and her own natural vanilla scent. How a monster could be so attuned to the delicacies of life was exactly the appeal.

I pulled out a pen and drew a map of the Harvard campus on my napkin. No place-names—no evidence to leave lying around the bar counter—just a vague sketch with all sorts of arrows and circles. Situational arrows. "If this, then that." If the bodyguards pull out knives, we demobilize them from their flank. (We kill them.) If the crowd is sparse, then we act early. Early—because a fatal shot to a bodyguard is not nearly as much paperwork as a fatal shot to a Harvard bystander. And by *paperwork* I mean prison.

"You gonna order another, Ryan?" The bartender pointed at my glass. "Or just fondle your library card?"

The bar was half empty but somehow I was taking up all her lucrative territory, nor drinking enough beers.

"Hey," said the bartender. "I didn't mean to kick you out."

I smiled politely and gathered my things.

"So, I'm wondering. Why do you stick with her?" the bartender asked, watching me.

"Stick...with...?" I didn't know what she meant. "My wife?"

"She doesn't love you anymore, right? I mean...I'm not being harsh. I'm just being honest...about what I see and hear."

Ah, just being honest. In my experience, people who talk about how honest they're being *aren't*. I think this bartender wanted to have sex with me.

I smiled, picked up my beer, toasted her in midair—trying to be suave, as it spilled down my knuckles—and headed for a distant booth across the bar. Myself. My novel. This beer.

The magic was gone, though. I couldn't reimmerse myself in the pages of the book about a journey through prewar Paris. And worse, I'd left my map at the bar—the map drawn on that napkin. Sure, I doubted anyone would pick it up and say, "Hey who's drawing tactical schematics of an assassination on Harvard's campus?" But the fact that I'd left it anywhere at all was a small but important sign that I'd started to lose what we in the business refer to as my edge.

Five years ago I would not have made even one single mistake. Now I was watching a yuppie couple pull up barstools precisely where I'd been sitting. Precisely where I'd been drawing.

I should've immediately gone to grab that napkin, just in case the yuppie was a cop, or a fed, or just even one of those annoying fans of the evening news who sees some report and proudly calls the 1-800 tip line at the bottom of the screen.

Five years ago I'd already be at the counter, clutching the napkin, maybe breaking some nice man's nose. But at this point in my life?

I watched the guy's lady friend nuzzle up behind his shirt collar and place a kiss upon his neck. They giggled about some joke they must've whispered to each other countless times. These two couldn't care less about my napkin. She hugged him again.

Why can't Maria hug me for no reason?

I stopped at a flower store on the way home. Desperate times, desperate measures. I bought her an orchid in a cubic vase.

When I got home and entered our creaky bedroom, Maria was asleep. I knelt in front of her side of the bed, and stared at her for longer than I'd care to admit. She looked so vulnerable. So lovable. The hundred fights we'd had that year didn't seem to erode her. She was still quite pretty in the right light. Her creases were coming, yes, but those creases were coming for us all, weren't they?

She wanted me dead.

But several minutes later I was in the laundry room, at 2:00 a.m., washing her butcher frocks so she'd have a dry frock for her shift the next day. It was something she'd always forget to plan for.

She didn't know I did stuff like wash and iron her clothes.

I crawled into bed at 3:15 a.m., taking one last look at the cover of *Le Parfum* for inspiration. I would be back at the Harvard courtyard at ten in the morning, executing my last assignment ever.

Retirement would pave the way for me to go to marital therapy. To be a better husband. To heal our romance. I rolled over toward Maria, hoping she might softly retreat into a spoon. She didn't. We were both unaware that by the start of the next evening, one of us would be dead.

CHAPTER 5

"LET'S SAY IT to each other one more time," I said to Milt.

"Really?" he groaned.

We were walking toward the main courtyard and already noticing cops. And cops were noticing us. Not outright. But we got glanced at. You don't want eye contact in my line of work.

"We converge from opposite sides," said Milt, beginning his summary of the pivotal six minutes of our plan. "You're the primary. I'm the cleanup." He was speaking in monotone, reciting memorized facts. "We shoot for the heart and keep the exit wound contained in his backpack to minimize the visual blood. If his bodyguards react to us, we shoot to neutralize. We exit opposite corners."

"No phones," I added.

"I said that."

"No, you didn't."

"We don't use phones." He gave me an annoyed look. "If

something goes wrong, communication is via email from a random computer at a random Apple Store."

"We don't rendezvous until after forty-eight hours."

"Right."

It was a traditional setup for us, in many ways. But this was far from a traditional hit. Shooting a kid? *Amidst* kids? How do you answer for that when you stand before the Almighty?

"Christ," said Milt. "It's raining."

I was praying for any hiccup to derail the day. I was. But things were well on their way to going wrong, and the bad weather was merely an appetizer for the bad news. When we arrived at the courtyard, we saw the essential issue: foot traffic had completely rerouted to the perimeter. Nobody was crisscrossing the middle of the yard. That meant our walking paycheck, Goran Mesic, would be in the mobbed side walkways.

We did check the weather. But there'd been only a forecast of "light wind with possible light drizzle." Now it looked like some classes were getting out early to handle the surprise downpour, which meant we were already behind schedule.

Our contingency plans could handle that. We were already in position, ready for Goran. What our plans *couldn't* handle was the fact that Goran was walking directly *between* Tweedledee and Tweedledum. Not in front, not to the rear. But *between* his two bodyguards.

Barely any of our reconnaissance would be of use now. I closed my eyes for a fraction of a moment. I took a breath.

I pictured the most chaotic possible outcome of the next hour and let its climactic moment unfold in front of me in slow motion.

People reaching for weapons. Witnesses diving for cover. Slow motion. Like an NFL replay. I tried to see where each step could go wrong, letting the frozen moments inform me how to re-choose the better step. *If the guards protectively shove Goran down to the pavement: I shoot all three of them. If Goran runs directly away: I let Milt handle them while I footrace the kid off campus.* When you think like a victim, you choose paths based on fear. Fear trumps all. Goran would panic at the threat *on* campus and think to run *from* campus. That would mean crossing Quincy Street. I could head him off if I circled around the library and ambushed from solid cover.

What a fun job—shooting kids.

I felt nauseous.

"He's twenty," argued Milt. "He ain't no kid."

I'd already wanted to leave this career. I'd been searching for a doable exit plan for months. I had a wife who would barely kiss me anymore. A dog who barely nuzzled me. Ulcers. A leaky roof.

My work was the culprit. My wife hated what I did. I'd come to hate it, too.

"Anyone under thirty is a kid," I said to Milt.

By 10:05 a.m. we were established in our positions at the upper end of the quad. I could see Milt and he could see me. We'd given ourselves strict orders not to use the cell phones. Phone records can be searched. Checked. Studied. Conclusions drawn. You just don't know what kind of paper trail a text message becomes, should the cops get hold of you. Or worse, should the Croatian Mafia get hold of you.

"Is this chair taken?" I said to the girl next to me.

"Uh . . . no," said the girl, puzzled. She was wearing a giant, thick scarf, the kind that would discourage unwanted attention.

She moved her bag. "Go for it," she said.

The patio had stayed dry under its awning. I sat down. I needed to look like I wasn't standing around waiting for a homicide.

At 10:08 a.m. I checked for Milt. But Milt was no longer there.

He was hustling down the steps toward the middle of the quad. Worst-case scenario getting worse by the minute. There was Goran, and instead of being at the outer edges of the quad, he was walking right down the middle, which meant he couldn't be more noticed. Yet before I could even *begin* to strategize a new plan, our frightfully obsolete *original* plan commenced on its own. *Blam! Blam! Blam!* The gentle acoustics of campus gunfire.

CHAPTER 6

THE SOUND OF bullets ricocheted off all corners of the courtyard—all—disorienting anyone trying to locate the shooter. Did Milt fire first? I dropped to the ground as two more shots pealed through the air. *Crack! Crack!*

I looked up to see the chest of the first bodyguard explode forward. But he didn't go down.

On the far side, I could see Milt spin around to square up against the second bodyguard, just as the girl in the scarf spun around to look in the wrong direction. I got my handgun ready inside the front pouch of my hoodie. Two stray bullets tore into the glass next to us in the window of the café.

"Get inside," I told the girl in the scarf. "Stay low."

Operating on pure panic, she ducked inside the bistro. She didn't take her latte, she didn't take her laptop. And, most importantly, she didn't take her phone.

I still had my weapon somewhat hidden. Did the bodyguards spot me or were those bullets that passed me strays?

Where was the kid? Where was Tweedledum? I could handle the onslaught of gunfire from the two bodyguards; what I couldn't handle was the deluge of Cambridge police officers who'd be arriving here oh so soon. Within two minutes eight seconds, if our research held up.

Do we abort?

The goons had spotted Milt across the yard. But they hadn't spotted me. Distraction might work in my favor. They were concentrating on dealing with him. They had no idea I existed.

I grabbed the phone belonging to the scarf girl and started to rush through the scattered crowd, sowing the seeds of our exit plan. I told each student I passed that there was a lone shooter out on Oxford Street. I kept repeating the phrase. *Lone shooter, Oxford Street.* Moving from one spot to the next. Didn't matter what they were actually seeing; they just needed a catchphrase. *Crack crack crack crack.* Bullets flew over my head as I journeyed from one huddled kid to the next, ducking into whatever makeshift foxhole I saw—a terrace chair, a planter, a bench, a trash can. I'd cower with him or her and bequeath unto them the mantra. *Lone shooter, Oxford Street.*

The trail I'd left while making my way over to Milt, who was pinned down near a set of steps, would lead to a flurry of 911 calls. Then I made my own call.

"Nine one one. What's your emergency?"

"I think they detonated a bomb at MIT," I said into the phone. "I can see it from my balcony window. There's smoke. This is an attack. This is—"

Then I threw the phone in the wet gutter.

Then I found the next foxhole. A trash can in front of a trembling engineering student. I crouched with him and shared that people had seen three guys shove a girl into a white van, with the license plate number "something something KHR-11."

"Something something KHR-11," he parroted back.

"Can you call it in? My battery's—" I completed my sentence with a shrug.

He understood. He began to call it in.

"You saw 'em, right?" I said. "Unreal, man."

Then I leapt up and ran around the corner, spotted Tweedledee, and let four rounds of my five-round .38 rip through the atmosphere.

Every kid saw me do it.

"Cambridge PD," I yelled to them. "Get down."

The kids got down. I ran to the next post and shed my hoodie. Layer one—shed. Crimson to blue. I went from a Harvard tourist to a Patriots fan. Scrambled eggs.

Milt put his own 911 call in, reporting that two foreigners were on the roof of a tall building shooting at cars and pedestrians.

All designed to tax the system. Resources would be spread out in every direction. Eventually the main catastrophe—our catastrophe—would get lost in the shuffle. Eventually we'd have our escape route smoothly paved.

But then the second bodyguard spotted me. He seemed to recognize my unique fixation on Goran. Like any skilled protector, he foresaw the threat.

And like any skilled assassin, I foresaw him foreseeing my threat. I fired two shots right at him.

He fired back at me. And then another shooter joined the game.

Goran.

And Goran shot well.

CHAPTER 7

MILT AND I both use revolvers. Revolvers don't leave much evidence behind because the shells remain in the chamber. It's a little unorthodox in today's game of maximizing volume and sheen, but I've been in the trade for eleven years, and aside from that one time in Sarasota, I'm proud to report I've never been questioned by the police.

Goran's bodyguard turned around and fired seven of his non-revolver bullets at me.

And missed.

Tsk, tsk. You have a Springfield Armory XD-S 9mm with flush-fitting mag. Capacity seven, my friend. Now you're out. The other guard got into a fistfight with Milt, which is worrisome on Milt's behalf. If you saw Milt try to jog on a treadmill, or try to hurry to beat a yellow light, or just try to bend over and pick up a nickel, you'd know that he is a poorly constructed human being.

He could get exhausted just putting on a shirt. And now he was tangled up with the taller, more muscular of the two enemies. Both he and Milt still had possession of their firearms, but both managed to grip each other's grip.

The guard mounted Milt and was about to force his trembling muzzle into Milt's rib cage. There were way too many pedestrians around for me to continue in stealth. I had no choice—I stood up, marched directly across the courtyard through the rain, and buried four bullets into Milt's enemy.

So now everyone around me was aware that I was a participant in the mayhem. *Possible male Caucasian. Early forties.* I could hear the APB in my head. *Dressed in blue. Carrying a Smith & Wesson 686 for some reason. Shots fired.* I had to assume at least half of these kids were recording video.

Milt's adversary was getting up. I emptied my last shot into him. The loud ricocheting of bullets had been sending everyone lower and lower to the ground, facedown onto the concrete. Good instinct. Does modern society simply know to get low when they hear gunfire?

Goran pushed himself up and, in an instant, sprinted toward the Humanities building. He was going *toward* the crowd, ultimately trying to head deeper into the heart of campus. This would be troublesome.

"Stay down!" I yelled for the benefit of bystanders.

By now the melee had lured two different helicopters. One: the news. Two: the law. They were swirling in the distance, in the wrong area, thanks to false 911s, but they wouldn't swirl stupidly for long.

Milt started firing at Goran, which was at the crowd.

"Hold fire!" I yelled to Milt.

Milt fired again. Two more shots that didn't find their target.

"We're not flushing toward the crowd," I said to him.

"We gotta contain!" he argued back. He was reloading.

"Not the crowd!" I yelled.

I didn't have a proper rebuttal. He was right. Forcing the enemies to converge on the crowd left us with the higher ground, left us with better cover from the concrete planters, and left them with no way to escape. But there was a throng of students down there.

"Don't lose focus," Milt warned from across the atrium.

Goran had already penetrated through the clumps of students—his human shield—and fled past the one building that leads to central campus. I immediately went after him, full speed.

"Help me!" shrieked Goran. "Help!" A useful thing to say: it cast me as the villain and himself as the hero.

But we were far past the crowd now, running alone. I was forcing him to arc around in one giant circle, back toward the bistro. I could've pulled the trigger on him, but didn't.

I wasn't sure why, but I couldn't. Instead, I outpaced him on the ground and finally cornered him behind a series of ventilator units, where he'd ducked down. He had his gun, but I had his flank.

I heard huffing behind me—Milt was finally catching up to the mayhem, rounding the corner.

But our satisfaction was short-lived. Goran was waiting for us. Deliberately. He was standing still, facing me directly. Holding the girl in the scarf, in front of himself. With his gun pointed at her throat.

CHAPTER 8

MY ANTAGONIST HAD the blunt muzzle of his Taurus PT 111 pressed deep into his victim's esophagus. Deep enough that she struggled just to breathe. I'm sure her adrenaline blunted the pain, but still, it had to hurt.

"Drop your gun," Goran yelled.

How he knew that this kind of move would work on a good citizen like me I know not. Because in my line of work, chivalry is beyond dead. Milt, for instance, already had his gun pointed at both of them, absolutely unfazed by the collateral cost.

Goran, smart chap—a credit to Harvard—fixated on me. Wisely, he knew I was in charge. "I will kill this girl," he said to me. "I will."

His nerves must've been blitzing. He was pressing that gun way too hard into her voice box.

"Do it! Shoot her!" yelled Milt. "Then I get to shoot *you*. Legally. With no fear of hitting an innocent bystander."

"The hell's wrong with you?" I whispered to him.

Milt was already fully engaged. "Don't wait!" he yelled.

The girl screamed, but both Milt and Goran were hell-bent on global destruction.

"I swear I will," said Goran.

"Stop swearing and do it!" yelled Milt.

I had to do something. I stood up straight, raising my arms and hands. The gesture of surrender. "Goran? You win, okay?" And I started to walk toward him.

"Whoa," said Milt. "No, no, no."

I wasn't listening. "You got the upper hand," I said to Goran. I lowered my gun. "I'm releasing my weapon... as... you're able to see... but I'm only doing it on the condition that you let me walk over and get the girl." I was already walking over. It wasn't a negotiation. "Then you can go free."

"Tell your fat monkey to drop his gun, too," said Goran.

"I'm gonna count to five, you dick!" yelled Milt. "If you ain't facing the concrete, I'm firing away. Girl or not."

"I *will* kill her!" shouted Goran.

"Good!" yelled Milt. "Five!"

I was only twenty feet away. I was within striking distance. The average reaction time for a high-stressed individual in terms of the kinesiological timing of motor neurons is point eight seconds. I can cover roughly ten feet in that amount of time. I'd have ten left to go.

"Please," begged the girl. "Please... just let me go."

Her words tore at me. Bottom line, three-hundred-thousand-dollar tuition aside, we were all just human beings that wanted to survive through Tuesday.

"Four!" yelled Milt.

"Goran Mesic," I said loudly. "I need to tell you something."

"Go to hell," he replied.

"It's about your family."

"My gun's in her mouth and if—"

"It's about your father."

He stopped. I'd gotten his attention.

"Three," said Milt.

I talked quickly and clearly for this next part. This was all I had left. "We were assigned to kill you, but we got a change of instructions just one hour ago." Here came the lie. "Your father and I were friends a long time ago. We worked in the smuggling game." Like all good lies, this one was based in truth.

"Don't..." he began. "The... Don't get any closer."

"Two!" yelled Milt.

"Milt!" I had to scold him without losing momentum with Goran. "Your father made an enemy of one of my associates. This was a disagreement we had about the IRA. But it was settled one hour—*one hour*—ago. And now we're all friends again."

I turned around to face Milt. I made sure my body was blocking Milt's aim.

"Friends," I said, while looking at Milt.

It was a show of submission to Goran. I had my back to him now. He'd see this as a sign of sincerity, a show of support for Rachel. Rachel was the name I'd given the girl in my mind—I needed to do that.

Otherwise, I'd lose a sense of where the fiction ends and reality begins: *Rachel is a hopeful sophomore at Harvard who might be missing a larynx soon. Goran is the guy who started to lower his weapon.* I could finally end this peacefully. I might even rope the kid up and put him in a warehouse somewhere and somehow earn half of my half of a hundred and fifty grand without going the distance.

"Okay," I said to Goran, seeing him cooperate. "Thanks for being—"

Blam blam blam!

Three shots. Milt had his orders. He was a good shooter. He had shot both of them.

CHAPTER 9

ASSASSINATION IS NOT the rosy little business everyone thinks it is. Dead kids in an alley shall serve as Exhibit A. We hustled to the parking lot at the far end of JFK Street. We needed a getaway car.

"Time?" I asked Milt.

The smart move was to steal a vehicle. We were about to steal three.

He checked his watch. "Four minutes forty-one."

"That's it? That's miraculous." We were so much faster than I had thought. That made the next steps far more comforting. "We start with a sports car, then we go sedan, then sedan."

We were restating our plan again. The first car would be the nimble one. The second car would be the one that blends in. The third would be the one that survives inspection. Each leg of the race would require a different specialty. Yet obviously, all three cars should do all three things.

Right then we primarily needed speed.

"We wipe all prints," replied Milt. His turn to recite the plan. "We check under the seats to make sure we didn't drop anything. We ditch out of sight from helicopters."

Ideally, you also scrape your gun barrels with a chisel and go to a gun range for an hour. This lets you pass a possible paraffin test, and restructures the forensics of your gun's bullets. The day before we'd carefully surveyed the array of potential getaway vehicles and singled out a candidate. A little Ford Festiva. The idea was to pick something that wasn't obvious, something that wouldn't be noticed in the Boston traffic lanes.

Milt pulled a Slim Jim from his coat and used it to bypass the passenger door lock, as I watched for anybody loitering on our level of the garage. Once the lock clicked, we jumped in the car and squealed out of the parking space. We were both in our XXL Patriots hoodies, which came off as soon as we were on the turnpike. Next they were sailing out the window to become road garbage.

"Can't keep that in the car," I said to Milt. I was looking at a stolen phone he had in his lap.

"Nobody's gonna track it in the middle of a circus."

"Toss it."

But he was already dialing. "Hi," he said to whoever was answering the 911 line. "Our emergency is we're chasing after an Asian guy on a motorcycle who shot two kids. He's heading south on Quimby Avenue and he's wear—"

I yanked the phone out of his hand and tossed it out the window.

"That's how you get someone killed!" I yelled.

"Better him than us."

I cranked a hard left and accelerated past the whizzing bushes onto a dinky little side street. Our nondescript late-model navy-blue Festiva swerved onto the main road.

"Don't signal lane changes," said Milt. "You keep signaling and it keeps drawing attention from cops miles behind us."

You fucking shot some kids, I growled at him in my head.

That's what I said to him in the uncut version of my autobiography. "You're staying sharp," I told him. "I appreciate that. You were cool under pressure."

"Thanks."

"And you were able to keep us under six minutes."

"Thanks."

That was the simple exchange we had.

Then, after a few moments, he added a small clarification. "Sorta."

"Sorry?"

"Sorta. My stopwatch says four minutes forty-one seconds, but I'm not sure exactly when I hit Start."

"What're you talking about?"

"We're good, though. We're on our way."

"How much time elapsed, Milt?"

"We're on our way. I don't know."

"Since shot number one. What do you mean you don't know?"

"That's the thing," he began. "The first gunshot came from *them*. And I had to duck for cover, so I may not have pressed the stopwatch button right away."

"When did you fucking press it?" I asked. This was bad.

"I don't know. Maybe after we killed Goran. As planned."

"After we . . . ? As . . . ?" I paused. "That was three minutes later!"

"We don't know that."

"By my own math I'm feeling like it was three minutes. Maybe more."

"If you can do all this math, why do we need a stopwatch?" Milt said sarcastically.

"How much time went by before you arrived in the alley?"

"Me?"

I had to get it out of him. "Tell me, Milt. You must've seen a number at some point. Think. How much are we adding to your four forty-one and my three eight?"

"We're on our way. I don't know. I guess it was maybe . . . five minutes?"

"Five? Are you serious? *That brings our total to thirteen fucking min—*"

Then I was drowned out by the sound of glass shattering, as our rear window exploded into shards. The car lurched to the side and almost lost traction, and the horizon ahead jolted upward for a moment.

Because we were being shot at.

A glance in the mirror confirmed my fears. Cops.

CHAPTER 10

"JESUS," SCREAMED MILT, staring at the Cambridge Police Department. "Since when do these assholes just shoot at us?" They were unloading rounds of fully automatic MP5s in our direction. "No questions asked…just 'Merry Christmas, here's five hundred bullets in your windshield.'"

They hadn't hit our bodies or our engine. But they'd hit Milt's pride, like flicking the ears of a rhinoceros.

I floored the gas and made our Festiva earn every ounce of its five-year, fifty-thousand-mile, bumper-to-bumper warranty. We were going 110 miles per hour.

Milt leaned out the passenger window and tried to shoot left-handed.

"Back window!" I shouted.

I could see a curve in the road up ahead. We were veering to the right. That meant we'd open up an angle of attack, starboard. Milt let loose a barrage from his automatic, and fate played its hand. The trash truck to our right slammed on its brakes and thirty-two tons of bad news careened over us, towering for what felt like the majority of my adult life, as the other half of its wheels went airborne just long enough to make me swallow my larynx.

Stray fire must've stripped the truck driver of control.

Which was only the beginning of our very special moment, as an oncoming bus, desperate to avoid the trash truck, skidded back and forth, only to clip the trash truck—*dink*—before devouring the first two police cars behind us.

Head-on.

FWAAAAmmmbbbwwaaAAMMM.

It was the loudest thing I'd ever heard, as the trash truck also flipped—an overturned behemoth that slid a half block down the street in front of us—yielding just enough daylight for us to pass on the inside lane, speeding through the gap just before it cinched shut.

The carousel had closed. The cops were behind us.

I knew what would come next: helicopters. If they anticipated which parking structure we were heading toward before we reached it, dear Lord, we'd be doomed. They'd prep their other officers and have the building surrounded with SWAT well before our arrival. I screeched the car to a halt at the far side of a drainage ditch. If nothing else, we had our plan. I knew that the ditch snaked back under the main road and led straight to parking garage number two.

"Down the ditch," I said to Milt. "Let's go."

We ran down the ditch and without incident reached the

parking structure, where we had to race up five flights of stairs. Our golden goose was parked on the fifth floor.

"Hurry!" I yelled backward.

"Hurrying. Jeez!" yelled Milt, fat jiggling, lungs wheezing, asthma attack imminent. He looked even worse once he saw the chosen car. "This?!"

"Hurry!" I was already getting in. I pried open the door and tricked the ignition within nine seconds total.

"A Volkswagen Bug?" His disappointment was at a crescendo. "Bright yellow? Please tell me there's a daisy on the dashbo—"

He got in and saw the daisy.

"We are *completely* visible," he whined.

"That's where we're hiding. In broad daylight."

I got in the driver's seat and busted the casing off the console. By my mental clock, twenty-three seconds had elapsed. I'd counted them out while envisioning the last few turns the cop cars would make to narrow our location down to this particular garage.

Stock anti-theft alarms are easy. They go off but they don't linger once the kill switch is bypassed. I had us on the road in eighty-one seconds total, from my hand first touching the door to my tires first touching the road. It wouldn't fully compensate for the overall tardiness, but every microsecond helped. The turnpike was more crowded now, but we were safer. After a massive shoot-out, would you flag the brightest, friendliest, *yellowest* thing on the road?

We passed oncoming police cars, one after another, with Milt sweating each one.

Mine was a different concern. A deeper concern. I may have found us a successful vehicle to get back to Boston, but I didn't have an answer to a very fundamental question. I turned to Milt to ask what had to be asked. "Who ordered the hit?"

CHAPTER 11

FIVE KIDS SHOT in the upper body. Three nicked in the limbs. One head wound. Two dead guards. One gutted female. And a young Mafia kid with his face missing. Today had been carnage on a level I had never signed up for.

"Who ordered the hit, Milt?"

"What?" he replied. Nonchalant.

He hadn't picked up on how intensely I needed my answer. I kept my tone casual, because there was nothing casual about the question.

"Who?" I repeated.

"This car smells like pumpkin spice condoms," said Milt. "Can't believe we're in this thing."

Deflection. This wasn't going to be easy.

"I can feel my manhood decrease by the mile," he said.

"Oh, miles? I measure mine in millimeters."

He laughed.

For those wondering, I am a fantastic actor. A trained actor, in fact, a theater major who had commanded the finest of stages in each of the three theaters on the Boston University campus, and who had voiced truth into the most stilted of classical monologues. The trick was to believe in what you were saying. I had that sort of brain. It floated between the wonderful realities of life and the vivid realities of fiction, and I rarely wanted to know which was which. I was performing for Milt.

"Who called the hit?" I asked him.

He didn't answer.

I'd quit stage acting when my wife got pregnant. The baby was stillborn. The doctors were helpless. Maria spent the next few years resisting the urge to blame me. That effort had worn off recently, but I couldn't deny that my unhealthy lifestyle was at fault.

"Goran Mesic, son of Ivan Mesic," I said, without sounding too *Lord of the Rings*-y about it. "Tell me why he was chosen to fall."

"You knew his father?" questioned Milt. More deflection. "I mean, I heard your big bullshit speech back in that alley. I assume it was big and bullshit. Was it?"

"How about I answer your question when you answer mine?"

"What difference does it make? A job's a job. We're about to be paid."

Concord Avenue directly west. Toward New York. Then left on Arlington, then left on the turnpike, past Fenway Park, back into Boston. A bird's-eye view of our journey would make it look like we were New Yorkers. The crisscrossing was to throw any bloodhounds off the scent.

Which made me think back to the morning. Why were Tweedledum and Tweedledee suddenly walking next to the boy? How did they know to do that?

"You're right," I said. "The paycheck's coming. Thanks to you."

He laughed. "And ain't you retiring on it?"

"I'm retired as of twenty minutes ago. Unless what just happened with the kid was based on a *feud*."

"Game at Fenway tonight."

"Was it a feud? Did someone order a feud? Just tell me."

"Three wins outa first," he said before finally murmuring some semblance of an answer. "I dunno, man."

He was a bad liar. I knew the sign. He got louder.

"I really don't know, Mike."

"Who *would* know?"

I knew Milt had read some real estate sales book that said that people tuck their voice in the back of their throat when they lie. So he compensated by being so confident and loud—*GOSH, I HAVE NO IDEA, MIKE*—it was like he was suddenly in a discotheque. "I got the info from the normal channel. Y'know how it is. Anonymous."

He was covering it up. Anything to hide the truth that I'd become aware of during this car ride. Milt was going to kill me.

CHAPTER 12

WHY DID I keep finding myself not at home? At the Alluvial Tavern I had my book open, beer poured, jukebox cranked.

"Another," I said to the general area of the bar. No eye contact.

Another arrived.

The bartender made no conversation.

How did I get there? I could barely recap it. I'd dropped Milt off at the ditch site. We'd parked our car, wiped the prints, then abandoned it in a bad neighborhood, where it would be stripped clean like one of those time-lapse nature videos where bugs reduce a carcass to nothing. Next thing I knew I was in a cave in the South of France. A little village called Grasse.

Well, not me, but Grenouille, the protagonist of *Le Parfum,* now learning that he himself has no odor. An entire novel about odors—and he finds out he himself has none.

"I can relate, pal," I murmured to no one.

I devoured pages and triple IPAs, one after another, never engaging with the gray-eyed bartender.

When my thoughts drifted to my day, all I could think was, *I hate shooting kids*. That's why I was at the bar.

"Check," I said out loud.

Once you name your self-deception, it loses its power.

I took a taxi home and got out a half block before my house. I'd enter quietly, hoping with all my heart that she would just—*just for once, Maria*—wake up when I came home. *Touch me a little.*

"Maria?" I whispered toward the closed door.

My house key clicked into the knob with an unusually loud gnash of teeth. The lock was grungier than normal and it scraped upon a stillness I hadn't felt in years.

"Maria?"

Having an absent wife is one thing. Having a house absent of the absent wife is another.

Was she gone?

I started to enter, quietly, striving to avoid excess noise.

"Maria?" I said, loud enough to be heard if she were up, soft enough to be missed if she weren't.

No answer.

"Maria?"

I crept toward the kitchen and turned on the lights.

Blood.

In large quantities.

There was blood all over our white linoleum. I reached for the gun inside my coat with a trembling hand. I could only pray that my wife wasn't the source of the . . .

I couldn't finish the thought. I knelt by the scarlet pool. It was dark, a spilled Merlot. I guessed by temperature that it'd been on the floor for at least an hour.

"Maria!?" I called out.

I inhaled the air in the kitchen. What had happened in the last hour?

All I could smell was my own breath—the faint trace of beer. There was nothing else to know in this kitchen.

"Maria!?" I let loose.

I stood up and ran from room to room. The den. The guest bathroom. The guest bedroom. No answer. I banged open every random door I could find. The closet. The laundry room. The hallway cupboards. I waded through piles of folded linen, books strewn, broken paintings, broken mirrors. A storm had come through this place. My gun's muzzle led the way.

I was ready to blast anything that moved until I found Updike—my dog. He was curled up, ears flattened, tail rigid, shivering with fear.

"Here, li'l man," I called to him. "Good? Where's your mom?"

Whoever had come through here must've been a tornado of violence. Updike was now a cowering wreck. Part corgi, part Lab, part Jack Russell—rarely does this hyphenated beast back down. Yet he stayed glued to the wall, quivering, looking like he'd seen a ghost, like he was still seeing one.

"Maria Amelia Ryan!" I yelled.

I took a step back from Updike. Poor guy—he looked eternally relieved when I retreated.

I don't know why I checked the bedroom last. I opened the door and there she was. My wife. Cut in half.

CHAPTER 13

THERE WAS BLOOD across the majority of the bed. There was spattering on the walls, even on our ceiling fan.

"Baby?" I squished the nearly inaudible word from my empty lungs.

There she was.

I grabbed her outstretched hand, the last remaining body part that was clean. A sliver of moonlight found its way through our window. With my horror was a tinge of fear.

I listened for breathing. Hers. Mine. The dog's. Was her killer here? I heard nothing, my gun aimed toward the closet. If anything burst out of those doors, I'd bury every bullet I owned in it.

But nothing would come that night.

"Baby, we have to get up," I whispered to her rigid body.

I gathered the front half of her, staring at her face, looking for a greeting, a nod of approval—that what I was about to do needed to be done.

"Babe?"

I carried her torso down to the basement.

"This is just for now, okay?"

In the basement, we have a Kolpak 1010, one of the first walk-in freezers available for installation in a residential home. No, she didn't get a Whole Foods employee discount. What she did get was the most consistent cooling flow professionally feasible. I opened the door without setting her body down, crouching awkwardly to get my left hand on the knob. She loved this freezer. It contained about forty pounds of top sirloin, thirty pounds of pork, thirty pounds of salmon, and now its owner.

As I left her resting, I don't know how I was able to think with such merciless objectivity, but I knew it was imperative to avoid calling the cops.

Cops would occupy my time. Contain me. They would try to prevent me from doing what I had to do next. I went upstairs and grabbed my shotgun. I grabbed a dozen shells. I grabbed my dog and his leash. Sadness was giving way to a new feeling, a very important one. The French word is spelled very similarly to its English translation. *Revenche.*

CHAPTER 14

I DROVE TO the one place I knew I'd find none of the answers I needed and even less of the satisfaction I craved. Shotgun in my lap, I drove to Milt's home.

Milt would resist my inquiries, but I had nowhere else to go. My fingers were trembling on the steering wheel. I was taking deep breaths to fend off a panic attack. I screeched to a halt and stormed out of the car, pulling my dog's leash. Shotgun in my right hand, Cerberus in the other. *Revenche.* Revenge.

"Milt!" I yelled toward the house as I started dashing up his steps. "Milton!"

He opened the door and I instantly bashed him in the stomach with the back of my weapon.

"*Oooph!*" said his diaphragm.

He tumbled onto his back while my momentum took me right into his house. I donkey-kicked the front door shut behind me. We were in a shady neighborhood, but not so shady that neighbors wouldn't take an interest.

Things got loud. Updike barked a few times at our commotion, then skedaddled into the corner of the living room, paws clawing with zero traction on the wood floor. I grabbed Milt by the scruff and shoved his crumpled, compliant body into the crook of his couch.

He was heaving for breath until he gathered his strength to say, “What the living hell is wrong with you?”

“You tell me,” I replied.

His face was mostly angry but now a little puzzled.

“She’s dead!” I yelled.

“Who?”

I shifted my tone a bit. Business mode. “I’m only going to ask you once, Milt.”

“Who’s dead?”

“My wife!” I yelled, then returned to the mode. “I’m only going to ask you once.”

His face was going into shock. Brilliant acting on his part. He looked authentically sad.

“Who ordered the hits?” I asked him.

“Wait,” he responded. “What do you mean? Maria? Your wife?”

“Stop pretending.”

“She’s dead?” He looked genuinely upset, more upset than I had anticipated.

“They obviously tried to kill me and ended up with her carcass. Who ordered the hit?”

“Uh . . . the . . . the hit on Goran? I told you I don’t— ”

“No! The hit on *me!*”

This silenced him. He stared at me, unsure if I was really

asking what I was asking. He stood up. He knew I'd allow him to do so. There was a protocol. He walked to his wet bar and poured himself a dizzying ratio of bourbon and water. Stalling.

"That's... That's crazy talk," he said, beginning to gesture toward me. "Why would anyone put a hit on this town's best mechanic?"

Just as he was about to drink, I smashed my shotgun through his cabinet.

"No more charades!" I shouted. Slightly overblown.

"What are you...? What are you talking about?"

"Milt, I swear to God, if you ask me one more question..." I raised my shotgun to aim near him. Not at him. Not yet. Near him. Hovering in his southeast region. "I'm the one with the twelve gauge. You're the one envying it."

"Jesus, Mike, yeah, of course, I'm telling you all I know. I just wanted to clarify what you mean by *charades* is all." He paused and realized he shouldn't pause. "The guy who called the hit was just a middleman. I don't have access to the top of the food chain."

"Who's the middleman?"

"The name? I don't know who it was"—catching himself again—"but-but-but I was told at the docks. What I was told was, uh, that place at four fifty-one. At the docks. I'm sorry about Maria. Is she okay?"

"Is death okay?"

He took this in for a moment. It was starting to sink in. He started to cry.

So I shot him.

CHAPTER 15

MILT WASN'T DEAD. Milt was dying. I sat on the couch with him.

"Milt," I said calmly. "I'm going to shoot you a second time. I shot you once. Just now. But I'm also going to shoot you again."

"Kh . . . h . . ." he said.

A twelve gauge will tend to make an argument one-sided.

"But before I shoot you again," I added, "I'm going to tell you something."

He struggled to breathe and burbled up blood.

"I'm going to tell you that, in my opinion, the second most vile thing in this world is . . . classism. I hate classism. That's number two."

"Call . . ." he said. "An . . . n . . . n . . . an am . . . bulance."

"Would you like to know number one?"

"Please."

"Good. Thank you. The number one thing I hate in this world . . . is . . . disloyal pricks who stick their log in another man's fireplace."

"Wh-h . . . ?" He found that surprised look again.

Milt was really a lot better looking than I'd allowed myself to think. I could see why Maria had slept with him. Some guys in my position would be angry—that his wife had enjoyed the very handsome qualities of another male, the sleek jawline, the broad shoulders. But not me.

"That means I hate your existence, Milt."

He hid his fat well. Some people can be fat but pull it off. Not me. That's why I jog countless miles per day and eat fashionable amounts of kale.

"You have shifty eyes," I said to Milt. "Your face points one way but your eyes watch stuff at a different angle. How cliché is that? At least be inventively repulsive."

He groped for air, with his hands, then said, "Call . . ."

"Would you like to hear my one French sentence?"

"Call the ambulance. I'll pay you."

Ah, the bribe offer. Right on schedule. "Really? How much is a dopey, no-good, cheating partner's life worth?"

"A hundred and fifty th—"

I shot him again.

He lay there inert. I'd aimed higher this time. The stomach wounds hurt. The chest wounds kill.

I drank his bourbon. I wanted to look tough, but his choice of alcohol tasted like buttered Windex. I spat it out and stood up.

"You may think this is over," I said, "but you're misunderstanding the rules. This isn't over. This is page one."

CHAPTER 16

I WAS DRIVING the speed limit. Updike was next to me in the seat. And my trunk was full.

Of Milt.

After thirty minutes of very focused driving, I arrived at what I now hesitate to call "home." The hardest part was getting him from his house to my car. Solution? Cut him in half. Just like they did Maria. Seemed only fair. I brought the first piece out in a suitcase, the second piece in a golf club travel bag. Each segment still weighed over a hundred pounds, so I'm not saying it was easy.

By now Updike was in sync with my erratic behavior. He himself became more erratic and, oddly, more cooperative.

"C'mon, pal," I said toward his area of the backseat. "Don't look at me like that."

He did. He looked at me like that. The eyes of canine judgment. I could see them in my rearview mirror, gazing at me.

We were going thirty-four miles per hour in a thirty-five

miles-per-hour zone. Cops do actually pull people over for going "too much" the speed limit. It's what drunkards do. It's what serial killers do. I'd already made up my mind at this point how I would handle the situation if I were stopped.

And I *was* stopped.

A cop lit up in my rearview mirror, visible just past the flattened ears of my nervous heap of a pooch. The new police cars have subtle, low-profile lights to fool you, to lull you into cop-oblivious behavior. I was pretty sure I was getting cited for running a light. What I wasn't sure of was whether my trunk had drops of blood on the outside.

I slowed down. He followed me to the side of the road. I parked. He parked. Then came that ugly fifteen seconds when they just sit there behind you. When his door finally did open, he took a long time to approach.

"I *will* kill him, Updike," I murmured out the side of my mouth. "You understand that, right? I'll kill him, if circumstances demand it."

Updike whined that signature dog whine and looked around for the nearest airport. I was sweating right up until the moment Officer Something-or-Other arrived at my door. Six two. One ninety. Mustache. He had a Beretta 9mm holstered. I calculated that I could have my own gun pointed toward his torso twice as fast as he could ready his.

If necessary.

"Good afternoon, sir," I said.

"License and registration," he said.

I complied and we traded the usual three minutes of

dialogue. He left with my license but stopped to look at my plates, which to me felt like he was looking at the trunk.

"There's no blood on there, Updike," I said quietly to Updike. "I checked. No blood. Okay?"

Updike looked backward. He knew the cop was trouble.

My finger had already laid itself upon the trigger of my .38 Special. I could open my door. I could loudly say, "Officer, my left hand is bleeding." He'd yell at me to get back in my car but for a split second he'd look at my left hand. He'd look for the blood, not the weapon. And I'd raise that weapon and power two slugs past the Kevlar, into the small clump of tissue just above the eye sockets.

"Sign this," he said, suddenly back at my window, ticket clipboard in hand.

I must've blanked out for a moment. While I was sitting there, fretting over what he was seeing on my bumper, he had already journeyed all the way to his own car and back.

I signed the ticket.

"Please drive safely," he said. "Life is precious."

Then he walked away.

Done. Thank you for that fortune cookie's worth of wisdom, sir.

When I arrived home—some two hours later, I think—I pulled out Milt: The Prequel and placed it near the rear bumper while I dragged out Milt: The Sequel in a second bag. I brought the complementary works of art down to the basement while Updike followed cautiously behind.

There wasn't enough room next to my silent wife unless I took out a few of the boxes, so I did. I slid them to the middle of the basement, where I knew they'd start to smell within days.

"In ya go, Milt."

I wasn't operating on a "within days" timeline. I barely knew what the next three hours would hold for me. And by the time I'd stashed Milt's carcass, I'd burned through at least one of those precious three hours.

Maria's body hadn't become rigid yet. She was cold, but still supple. Tears welled in my eyes. As much as our romance had dwindled lately, I'd still cried about her every night, softy in bed, or loudly in the shower, or even louder in the car.

I started to caress her cheek with the back of my hand. Then I stopped.

I missed my wife. I couldn't believe somebody had done this to her. Had done this to her, when we were so far from where we should have been. My retirement would've solved everything. I wiped my tears with the inner elbow of my sleeve, sat on the stack of sirloin, and pulled out my cell phone.

"Thank you for calling Whole Foods," answered a chirpy voice. "This is Amber."

"Hi, Amber," I replied. "This is Maria's husband, Michael." She said hi back. "Just a quick heads-up: she's got the flu... and yeah... didn't wanna introduce it to you guys... so... she's gonna stay home for a couple days."

We traded a few useless remarks about how, *gosh, something sure is goin' round lately* and *Stay warm* and *Belichick always tells his team to drink fluids* and I hung up. At first I'd had Milt's upper body on the ground with his lower body hung by the hook. But Maria's cadaver had gotten bumped in the shuffling and slowly rotated toward his.

As much as I resented the current population of this meat locker, I couldn't let them sit there like savages. So I fixed Milt, nice and neat, and let his wobbly head sort of stare at my wife.

"You'd like that, wouldn't you?" I said to his unblinking eyes. I turned to Updike. "C'mon, li'l man."

CHAPTER 17

IF I WAS GOING to enter the docks in daylight hours, I'd need to be ready for a bloodbath.

Milt had said 451. I was pretty sure he meant shipping berth number 451, which was a drop site run by a man named Big Byron. I played the waiting game, sitting in my parked car across the street from the wharf entrance, after hours, staring at a torn photograph of Maria, until a bright-red Escalade pulled in.

Byron. He was that guy. The polyester-track-jacket, medallion-against-a-hairy-chest guy.

"Do you even *try* not to lure feds?" I said quietly.

I'd never seen him in person. For all I knew, he could be black or Asian or young or old. Or, worst-case scenario, not even in the car.

But after a few turns, the rear passenger window lowered an inch and out came an empty can of Red Bull, bouncing to the road behind him. Confirmed: he was in that vehicle. So I followed at a professional distance as his driver took him to the far end of the shipping yard.

I stopped my car behind a tall heap of loading pallets, the only place where I wouldn't be detected by my prey. I was past the point of self-preservation. Every fifteen minutes, my mind would remind me that Maria was gone. I'd cry for a half minute, force myself to forget the thought, and clear my head.

A bloodbath? So be it. I'd already shot one person today. By tonight, why not make it two?

I got out of my sedan and quickly but casually walked toward the first empty doorway I could find, just in case the pilot of the red Escalade was eyeing me from a distance. I doubted it. Guys who install fake chrome aftermarket hubcaps generally don't hire drivers who check mirrors.

I ducked into the shelter of the doorway, counted to ten Mississippi—pretending I was a delivery guy—then headed back to my car, glancing nonchalantly toward the Escalade about a half mile down the road. There it was. Unattended.

Knowing this was my one chance, I sprinted toward my goal. I covered about a half mile in five minutes. When I got close enough to see where they'd entered, I picked up the first rock I could find.

They'd gone into a small warehouse for berth 451. I channeled my inner Cy Young and flung a wild pitch up and over the two-story warehouse so that my rock would land, hopefully, on the far side, on a stack of hollow barrels. Or on something just as loud.

It hit a tin roof. *Whaunk!*

I entered.

CHAPTER 18

I HAD NO idea what to expect inside. There could be thick Slavic dudes in turtleneck sweaters, itemizing a table full of weapons, with additional machine-guns aimed at me. There could be an unchained Rottweiler trained to attack. There could be a missile silo.

Once inside, I saw, happily, that only one inhabitant was visible: the rear end of a guy in overalls, heading away from me, out the back door. The rock had worked.

I didn't catch sight of Byron, but I still didn't actually know what Byron looked like. I was operating on pure instinct. He would be ugly; his guards would be uglier. That was my theory. Find the handsomest guy in the room—and shoot all his friends.

The first person to reemerge from the back hallway was the overalls guy, a 175-year-old man whose osteoporosis bent him clean over like the handle of a human umbrella.

"Can't shoot someone like that," I mumbled to myself.

The old fella looked up, glanced at me, glanced at the

weapon in hand, and proceeded to do absolutely nothing different. He kept shuffling toward his corner of the room, where he picked up a broom and started sweeping. It was as if this place had been stormed by gun-toting enemies at least three times a week for the past decade.

I couldn't hear much because there was static-ridden music blaring from his radio, the lyrics in what I could only guess was Croatian.

I put my gun back in my pocket. Maybe this would be more of a diplomatic mission than I had thought.

"Who're you?" said an abrupt voice from behind my left shoulder.

This was trouble. I hadn't turned around yet but my eleven years as a trained killer told me his intonation was trouble.

"Hey," repeated the voice. "Who the hell are you?"

Showtime.

CHAPTER 19

I HAD NO response to his question, and no idea if the voice behind me was from *one* lone guard approaching me from my flank or from one of *several*.

I'd failed to hear his footsteps—tsk, tsk—letting the radio drown them out. After a moment, I finally turned to face my hosts.

"Who am I?" I restated rhetorically—anything to throw them off guard for even a split second.

I was now facing two men.

"I'm . . . here," I began, "because I was hoping to buy a . . . a . . . um . . . y'know."

They could think I meant drugs or guns or girls. I was dressed like a middle-class American male, easily in the market for any of the above.

"Wrong place, buddy," said the second guy.

"I need a gun," I said. "I need one as soon as possible."

He laughed. "As soon as possible?"

I could tell he was underestimating me. Good. Maybe

he'd assume I was a loser seeking revenge on my cheating girlfriend.

"How much you pay?" he mused.

I needed him to move several feet to his left. I edged to my right so that he'd subconsciously counter. I'd enacted this geometry before, this knight's move.

"Pay?" I said.

"How many thousand you gimme?" He laughed. "What you do with gun?"

"What I do with gun . . . would be something *like* . . ." I let my sentence linger until just the right amount of time had elapsed, then quickly raised my revolver. "*This.*"

And fired four shots at the two men. *Blam blam blam blam.*

Shamefully trite, I know.

Blam. Plus an unplanned shot at an unseen third guy who'd been kneeling to pick up trash off the floor, who'd just now sat up to see what was happening.

It was a barrage in three cones of attack, each grouped around the upper torsos of my opponents. Itemized: I hit one aorta and two lungs. The first thug fell to the ground while the second fell to his knees, clutching a geyser of blood from his neck. The old man with the broom, still sweeping, who maybe was deaf now that I thought about it, didn't flinch.

My intended victims all dropped as scripted, except for the third guy. The memorable performance was from the third guy.

First he stumbled to his feet, then backward through

the open quay doors toward the lip of the dock, where he teetered on the edge. Then he futilely grabbed for the hull of the nearest trawler. This positioned him precariously over the water, balancing... balancing... until, *ploosh,* he fell in.

I trailed him all the way there, more out of curiosity than bloodlust. After a mutual moment of awe, he stopped splashing. He looked at me, then looked at what was on the dock, merely one lunge away from his hand.

I had my revolver up and ready. He was weighing his reaction time. He had to confirm that he was fast enough to scramble for his weapon before I could discharge mine. The not-so-trivial factor in this arithmetic was that I'd already fired *all five* shots of my five-shot cylinder. I was out. I was pointing an empty gun at him.

"Try it," I said. Pure effrontery, pure bravado.

Could I sprint to his gun before he could arm himself with it and fire at me? Based on physics and standard NFL forty-yard dash times, no. He was too far from me. He'd win.

"I hit your buddy in the carotid artery from fifteen yards away." I said this with a voice full of swagger. "You're only *five* yards away. And much more predictable." Could he know that my Smith & Wesson didn't have the capacity for a sixth shot? Was he even counting? And while we're at it, why, Michael, do you carry a gun that holds only five rounds? I pulled back the hammer for philharmonic emphasis. "Don't make me sink you."

He bobbed in the water for a few seconds without

speaking. I could see the math taking place in his head—he was desperately weighing his probabilities. Everything, including that I might be out of ammo. Everything, including his gradual, eventual recognition of my face. He didn't announce it yet but he soon knew exactly who I was.

"I'm not grabbing the gun," he suddenly said; this came with an opening of his palms to demonstrate complicity. I went over and scooted his pistol out of his reach. Then I positioned myself to help him up. The last thing I wanted to do was save the life of a guy who was guaranteed to hunt me down within a week, but what choice did I have?

"You're Byron, aren't you? Can we talk?"

"Go to hell."

"I would prefer we don't antagonize each other. Are you sure we can't talk?"

"Go to hell."

"Fine. If you need negative stimulation, I'm going to show you something that will scare you."

"Go to hell."

He was being combative. So I decided to do this the ugly way. I showed him a picture of my wife.

CHAPTER 20

"YOU SEE THIS?" I held up a small wallet-sized photo.

"Help me get out," said Byron.

"You see this?!" I shook my favorite picture of my wife at him.

It didn't make sense that the big boss had been kneeling to pick up trash off his own floors. The old Croatian fossil in the warehouse kept cleaning. The two dead bodies in the entranceway seemed very dead. And Byron was still treading.

"Her name is Maria Amelia Ryan," I said. "She's beautiful and she's vibrant and she's dead."

"I get it."

"No, you don't. She's dead because of a name and I don't know who that name is." I aimed my gun at his forehead. I was crouched down tight enough that from a distance anyone would think I was just tying my shoe. But there was still no one around this stretch of the quay.

"Suppose... Suppose I... I had a name to give you. You want a source, right? The Goran boy. Right?"

"Who ordered it?"

"I can help you but . . . you're gonna kill me anyway, so the longer I . . . the longer I . . ." He winced from internal pain before eking out his point. "The longer I hold back, the longer I stay alive."

He tried to climb out. No luck, too steep. He took another moment to catch his breath before returning to the negotiation table.

"So why don't w-we try a deal?" he said, wincing. "Let's find a way . . . to guarantee . . . my life . . . and I'll tell you a name."

"No."

He stared at me.

My single syllable arrived with such finality that he lost all his leverage and could only gawk back at me. Two men locking eyes. I wasn't trying to scare him. I'd always wanted my enemies to regard me as respectful and polite.

"Wait," he said. "Wait, wait. Look, I could lie to you, but I'm not gonna lie, I'm just gonna come clean and tell you *I don't know* who ordered the hit."

"You probably just have one functioning lung," I told him. I could see that his wound was pretty bad. "That's hardly a game changer. You climb out, you rest for a month, then you'll regain full health. The catch . . . is . . . you can't climb out without my help."

"Go to hell."

"Eventually, yes. But I'm looking for an answer."

He didn't provide one. He was going to die very soon.

"I'm asking one more time, then I'm walking away to let your blood drip into the Atlantic."

"No! We negotiate."

"I'll tell you what." I flipped my cylinder out to reload. I left one cartridge in my hand for dramatic effect. One cartridge. I did all of this very slowly and with a certain panache. "I don't negotiate but... Do you like strategy games, Byron?" I placed the cartridge on the pavement between us. "This isn't exactly Russian roulette." He was petrified. "See, instead of four empty chambers and *one* bullet... I have one empty chamber and *four* bullets." I spun the cylinder with a classic silent whir. A Wheel of Misfortune. I snapped it in, then abruptly pointed the gun at him and, with no overture, immediately pulled the trigger.

Click! Empty.

"Aagh! You're insane!" he said, heaving for breath. "You're insane. I heard about you."

This got my attention. I lowered my gun. I lowered my voice. "I'm not insane. I have a love of literature and grain-fed meat, but insane? Not true."

I spun the cylinder again.

"I'm telling you," said Byron. "I don't... The..."

I aimed the gun at him.

"I don't know!"

I pulled the trigger again. Click.

Miraculously, I mean quite miraculously, the hammer had clicked on what was the lone empty chamber yet again, twice in a row. The odds of this were astounding. Twenty-five to one. At which point, at last, to everyone's relief, Byron decided all bets were off and spoke rapidly and earnestly. "Okay, okay, okay, wait, okay, listen," he said.

"There was only the initial communication from the lady at the county, that's it. That's it. Okay? Nobody told me the source because it's political, okay? Because Croatian business is absolute, okay? And none of us can risk being part of something inside the family."

"Hang on."

"None of us can. Okay? That's why we don't ask."

"Hang on," I said. "The lady at the county? What does that mean?"

And then he told me all I needed to know. "City, I mean. Not county. The city council. Allison. That lady who handles the docks. It comes from her."

"Allison? Why the hell didn't you say that?"

"I thought you wanted the source."

"Allison O'Hara? I just wanted to know who told you."

"Ohhhhhhhh, thank God," he exclaimed with profound relief. "Thank God. Then please, please, yes. Help me up."

"No," I replied. I shot him. "Time for me to buy a bigger fridge."

CHAPTER 21

CUTTING UP CADAVERS is gross. Truly. I've seen it in TV shows and I get ill just hearing a character *talk* about it.

I left the dock, and left the old osteoporosis fellow alive and kicking. Was this stupid? Of course. But it was my guess that the gentle relic wasn't here in the US with the best of paperwork. He would maintain his low profile.

Then I was heading home with a car full of three dead bodies. I had propped the trio upright in their seats so that to anyone else on the road it'd seem like they were just drunk passengers. I was driving home with all the evidence against me in one place.

"This is for Maria," I said to my carpool as we first hit the road.

"This is for Maria," I said again as I dragged each body to the door of our Kolpak 1010 freezer system.

I had to remove some more of the cardboard containers—a stack of at least four hundred dollars' worth of Whole Foods premium cut.

Couldn't let it all go to waste, so I used some of the grass-fed beef to make dinner for Updike. Real dinner. Candlelit. Folded a linen napkin into his collar. Put a quilted cushion below his hind feet. He deserved it.

He sat upright on the chair, two paws on the edge of the table. The whole thing was defying every domestic rule imaginable for him. He stared at me, riddled with canine insecurity. *You sure about this?*

"It's all you, buddy," I said. "Eat up."

He bent down and nibbled, then stopped to look up at me. Still hesitant.

"C'mon, have confidence, pal." Me telling him what I needed to hear. "Life's about confidence."

He nibbled again. Eyed me again. Nibbled more. Eyed less. Then soon he was burrowing his head in the bowl. I sat there and smiled at the first pleasant tableau I'd beheld in weeks. I'd tried to distract myself with my book, right there at the table. *Le Parfum.* But after two attempts I couldn't distract myself. Each sentence only served to remind me of the urgency of the next step. My next step. Her.

Allison O'Hara.

Allison was a "fixer." Why would a fixer be a link in this food chain? City council was the title she threw around town, but what Allison actually did was troubleshoot the docks—the dingy, violent world of the Mafia shipping trade, smoothing out whatever kinks the "family" might encounter. I would've never connected a lady like her to a Harvard kid.

This was my brain at work, searching for a way to get

to her. Did she hike alone in the woods? Did she walk to church on Wednesday nights through a dark parking lot? I had to discover the best opportunity. I even searched my house for explosives to use on her entourage. Didn't have any. Getting to her meant getting past her legion of stewards, which she would have armed to the hilt. But my dinner with Updike gave me an idea.

CHAPTER 22

ALLISON ATE AT Tidal Moon every week—one of those fancy restaurants with no name on the front, no advertising in town. It had wooden interiors, leather chairs, and real towels in the bathroom, handed to you by a real human immigrant.

Tidal Moon was Allison's venue of choice for girls' night out. For a bachelorette like her, who led a carefully marketed life—Louboutins, Dolce bag, Chanel blush—a midweek meal was legitimate PR.

I was lurking in the alley behind her restaurant.

I'd waited a couple of hours for her chauffeur to pull up and drop her off at the back entrance. That moment never came. It was already 9:15 p.m. I'd been confidently eyeing her bodyguard, who was chain-smoking in the back, and after crouching in the shadows long enough to cramp both my upper thighs, I finally walked over.

But there was nobody there. I'd been eyeing the silhouette of a torn tarp, wafting in the wind.

"Gotta be kidding me," I said to myself.

I retreated back into the shadows until a new bad plan presented itself. The sous-chef opened up the back door to the main kitchen and propped it open while he walked out a bag of trash. "Dinner," I said to myself and entered the restaurant.

I didn't have a tie but I did have on a decent dress shirt. I unbuttoned the top buttons, tousled my thinning hair, flung my thirty-nine-ninety-nine-dollar Mervyn's jacket in the trash, and thereby resembled the general douche who ate there. An unmolested walk through the busy kitchen led me to the dining room, where a cluster of intimate dining tables stood between me and my target.

Allison.

Designer heels and a minimal amount of cocktail dress—she wasn't here to be sipping a Bordeaux, she was here to be *seen* sipping it. Hiding herself at a remote table to seem like she didn't want attention, yet likely going to the bathroom at least thrice an hour so she could parade past fellow diners.

"Caution, Mike," I cautioned myself.

I could see that she was seated with the young wife of our young mayor. Evenings like this were a business move for Allison and I was about to thwart it. A passing busboy was all I needed. The first one to glide by held a tray full of several unfinished soup bowls. I nonchalantly dipped three fingers in the brightest-colored bowl. And thus equipped, I walked over to Allison's table.

I approached her friend from behind. "So sorry to interrupt," I said with neighborly grace, "but I think they just spilled something on you and . . . I'm kinda worried it'll set in." While leaning over to say this, I'd placed my sullied hand upon her shoulder blade and smeared a free sample of *crème du tomato* on her clothing. "This is silk, isn't it?"

"Oh, my God, are you frickin' serious?" she said.

"Without ice water," I said, "the stain is . . . eternal."

She was wearing a Ralph Lauren jumpsuit. Retail price twelve hundred ninety-nine dollars, I'm sure. She would have to completely disrobe to clean it.

She didn't even thank me.

"Unreal," she said, getting up, ready to fire whoever she could fire, marching to the restroom, where she would soon be half naked and scrubbing and cursing.

Allison barely had a chance to process any of this before I sat down in the newly open seat so deliberately, so casually, that the most she could do was launch the "Wh" of "What the f . . . ?"

I placed the napkin in my lap and picked up a menu.

"I hear the duck's good," I told her without looking up. "Me, I avoid fowl."

I paused to truly read the menu. I actually *was* hungry, and the array of entrées that each cost more than my jacket back in the trash can were described quite appetizingly. That's when she piped up.

"If this is a game," she said in hushed syllables, "I'm in no mood."

"Being in no mood is itself a type of mood."

"I have people who can hurt you," she said. "They're in the lobby."

I looked up at her for the first time, my stern countenance prepared. I'd resolved to hide any attraction I'd feel for her once I actually saw how pretty she was, face-to-face. But when it finally happened, I had no chance.

She was all I feared she'd be.

"Is everything okay here?" said the waiter.

He must've caught sight of our fracas from afar because he was suddenly at my side, attentive to Allison's demeanor.

She kept looking at me and neither smiled nor frowned. "Everything's fine," she said to him.

The waiter glanced at me, then glanced back at her. "Are you...?" he began. "Are you sure that you...?"

...don't want our staff to beat him to a deep-fried pulp?

"I'd like you to get him a drink," said Allison, dispatching the waiter with the following: "He'll have a triple IPA. With lime. Quartered."

CHAPTER 23

SHE KNEW MY drink. Jesus Christ, she knew it. Which was both hot and terrifying.

"Look," I said to her, "I'm not here to drag this out."

"You're a moth," she said. "You're hovering by the flame because you have nowhere else to look. Get out of the house."

"It's not that simple."

"Get out before I have you singed."

"I thought you wanted me to stay. You just told the waiter—"

"I *wanted* to avoid a scene."

She was right. I had nowhere else to look.

"Listen," I said. "I don't know why Goran Šovagović Mesic was a name that passed across your desk . . . and part of me doesn't care . . . but whatever the reason, you're gonna tell me who put it there."

She wasn't listening. She was glaring at me—bored, annoyed.

"Or I make calls," I whispered.

That's when her face suddenly lit up. And the calculating woman subsided as a tiny laugh bubbled out of her.

"Wow," she said, sitting back in her seat. "You really are at a breaking point, aren't you?"

"What? No."

"The legendary Mike Ryan. The contract killer. At my table. Trying to play it cool but...isn't quite..."

I couldn't move.

She leaned back in to say, "It's okay if you're losing your good judgment."

"I am not."

"Prove it."

She sat there a moment to let her remark incubate. Prove it?

Then after a smirk, she relaxed, reclined, and recrossed her legs, letting her calf graze my shin, which she pretended not to notice.

"Follow me," she said.

She got up. I had to hurry to stay with her, her long legs striding forcefully across the marble.

The next minute was a blur.

"On my tab," she said to the maître d'.

This woman rendered me a heap of gibberish. I struggled to decipher what was happening as she stopped near the valet to chat with some guy—her chief goon, I think—who then maybe went to look after her soiled girlfriend.

Allison took me around the outside of the restaurant, guiding us toward the riverfront. She was taking me to the park behind the main road. It was late but the public restroom was still lit.

We entered the women's side and she bolted the door behind us. We were alone.

I spoke first. "You certainly—"

She slammed me up against a wall.

If this was a kiss it was going to be wild and decadent. My eyes involuntarily closed. My mouth involuntarily softened. "Respect was invented to cover the empty place where love should be," Karenina said unto Vronsky. I then looked up to find that, yes, Allison's lips were hovering inches away from mine and that, yes, also, well, okay, she now had a gun in her hand, pressed into the softest part of my heart.

CHAPTER 24

I'VE BEEN HELD at gunpoint before. Instead of thinking quickly or wisely, you fixate on one lone, pervasive thought.

You can't believe it's actually happening.

"Back up," said Allison. "Get on your knees."

"If you're . . . If you're gonna kill me . . ."

"Now!" she shouted.

I couldn't believe this was happening. She nodded for me to move toward the rear. My spine complied. My mind raced clumsily for a way, some way—despite the indications that I truly was losing my edge—to reduce her control of the situation.

"Am I here to confess?" I asked.

I could guess what she'd told her henchman just now: to get permission from the top. Permission to kill me.

So I blurted out the only thing that could catch her attention. "You had sex with him, didn't you?"

She had no reaction.

"Goran," I specified. "You had sex with Goran."

She didn't respond right away, and by *right away* I mean there was a trillionth of a second too long in her eye contact with me as her brain improvised her retort.

"No," she said.

Wait a minute.

"Why would you even think that?" she said.

She was lying. I had completely, idiotically, randomly stumbled upon the crux of her only position on this chessboard.

"He's a good-lookin' kid," I said. "He has money. Adrenaline. Yet would still be a bad decision on your part. A decision that would need...I dunno...cleanup. I'm not saying you were the first hand to stir the pot. I'm saying you were willing to approve it." I'd found it. I needed to get her to overthink. "Because let's be real, Allison: the request would've had to go through you. Which you would've had to, under normal circumstances, veto."

She contemplated my tone. She was mapping out the various routes for our predicament. She could smell my conviction. She knew that denial wouldn't work.

"Did you tell anyone?" she asked.

That's what she wanted. That's why she'd brought me here—so she could survey the damage she'd done. That's why I wasn't dead yet.

"I get it now," I said. "The IRA and Croatian Mafia. Literally in bed together." I'd connected her two worlds through the back door.

"Whether or not *any* of this is true, I need to know if you've told anyone this stupid theory."

"I've been on your side of the interrogation table, Allison." I started speaking with just enough smugness to enrage her. "In fact, I was just interrogating someone this morning when—"

"Did you tell anyone?!"

Blam.

She'd leaned in too close and in a dizzying flurry of fingers I'd grabbed for her gun so that, within an instant of our two sets of hands gripping one tiny weapon, I discharged it.

We were now tugging on it. Both of us.

Not sure yet where the bullet had gone. My muscles were flooded with adrenaline. Our web of limbs hit the wall, her grip versus my grip. She elbowed me in the jaw, sharp jabs from her 130-pound frame, until I was soon pinning her back. Three of our four hands now held "our" gun so that it was aimed at the side of her head while our fourth hand—my left hand—was free to grip her chin.

I was winning the battle and she knew it. So, quick thinker that she was, she flipped the script.

Her body changed, she stopped trying to kick me, she stopped trying to elbow me, she popped her palms open in surrender. She started to laugh.

"I have something," she said.

"Don't move."

She didn't move. She laughed harder. The bullet had pierced her tricep. Our faces were inches apart.

"What's so funny?" I asked.

"I have something that will change your mind."

"Tell me who ordered the hit."

She smiled.

"What?" I growled at her, searching her disposition until I started to see, with growing dread, that maybe the battle's winner wasn't me. "Wait. Where did your driver go?"

"To get me leverage."

"Where exactly did he go?"

"To get your dog."

CHAPTER 25

"MY DOG?!" MY blood was boiling. Allison was playing a very dangerous game. She didn't know how irrational I could be.

The self-preserving move on my part would be to comply. She was assuming I'd be self-preserving. "I know what's wrong with you," she said.

"Back away from me!"

"Listen to me, Michael Ryan. I know *exactly* what's wrong with you."

"Turn around! And face the wall! Hands!"

She couldn't possibly have my dog. He'd be too fast. He wouldn't trust the front door.

"I know why you can't function anymore," she said.

"Hands against the wall!"

I didn't care if they found the basement and the frozen bodies. I just wanted Updike to run.

"I swear to God," I said, "if you hurt one single . . . !"

I slammed her backward against the mirror.

She was freshly invigorated. She spoke with new strength. "My phone is going to ring when the animal is in the possession of my driver. Before that happens, we will reverse roles and you will give me back my gun. You're strong, Michael. See that? I know you. I know you had trouble in your marriage. She didn't appreciate you."

"You're sick."

I spun her away from the mirror, then shoved her back toward it, so her chest slammed against it, so my chest slammed against her.

Yet she remained in control. "You can come out ahead here, Mike."

She'd probably had hundreds of enemies beaten up in hundreds of lobbies and parking lots, but I, for some reason, must've stood out as one of the rare victims who required personal attention.

"I won't kill your dog unless you make me," she said.

"Who ordered the hit?"

"I won't unless you ch—"

Blam! I fired the gun and blasted a bullet into her hamstring.

She winced deeply, yet seemed to disrespect the pain. Her eyes searched into me.

With two bullets in her body, she seemed to understand me just ever so slightly more.

I'd just won the war.

"I admire you," I said to her. "You brought me here alone, *alone,* because you needed to defy a broken system. Stay still. You were never actually going to get your so-called leverage—leverage you only happened to mention after you lost control. I admire you, Allison, but you're done. Tell me who ordered the hit."

She took one last strategic breath. She didn't have my dog—I saw it in the way she flinched. It was a shift in dominance. She eyed me, searching for a promise that I wouldn't kill her.

My question lingered in the air. She decided to answer it. "His brother."

CHAPTER 26

HIS BROTHER?

There it was. The fruit of my entire day's work.

"His brother paid me to arrange the kill," she said. "The son of Ivan Mesic called me to request a public hit."

Ivan fathered a son who would request the murder of his other son. It would've been ghastly to hear if it didn't make sense. In this business, the idea of an intrafamilial feud felt sadly obvious.

"Okay?" she said. "Now, why don't you . . . let me leave this room . . . so that I can then live in healthy fear of you . . . so that you can then go home to your wife?"

"My wife?"

"She needs you."

"My wife is . . . uh . . . well . . . She's dead."

"What?"

"She was sliced in half."

"Who'd be stupid enough to kill the wife of a relentless maniac?"

"The maniac himself."

It felt good to say.

"Please let me go, Michael. You're smarter than this."

"I killed my wife, face-to-face, just like we are now."

"I don't believe you. I don't believe you're that far gone."

So I ended the conversation with a parting gift. I shot Allison O'Hara for a third time, gun pointed at her head.

"Yeah," I said to her as she slid down the wall, dead, "neither did she."

CHAPTER 27

IT FELT GOOD to admit it.

"The maniac killed his own wife," I repeated. It was Allison's phrasing. Maniac? That's a bit flattering. Maniacs are go-getters, highly motivated, athletes, CEOs. I was none of that. I was just a guy driving the divinely sensual corpse of Allison O'Hara to the parking lot of the Alluvial Tavern. There I would leave her curled up with my spare tire as I sought one final beer.

"Triple IPA," I said, taking a seat. "No lime."

The instant she saw me, the bartender seemed to know I'd just had an encounter.

"You have a new lady?" she said. An accusation more than a query.

"Yeah, she's in the trunk of my car."

Ms. Bartender pushed a beer toward me and left it halfway out of my reach as she went back to the kitchen. She hadn't liked me in general; now she didn't like me specifically. I pulled out two books, one of which was of course *Anna Karenina*. The other was *Le Parfum,* its final chapters dog-eared so I could relive their glory.

Within minutes I was done and closed the book—an act that cued the bartender.

"I just want you to know," she said, returning uninvited. "I think you're manipulative. I think you tell people what they want to hear. Including yourself."

I toasted her, midair. I had no rebuttal. She toasted back with her favorite finger.

I opened *Anna Karenina*. Chapter one. I read the overture to the greatest mirror ever held up to social chaos. Then I left the bar and drove Allison's remarkably cooperative corpse to the home built on top of my basement. The front door was locked. The front porch was fine. Nobody had been there. Nobody had come for Updike.

"I tip my hat," I said to the cadaver in my arms. "That was quite a bluff."

From inside came a few happy yips, and once my chin was within reach, he greeted me with licks until I hugged him tight enough to force that wiggle that dogs do. Where they flop their head around and try to break your nose, then do a lap around the room to boomerang back.

We don't deserve dogs.

I hoisted Dead Allison onto my shoulder and brought her down to the Kolpak 1010 freezer system to be the sixth inductee in my hall of fame. Maria, Milt, Byron, Byron's two friends. Everyone was rigidly in place. It was a little scary to turn on the light—I'm not impervious to being spooked by ghosts, and so forth.

"I was loyal to you," I said to Maria. "Allison made advances on me but I remained loyal."

Maria didn't seem to believe this.

"Yet," I said, "of all the people in the world for you to betray me with, you chose a man who was *out to get me?!*"

I waited for a rebuttal. None. I left the freezer. I walked upstairs to grab Updike's leash. He needed a walk. I needed a walk. We had things to discuss, he and I, and once outside, once there were a few blocks of chilly night air behind us, I told him the truth.

"I just want you to know...that...what happened to your mom...wasn't something I wanted."

I let that admission hang in the air. I almost had the feeling someone was following us, but I felt that way a lot lately.

I lowered my voice regardless. "I'm, uh, I'm sorry she's gone."

We walked in silence a bit. He peed on three bushes.

"What I'm trying to tell you is, I did it in self-defense. She was trying to murder me. She and Milt, they were conspiring to..." I stopped. Again I heard someone following us.

Had to be pure paranoia. Updike would've growled long before I would've noticed anything. Although there was now something oddly enticing for him wedged in the side bushes. Nothing unusual—for a dog to stop for a sniff—but it did seem peculiar that someone had left what looked like a piece of raw steak by the sidewalk.

"What is *that?*" I said to him.

Updike is never opposed to a second or ninth dinner, so he wasn't going to question it.

I only had to look up to see the explanation.

Two guys in ski masks.

CHAPTER 28

UPDIKE SAW THEM, too. He instantly took off for the closest guy, top speed.

"Updike, no!" I yelled.

The man saw the snarling little jaws and hopped up the slope of the nearest front yard, then sprinted around the back as a midsize dog pursued him deep into the shrubbery.

"Updike!" I started running.

And soon the other ski mask guy was running after me. We all emerged through the foliage in a footrace down the alley. I didn't have my gun with me, which was stupid, and there weren't any places to duck into, so it would be a clean shot for them.

"Updike, no!" I yelled.

My main concern, only concern, was my dog. When I rounded the corner I saw no sign of him or the first guy who had pursued him. I had to assume this was a good thing. Maybe his canine GPS would guide him home.

And then they'd know where I lived, if they didn't already.

I should've been rifling through my mental list of who could possibly be chasing me, so I could make a plan, but that line of thinking was cut short when I was put in a choke hold from behind.

The assailant had come out of nowhere. He must've dropped his knife or his pistol, or whatever he had, because he chose to grapple me. His partner arrived just in time to participate.

I'm not a huge guy. But I'm scrappy. We fought hard. One guy in front of me. One guy choking me from behind. The ideal maneuver here would have been for me to exploit the grip of the guy behind me by flinging my legs upward and kicking the chin of the guy in front.

"Stay still!" shouted one of them.

The time was ripe. I leapt upward from my half squat and launched a karate kick at the forward guy.

And missed.

Absolutely missed. Airballed, then came crashing down on the ground in a heap of athletic shame. However, it was a fall that also brought my primary assailant down with me.

"Ooooooph," said everyone.

We were all stunned. The guy in front had his gun, but because of the new tangle, he had no clear shot. So I had a moment to kick toward his jaw. Another Michael Ryan kick—my foot naturally caught his kneecap instead. I'd somehow neutralized both my opponents in two sad moves and seized my first chance to scramble off.

I could hear them follow.

I didn't want to head into my own backyard but that seemed like the only way to get my hands on a weapon. I hopped my fence, sprinted through the tall grass (that Maria used to complain I never cut), and prepared my shoulder for the impact that was coming as I busted down my own back door.

I'd stashed weapons in my house for emergency purposes: the shotgun was upstairs, the revolver was upstairs, the Taser was upstairs, and the Glock 19 with laser sight was in the kitchen cupboard, where I was heading, full speed until I collided with a third ski mask guy. Who elbowed me in the throat like only a professional would.

And knocked me out cold.

CHAPTER 29

I WOKE UP gradually, minutes later, on the floor of my kitchen. Hours later? With the vague sound of barking in the next room. A blurry ceiling was the backdrop to three faces now looming over me.

The ski patrol had assembled and they had guns, aimed in my direction. I had nothing. I felt like crying. What had I done right this week? This year? All I had left to embrace was the four-legged idiot barking in the next room, and I couldn't even keep him safe. My hands—I extended them outward slowly in the surrender position.

I almost wanted to make a quick, staccato move and bait these men to end it all, just as long as they'd subsequently open the door for my dog.

"Just do what's right," I said to the ringleader.

He didn't move for a second. He was hovering something gold over my body.

"Just do—"

"Michael Ryan?" he said.

He let that gold thing fall from his hand so that it wafted downward and landed directly on top of me. It was an envelope. Then he bludgeoned my skull.

CHAPTER 30

THEY'D LEFT. I didn't see them go—I woke up and they were no longer in my kitchen. I'd blacked out after the fancy envelope was tossed onto my chest. I didn't hear Updike barking anymore, but at this point I wasn't worried. I felt his presence.

"I already hate whatever this is," I mumbled to myself.

I did a half sit-up to inspect the envelope before touching it.

I read what was written on the front. "To Ryan."

No return address. I tore it open to find a greeting card inside that looked like a wedding invitation. It was a banquet announcement printed in Croatian except for the scrawl at the end.

"I . . . expect . . . you."

I could barely decipher the rest of the scribble but I'd already anticipated who it was from. His name was at the bottom. My former boss.

Ivan Mesic.

The man who ran Boston's slice of Croatia. The man whose son was dead on a Harvard campus. Ivan the Terrible.

So why had he sent three guys in hoods to almost kill me? The "kill me" part wasn't surprising. The "almost" was.

I checked on Pupdike. He was fine. They'd shoved him in the bathroom and shut the door. I showed him the envelope. At this point, he deserved to be fully informed. The invite had beautiful calligraphy and the location was one I knew. Bay Standard Hotel. Saturday evening. Formal attire.

"That's where I'm going," I said to him.

He sniffed the envelope without comment. It was likely I'd be walking into my own tomb, but I knew I'd have to go.

They wanted to kill me. And I wanted them to *want* to kill me.

CHAPTER 31

THERE WERE SECURITY personnel standing along every wall of the ballroom. Not just chiseled, Slavic men in dark suits on headsets, but cops. Ivan-owned Boston cops. Bribes ran deep in these woods. Croatian money meets IRA money and it converges on the shores of Boston Harbor. Allison had presided over that junction, and though her death would jostle the local hierarchy a bit, its effect would be nothing compared to Ivan's upcoming expansion.

I mean, look around. He was starting an empire.

"Your coat, sir?" said the porter.

So this was high society. A garish hotel crowd with gold balloons, gold ice sculptures, gold-colored champagne on gold trays, gold caviar, gold-dusted prawns, and all of it carried by gold-painted supermodels.

"Your coat?" repeated the porter.

In every direction I looked there was a steady stream of plump tuxedos and skinny women. Prosecution of the sex trade was at an all-time high but clearly Ivan's business was thriving.

"Mr. Ryan?" said a voice approaching from the side.

It was the concierge. I didn't know I was recognizable. I felt like the scruffy middle school kid who'd snuck into prom.

"I trust you'll spend some time enjoying our open bar and gourmet buffet," he said, then gestured. "When you have a moment, we'll show you to the waiting room."

"S-sure," I said, unsure.

I pressed my forearm against the lapel of my rented tux, subtly dragging it down my chest to test for the bulge of my gun. I couldn't imagine I was the only one in this room packing heat right now, but I didn't want to be identifiable as such. They literally had Boston PD with rifles guarding the front. Rifles.

"There he is," murmured someone next to me.

Everyone in the crowd began fussing over whatever was taking place above us. Visible on the balcony, an entourage of bodyguards and underfed women was flanking the small-statured, big-knuckled Mr. Ivan Mesic himself. He was now flashing a syndicated smile for the guests below.

"Really?" mumbled a random guy next to me. "So this is how the underground keeps a low profile?"

I looked over. One of those sideways talkers—some guy who couldn't wait to state his disapproval of whatever social blemish was in front of him. He didn't know who I was other than that I looked like someone who'd enjoy gossip. I wouldn't. Which didn't deter him in the slightest. "Maybe writing a ten-million-dollar check to city hall to quote, unquote 'assist the fight on street crime' is what keeps him so anonymous."

I didn't answer.

It didn't matter. "City council each gets a cut," he continued. "Police gets a cut. Bureau gets a cut. And then guess who? The dockworkers get a cut."

"Bravo!" yelled the crowd after whatever Ivan had just said.

"Because at the end of the day," continued my barnacle, "it's all about the docks. It's about cargo. Cargo standing next to us in six-inch heels." He laughed, then scooted even closer to say even more laterally, "But I ain't complainin'."

Please don't touch me.

I'd worked for Ivan Mesic in the past, but human trafficking hadn't been in his repertoire back then. There were marketable women everywhere. His dukedom had broken new ground.

"Croatian people've had a rough go," I murmured back to the guy.

He wasn't listening. Ivan's rousing speech was coming to a crescendo. The crowd was caught up in it, my barnacle included.

"If at all!" yelled Ivan—the punch line to whatever anecdote he'd just roused his audience with. *"If. At. All."*

"Tonight is your night!" continued Ivan. "My way of thanking you! So let's rock!"

Applause and cheers erupted. He certainly didn't *seem* like a grieving father, did he? I turned to head toward the nearest source of beer—anything to placate the drying disdain in my gut—only to collide with the tiny concierge.

"Mr. Ryan," said the concierge. "It's time."

We rode in a private elevator on the far side of the building. Two quietly angry-looking men stood on either side of me while the wiry little concierge stood in front.

"Shan't take but a moment," he said.

We didn't go to the top floor. We went to the bottom, where we entered a large laundry room. The staff was immediately removed.

Dismiss the witnesses. I get it.

I kept my hands visible and benign. I knew the guards would take my gun from me. I knew they'd frisk me for a second piece of hardware. They did. And found nothing. Ivan then entered the room with two guys behind him, which made five henchmen total, which, along with us, made seven—seven grown men in a crowded laundry room.

CHAPTER 32

"MIKEY," SAID IVAN. "Thank you for coming." He had a very disarming sweetness to him. You don't scale the top of the criminal mountain without charm.

"Ivan," I said. "Pleasure's mine."

"You're teasing me but that's good. I appreciate the effort." He clapped his hands once. "So... do you know why you're here?"

"Uh..." I droned. "Execution?"

"Of?" He looked genuinely perplexed until he suddenly threw his head back in gleeful epiphany. "You?! Hahahahahaha." The signature Bond villain laugh. Where did they all learn this? "No, no, no, Mike, c'mon." It was the first time tonight he seemed even remotely happy—briefly—and then he got serious again. "I'm not here to harm you. I'm here, believe it or not, to offer you... yes, offer you... a lot of money. A *lot* of money."

I had no response.

"This room is crowded so you have witnesses," he said. "I'm making a business proposal."

I had nothing to say. I hadn't expected this.

"My son has been murdered," said Ivan. "I don't know who did it. I don't care. I just want the individual dead."

He summoned yet another goon into the room. Maximilian. I didn't actually know if that was his name or not, but I'd never seen someone look more Maximilian than this two-legged tank. Maximilian carried a large duffel bag in each of two gargantuan hands.

"Here is one million dollars in US cash," Ivan said. "I'm showing it to you because you need to know it's there. Incentivizing."

Maximilian unzipped both bags. Inside were stacks of our cherubic Mr. Franklin.

"Find out who killed my son and kill him. On the spot. No questions asked. No torture. No theater. Just kill him wherever you find him. I don't care if he's clutching his newborn daughter. Midbaptism. Inside the goddamn Vatican. Make him dead."

He took one step closer to me to emphasize his conclusion.

"And the money will be yours."

CHAPTER 33

ONE MILLION IN cash. That would be my new retirement plan. I'd previously regarded a mere hundred thousand as the gateway to a new life, but one entire *million?* It'd be a six-digit funeral pyre to singe every inch of my old self. And a lifetime supply of fine cuisine for my dog.

"Thank you, Ivan," I said. "I'm in."

Maximilian squatted down, paused, made sure I saw the contents—I did—then zipped up the duffel bags. Ivan turned to me. I'd thought our time here was done, but no, this wasn't a deal that ended on a handshake. "Beautiful," he said. "But first . . . But now . . . Please. Yes? You join me for a drink. Yes?"

Tearful nights were etched in his face.

"One drink?" I said.

"Please. It's very Croatian." He missed his son. I could see it now, in his eyes.

He and his entourage ushered me up to the hotel's back ballroom, which had been set up as a temporary casino for that night. They'd brought in luxury gaming tables for blackjack, craps, and even roulette. Ivan walked with me to the middle of the hoopla, glad-handing fifteen different business associates along the way. Then, amidst his smiling and waving at the elite, he mumbled, without looking at me, without breaking character, a rather terrifying sentence. "Mike," he began, "you . . . uh . . . *you* didn't have anything to do with the death of my son, did you?"

He didn't stop his stride or stop his parade wave. Which meant he was *completely* paying attention. I had but one chance to answer this correctly or be decapitated.

CHAPTER 34

MY BLOOD RAN cold. "The hit on Goran?" I said, for needless clarification.

"Yes." *Don't be casual, Mike. Don't be rigid.*

"Whoever pulled the trigger... won't be alive by the end of the week."

My voice trembled, I knew. I didn't feel convincing. I kept doing the one thing you shouldn't do when you lie: visualize the truth—the alley where Milt blasted six flesh-eating rounds into two twenty-year-olds. Worse, I was visualizing the kid's only brother ordering the hit.

"I'll make sure of it," I said.

The brother's name was Vassotav or something, I thought. I vaguely remembered Ivan mentioning him years ago.

"I know," said Ivan. "I know you will. I offered the job to a few other mechanics but you're the only one who has the *jaja.*"

He turned to his posse expectantly.

"We're here to enjoy ourselves," he said. A tray of glasses of plum brandy had arrived for us to pluck from.

"*Živjeli,*" said the group.

"*Živjeli,*" said Ivan.

"God help me," I said to myself, under my breath, before gulping down the two-ounce serving of battery acid.

I thought about the prospect of locating my new target. The brother. Varrotav. Or whatever his name was. He could've been anywhere in Boston. *If* he was even in Boston. If he wasn't, he—fitting the infamous playboy reputation I remembered—could now be anywhere in the world, behind a swarm of machine-gun owners.

A second and third round of Croatian liquor were soon sloshing inside me. My mental facilities dulled. The golden glow of the room became a haze. Music blended, and details became friendlier.

Ivan had tallied a seventh or eighth glass of his national blood. His arm was soon around me, bodyguards in Armani suits following us without smiling. We headed toward a back room and a private card table.

"I would like to introduce you to someone," said Ivan. "Someone who may be of help in your endeavor. Someone who insists that tonight we celebrate life itself."

Ivan jovially pointed to the chair at the far end of the poker table. Seated in it was a young man of about twenty-three years of age.

"This is my other son, Vatroslav," he said.

Vatroslav. That was the name. He said, "You should join us, Michael. Our game is under way."

My search was over before it had even started.

CHAPTER 35

I HAD TO focus on the basics. *All the variety, all the charm, all the beauty of life is made up of light and shadow.* When I get nervous, I mentally sift through passages of Tolstoy, hunting down a remedy for the feeling. Not sure where it had gotten me this time. Light and shadow?

I sat down with Vatroslav and Ivan for a bone-chilling game of five-card stud. I paired two sevens on the very first hand.

"Raise," I said.

I'm no fool. You don't walk into a room like this and expect an honest deck.

"How much?" he said.

Vatroslav Mesic. Shorter than his father. Equally hirsute. Much more cunning.

"Fifty bucks," I said.

I wasn't playing to win. I was playing to look like I thought I could. To determine whether or not *he* knew that I knew. Could he have found out I'd talked to Allison? Could he have found out I'd killed her?

"Call," said Ivan.

"Call," said his son.

If he were ruthless enough to order a hit on his own brother, what would he do when he learned that his father had just purchased his demise?

The next cards were dealt. A couple of jacks landed elsewhere and I got no help from an eight of clubs. They could think I was on a straight draw, but that'd be a sucker's play. Nobody smart would fear it. They'd just bet me off.

"Mike always overthinks the numbers," joked Ivan.

Watching him, I calculated there was no way he knew "it" was a family affair. I'd seen every strain of lie that the Boston criminal population ran on. No one's *that* good. If you're aware that your own son killed your other son, you don't relax the way Ivan Mesic did.

By the advent of the final card, I'd failed to improve my sevens. They remained a dull working-class duo, no more, no less. Yet in a game like five stud, virtually any pair will earn you the win.

"I raise one hundred fifty," said the brother.

"Call," said his dad.

"I'm out," I said.

"No way," said the brother. "Really?" He was genuinely lamenting the lack of competition from me. "C'mon. I'll spot you the money."

"Sorry," I replied. "I can't."

"A loan. An IMF loan," he joked. "Developing nations."

We weren't playing for a big sum, but it was definitely beyond my disposable income bracket. The irony of seeing a million dollars downstairs and coming to this room to fret over a couple hundred was not lost on me.

"I can't accept your generosity," I said. "I don't have the cards and I don't have the cash."

"Why do I seriously doubt *you* don't have cash?" joked the brother. His eyes lingered on me, the word *you* slightly elongated.

Jesus Christ: he was talking about the hundred and fifty thousand I'd been assigned. He didn't know about the million. He was talking about the bounty he himself had put on his own brother.

This was beyond reckless. Ivan was sitting right *next to us*.

"Stop flirting," said Ivan.

Luckily, Vatroslav's father's bloodstream was basically syrup at that point. He was swaying just trying to sit still.

You seriously doubt, kid?

The son's remark echoed in my head. It was a daredevil's move. His father could expose both of us, right there at the table. I didn't even want to glance toward him. There were four armed guards stationed in the room with Strojnica ERO imitation Uzis. Ivan could signal his platoon to eviscerate us. He could, but again, the alcohol. Ivan suddenly giggled. He drunkenly said, "Fold."

Ivan could've stayed in the hand for free. But he didn't. Vatroslav was left alone to show us what turned out to be, indeed, his pair of eights.

I didn't know what dollar amount he'd wanted me to gamble and lose, but neither of us were happy with the outcome.

"Good hand," he said.

"Good deal," I said back.

My heart was racing. I got up and bowed my head to Ivan, a nod of respect, needing to be out of there before I sank into a vortex of anxiety. Ivan of course grabbed my forearm before I could rotate toward my escape route. "My sons are *ev*-verything to me," he said.

"Understood," I said.

"Find the bastard who tore my boy from me and tear that bastard from this planet."

"Understood."

"For that," he said, "I'll be v-very grateful to you."

I glanced at Vatroslav, then looked back to the father and gave him my vow. "I'll kill him, Ivan. I'll kill him when he most expects it."

CHAPTER 36

THE PRIZE WAS one million dollars. I began to tell myself I'd buy a new house. Sell the old one. Move on. A departure from a home whose every nook reminded me of a woman I could no longer touch. My second thought was a daily array of gourmet bones for Updike. It was around 2:00 a.m. when I finally returned to my porch.

"Sell," I said to myself. "Last job. Then sell."

Before sitting down at the poker table of life, mere hours earlier, I was plotting how my week would be devoted to tracking my target—bribing dance club owners for intel, scouring brothels, conducting a statewide manhunt. But Vatroslav—the son, the brother, the killer, the bastard—had been seven feet away from me. And judging by the final smirk on his face, he wasn't about to run.

"Hey, little man," I said to Updike. "Lemme check on our tenants, okay?"

Updike had greeted me at the door, tail whapping against whatever made the most noise. Together we went downstairs to the Kolpak 1010 freezer system to tell Maria the latest news, and to tell her yet again that I was sorry things had gotten so dire. I took a preparatory breath and opened the freezer door to confront the imagery. Nothing had changed. Everyone—all six of my guests—had remained in the exact same positions with the exact same facial expressions. They even smelled the same. A faint odor of lemon.

Maybe not surprising that no one had moved. But then most people have never stood in front of a dead spouse and dead backstabber, propped up next to a dead heap of middlemen.

"Can I trust you to take care of Updike?" asked Maria. There I was, checking the frost levels, inspecting the outer air ducts for incriminating odors, and reducing the risk of an alarming spike in my electric bill. These weren't the idiosyncrasies of a madman. This was professional survival. I even scrubbed the upstairs flooring, in every room—took several hours, despite a severe lack of sleep—to keep the place pristine. I slid both house keys onto a special key ring and inserted the key ring into the penultimate chapter of my copy of *Anna Karenina,* as a bookmark.

"To answer your question," I said to Maria, "Updike trusts me. He trusts me to hold one principle above all others. Loyalty."

I closed the door and locked it. The dog and I left on schedule.

CHAPTER 37

IF VATROSLAV WASN'T staying at the Bay Standard Hotel, he was probably hidden in some equally grandiose lodging on the trendy side of town. I had a list of candidates, but instinctually the Bay Standard felt like the place to start.

The day was moving fast. I entered the lobby wearing a bulky Patriots hoodie and a Sox cap. I stood by a column and made a phone call to the concierge desk just yards in front of me. It was a trick I'd learned a few years ago while tracking down a stubborn target in a six-day, five-night self-barricade in a suite whose room number I'd never had.

"Bay Standard, this is Tangelo," said the voice answering my call. "How may I provide you with award-winning service?"

"Tangelo," I whispered into the phone. "Please listen closely..."

I told him I had a thousand dollars in cash for him if he'd pass on a warning to one of his guests. I told him that guest was Vatroslav Mesic. The catch was, I already knew what Tangelo would do.

Tangelo would refuse. If something bad were to happen, and a particular mob boss were to find out, Tangelo would face early termination.

Tangelo would realize all this midconversation. We'd then hang up with nothing gained.

I knew all this before dialing.

The real value for me was what Tangelo would do after our call. He wouldn't use the phone to warn his guest. He'd visit his guest in person. And that would be my chance to follow him.

"May I place you on hold a moment?" Tangelo said.

"Okay."

I felt good. I felt like I hadn't lost my edge.

But Tangelo didn't walk anywhere. I watched him. He didn't even initiate a new call. What Tangelo did was give some squirrelly-looking valet two sentences' worth of instruction. Then that valet came straight toward my column, and straight to me.

"Here," said the valet, and he held out a parking permit.

I had no words prepared.

They knew I'd come here? And would stand by this column?

"Mr. Ryan," said the valet. "It's for you."

"S-sorry?" I said, taking the paper from his hand.

But he left without discussion. My ruse had been outrused.

The parking permit was for something called the Osiris

Heights Condominium Complex. I'd never heard of it, but it sounded like a stack of McMansions built in the past twelve minutes, stocked with rich bachelor kids from the Mediterranean.

This thing in my hand was a not-so-subtle hint that my target was there, awaiting my arrival. He'd anticipated my gambit and was taunting me with a formal invitation to mimic his father's formal invitation.

"Vatroslav," I mumbled, "I salute the move."

Any self-preserving man would skip the million dollars. I'd be dead upon arrival. But, as we are learning, I am no self-preserving man.

CHAPTER 38

ONE HOUR LATER, with no stops at any taverns, I would be parking my car down the street from those Osiris Heights condominiums. I would pull into the loading zone of a nearby public library, a half street down from the target building, perched on a river just across from Boston's skyline. To the left, the endless Atlantic. To the right, the Cradle of Liberty. If you're going to die, you might as well die with a view.

"Stay here, pup." I scratched Updike's chin, then put my Bruins beanie on. I kept my Patriots hoodie snug. "I'll be back in nine minutes."

He whined.

"I'll do what I gotta do and I'll leave, okay?"

He whined.

We'd parked a block away to facilitate any possible stealthy arrival. They knew I was coming but I still needed to pretend I had a chance. On the brisk walk toward my doom, I rehearsed.

The first line of defense was likely the front desk staff. Honestly, what was I supposed to say? "Hello, my name is Guy About to Die Upstairs. Would you please inform Mr. Riddle Me with Bullets that I've arrived? Thank you. I'll wait." Every single minimum-wage-making individual I'd encounter would have been briefed on how to *handle* me. In fact, it was likely that one of them—the plumber, the maid, the cable guy kneeling by a toolbox containing a Beretta M9A3 with suppressor—would be the grim reaper. I'd be killed when I least expected it, while most expecting it.

"Mr. Michael Ryan to see Mr. Vatroslav Mesic," I said to the front desk staff member.

"He's expecting you," said the front desk staff member.

That's how it was going down. Seconds later I was alone in the elevator, watching the numerals climb to "PH." I should've had my gun drawn, ready to fire away at whatever might appear beyond the sliding doors.

I didn't.

I had a bottle of Kamešnica plum brandy. The one errand I had run along the way.

The elevator nestled to a stop and I walked into what felt like a carpeted air lock. *Thought I killed you at Harvard,* I said to myself upon seeing him. No, but all these bodyguards looked alike.

Vatroslav gestured for me to hold still, then had me slowly pirouette for him while his massive hands groped. He discovered my Smith & Wesson revolver—they always do—and took it.

What a joke of an apartment.

Picture three point eight million dollars spent as idiotically as possible on decadent all-white postmodern lowest-bidder neo-conformist decor. Wherever you looked you saw a bad decision. The odd walls. The couch from outer space. The rug with a Nike logo on it.

Then there was Vatroslav, standing by the distant window. I almost expected him to be in a velvet robe and monogrammed slippers, casting his gaze toward the bay while quoting Sun Tzu before snapping his fingers to have my throat slit from behind.

He was in jeans and a track jacket. Didn't even dress for the part.

"You actually showed up," he said.

"Figured you had questions that only work on a second date," I replied.

"Yeah. How *did* you know I had a pair of eights?"

He was as boring as I'd hoped.

"Seriously," he repeated. "How?"

Off to the side was a barefoot supermodel at a glass dining table busying herself with her phone. Part of me felt relieved to see her there. Her presence meant I might not be shot at. But after some good ole-fashioned pessimistic thinking, I remembered that imported sex trade girls are shown as much violence as possible as often as possible, so that they have motivation to cooperate. The guy behind me was armed with a delayed-blowback Croatian VHS-2 assault rifle. I made no eye contact with him. I crossed the room and sat in an armchair and started to undo the cork on the bottle I was still carrying.

This was way ahead of schedule. I'd meant to uncork it at the most strategic point in the upcoming banter. I stopped.

"Really?" said young Vatroslav. I couldn't tell whether he was impressed or insulted. "You sit down in my chair, you give up your gun, you keep your back to the man with the VHS-2, you ignore my question."

He said all this after observing me just doing nothing for a full minute. He was oddly patient despite his youth.

"This is not the skillful Michael Ryan I know of."

"He's retired." I finished opening my bottle, then took a Balkan-sized swig. When in doubt, talk about yourself in the third person.

Vatroslav came over and sat in the armchair opposite mine. I was in doubt. Terrified. He was somewhat bewildered by my actions. So was I.

"You're not on suicide watch, are you?" he asked.

I took another swig. The alcohol content of this swill was gut-wrenching. Kruskovac brandy, they called it. I set it down on the ottoman between us. I felt ill. Vatroslav snatched the bottle and sat back with it, then looked at me, then patiently rotated the label in his hand to read the good news.

"Jesus," he said. "This is a three-thousand-dollar Kamešnica."

"Tastes like congealed urine."

"Urine? I should kill you for saying that." He drank some. "But I'm going to kill you anyway." Then he drank more.

We didn't talk for another painful minute, after which I

cleared my throat and began. "Do you know the ending of Patrick Süskind's *Le Parfum*?"

"What?"

"It's a book. There's a passage in the middle. *'Se rendre parfaitement inintéressant. Et c'est tout ce qu'il voulait.'*"

"Why is this warm?" Vatroslav said. "Brandy is supposed to be the temperature of dawn."

"'He succeeded in being considered totally uninteresting. And that was all he wanted.'"

Vatroslav stared at me, embarrassed for me. "Do you have any women in your life who don't find you dull?"

"Do you have any women in your life who don't come by shipping container?"

I was fully invested.

He stood up and nodded to his thug. His thug stepped forward, machine-gun in hand. I should've left a handwritten note on my dashboard for whoever might find my dog in my car. I should've parked in a more visible spot. I should've found religion. I should've gone to couples therapy. I "should've" a lot of things. I should've been a more interesting husband.

CHAPTER 39

"LISTEN TO ME, Michael Ryan," said Vatroslav. "I built Boston. My family put serious money in this town." I didn't interrupt him. "We provide the most important product anyone here could want." I didn't remind him that a family donating ten million bucks to a city that does three hundred fifty *billion* dollars in business does not an empire make. "My brother...My brother got in the way of that."

Ah, yes, one son to nail women, one son to sell them.

"My brother," he continued, "was interfering with the natural evolution of this city's commerce."

"Your brother was in *school*. To avoid being as dumb as you."

My gun lurked well behind me, somewhere, maybe on a shelf in the foyer. Vatroslav was getting angrier. He began to pace back and forth, still drinking from my bottle.

"Why are you calm?" he said. "I can kill you. I *will* kill

you." He looked at me. I looked at him. The girl was now looking, too. At us. Vatroslav's question was not rhetorical. Everyone in the room felt the shift.

So I answered him by pointing my index finger at the liquor in his hands. "That," I said.

He didn't get it at first.

I told him. "It's poison."

He laughed.

"It's tetrodotoxin," I said. He stopped laughing. "Fast-acting. I added it before I got here. Tetrodotoxin numbs the spinal cord, then the heart."

He was listening now.

"Impossible," he concluded. He was putting two and two together. He was doubting the math. He looked at the brandy, then looked at me. "You drank it yourself."

I nodded to the bottle again.

"You drank it yourself!" he repeated.

"Thought you said I was on suicide watch."

He contemplated me for a long time. There was no twitch in my iris at this point. Full commitment.

And it painfully started to make sense, the possibility of a hit man who'd ensured mutual revenge.

"Guard!" he suddenly yelled. He grabbed his phone. Tetrodotoxin takes merely minutes to act. He dialed 911. A second guard ran in, ready to shoot me, but the prodigal son had a more urgent directive for him. "Get me the family doctor!"

"B-boss," said the guard. "What happened?"

"Get me the fucking doctor!"

We then heard the 911 operator answer through his phone.

"I've been poisoned!" he yelled into it. Then he ran to the bathroom.

I remained in the armchair the whole time. The guard had no idea what to do with me. He wanted to shoot me, he wanted to ask me questions, but most of all he wanted to *not* have the last remaining son of a two-son emperor die on his watch.

From a distance I could see Vatroslav through the open bathroom door. He was bent over the sink. He began dry-heaving as hard as he could, having grabbed a toothbrush to gag his tongue. Not much welled forth.

"Where's the medic?!" he screamed. Then he burst out of the bathroom and scurried down the emergency stairwell. Twelve flights of stairs to the ground floor. Followed by his second guard.

Gone.

Exited.

Both of them.

Alone with me now, the other guard had a serious dilemma. He could a) chase his boss, b) shoot me, then chase his boss, c) preserve me as the only source of valuable information on how to save his boss and *then* chase his boss, or d) yell.

"Glupi majmune!" he yelled, then punched a wall. He was malfunctioning. *"Idi u pičku materinu lit! Što si učinio?!"*

"Okay." I didn't know what all his words meant, but it couldn't have been a recipe for baklava.

"Što si učinio?" he screamed at me. *"Što si učinio?"*

He threw a lamp, then kicked over a desk, took a breath to gain some practical control of himself, then marched over to me.

"You poison him?!" he asked.

"Us," I corrected him.

He looked at me like I'd fallen from a passing asteroid.

I pointed to my mouth. *Us.* I opened my mouth. I showed him. Then he leaned over me to inspect this nonsense. What you are talking about?" he asked.

"I'm talking about . . . *this.*" And that's when I grabbed his gun. He had leaned in just close enough, just carelessly enough, to allow me access to his muzzle.

My left hand took the stock, my right took the barrel.

"Odjebi!" he roared.

He outweighed me by fifty pounds, yet from my seated position, gravity favored my effort. His weapon wound up pointing back toward him. His instinctual effort to reclaim it led him to slip his finger off the trigger, so that *bratatatat.*

Should have chased his boss.

CHAPTER 40

CLOCK TICKING, THE next step was to fetch my target. I had to assume the neighbors were now a logistical factor. Few things earn as much attention as an assault rifle going off behind cheaply built walls.

I stood up and saw the supermodel standing within striking distance of me. She looked like she was experiencing every emotion imaginable.

"I'm not here to hurt you," I said to her. "I just need th—"

Wham! She kicked the dead guard in his bullet wound. *Wham!* She kicked him again. Kick after kick. When she had finished, she looked up at me, panting.

"Hospeetal is there," she said, pointing across the city block in front of us.

She was looking out the window. There was a giant street and then a hospital visible in the distance.

"I tell you fastest way," she said. "First you go courtyard. Then—"

"I know," I said. "He'll try to cut through the library."

I'd mapped the route several hours earlier. Poison was the only way to get him out of his eagle's nest. I knew I had a very low probability of killing him inside this palace, but I figured if I could lure him to the streets, the playing field would level itself out. My Smith & Wesson was on the kitchen counter. I grabbed it and handed the VHS-2 rifle to our newly liberated female army of one.

I swear this woman was ready to adopt me.

I started to show her how to use it. "You just need to pull the knob t—"

Chkkkchk. She yanked back the charging handle.

"I know," she said. She pointed me toward the elevator.

Seconds later, I was heading down. My bet was there'd be someone waiting for me when the doors opened, but nope, the lobby was empty. I was sure our fireworks had been heard, but somehow this entire operation had aroused exactly no one.

I stepped out of the elevator just in time to see Vatroslav down the block, disappearing into the hedges toward the library.

"On schedule," I said to myself somewhat smugly.

Bratatatatat!

A hurricane of bullets shattered all the glass in the lobby. I was being shot at from the other elevator, two bodies visible.

I ducked behind the front desk while firing two quick shots toward my rear. I don't think I hit anything useful but I certainly made my point. They crouched low. I crouched low. Mutual suppression. They didn't do me the favor of collaborating with each other in English.

What if I crawled *toward* them?

There was a row of tall indoor planters and a door to the parking garage.

One warning shot from my revolver—*blam*—which elicited a barrage of wrongly aimed retaliatory fire, and off I went. Once I was close enough to the door, I lunged for the knob, twisted it open, and burst through. I then pulled it closed behind me, just as incoming bullets lit up the frame. The finishing touch was to jam the hydraulic arm up top—the skinny metal thing that slows down big doors. By grabbing it and doing a mock pull-up, I managed to bend its elbow downward, which bought me an extra ten seconds of exodus. A lifetime in this business.

I sprinted out and took a shortcut across the lawn to see the tail end of Vatroslav's flight. He'd sprinted across the sloping lawn and opted for a path that led to a locked gate, leaving him no recourse but to come back the same way, back up toward the main steps, and up to the front entrance of the public library. Enough time for me to catch up.

"You got a back door?!" he roared at the librarian he encountered.

I managed to catch sight of his frantic path toward a utility door.

Mmmmmmm. I knew where that led. The subterranean level, full of old, archived, out-of-date, ugly, gorgeous editions of every book imaginable.

Thank you, city of Boston, for conserving these valuable books. Vatroslav had cornered himself in a labyrinth of good ideas.

CHAPTER 41

HIS PANIC WAS increasing. I could hear it.

"Titles are listed by author," I bellowed out. "Not subject."

I was starting to relish the news I had for him. He couldn't see me but he could feel my voice come from every direction at once. The muted reverb was unworldly. Perfect for stifling the sound of a .38 Special.

"Get me out of here!" he yelled.

He rounded his final corner and arrived squarely in front of me, face-to-face, out of breath.

"The poison!" he said. "The poison is taking effect."

"No, it isn't," I replied.

"Christ, you don't feel the numbing?"

"I don't. And would you like to know why?"

"Move!"

He tried to get by me but he was so out of breath he didn't have the agility needed.

"Because there's nothing *to* feel," I said.

He stopped struggling.

"The bottle of brandy contained pure brandy." I had his full attention now. "I never added a drop of poison."

"What?"

"The mind is a powerful drug, my friend. Today you're learning it. I spent eleven years and one terrible marriage learning it. Pretending she wasn't trying to kill me."

"Wait. What?!"

"And now I'm here to kill you."

He looked at the gun in my hand, aimed his way. He wondered if I really wanted to fire it in a library. That was the beauty of the stacks—a fact I decided to elucidate for him.

"Worth mentioning," I began. "I have a noisy weapon in my hand but we're surrounded by thousands of sound-absorbent pages."

"My father will gut you." He spoke with as much venom as humanly possible.

I took out my phone. If he wanted to go there, sure. "I'll let you personally *help* him find out."

"Father!" he cried.

"Hang on, I haven't dialed yet."

I dialed.

"You'll never get away with this," he said.

"I'm gonna wheel your corpse out on a book cart. In broad daylight."

It was true. I'd probably shroud his dead body under a large floor mat and roll the whole mess out the back gate, right to the trunk of my car. I'd then drive the corpse to my house, where I'd lay it inside the Kolpak 1010 freezer system. I'd go to Ivan and give Ivan the house keys. Maybe Ivan would be kind enough to dispatch a team of people who'd make disturbing situations disappear.

"Yes?" said Ivan's voice on my phone.

The trail of evidence along this ten-person graveyard was way too damning for anyone to tolerate. A man like Ivan would be only *too* willing to dispose of the aftermath.

"Ivan," I said into my phone. "I'm here with the man who ordered the death of your beloved son."

"Father," cried Vatroslav toward my phone. "It's lies. He's lying."

There was a pause.

The kid repeated his plea. "Father, please. It's all a lie."

It was enough to paint the entire picture for Ivan. The feud. The handsome, Harvard DNA versus the jealous DNA. I could *hear* him at the other end of the phone, weighing the implications. *Michael Ryan has never once missed—or misjudged—his mark.*

"Father, get me out of here!" cried the son. "Father!"

This ushered in an epoch of a pause.

Until Ivan quietly spoke. "You know what the job is," he said. Then hung up.

"Father—!"

Blam.

Eight. Eight victims in three days.

The gunshot was a lot louder than my previous essay on acoustics would've had him believe. I didn't care. Vatroslav Mesic was gasping quietly for his last breath. I stepped forward and half knelt to him. I estimated I had twenty-five seconds before the closest librarian would hustle over to look into whatever lofty book had dropped.

He tried to grab my gun. Futilely. He had no strength. Fifteen seconds.

"I don't want to spoil it, but at the end of *Le Parfum*...the villagers get their vengeance on the villain."

Eight seconds. I took hold of each of his limp forearms.

"The line is, 'For the first time, they had done something out of love.' Which is saying that they did what they did out of compassion...which is saying that brutality can come from *love*...which, let's be honest, is not possible for any of us."

I started to drag his corpse toward the nearest book cart.

"But I've enjoyed pretending otherwise."

DEAD MAN RUNNING

JAMES PATTERSON

WITH CHRISTOPHER FARNSWORTH

CHAPTER 1

DR. RANDALL BECK sat in his office and looked across the coffee table at his patient.

Todd Graham was a big man who looked small. He hunched on the overstuffed couch, arms curled in tightly to himself. He looked cold. He looked scared.

You'd never know that a few months earlier, Graham had been one of the top men on the Metro PD's Emergency Response Team—the Washington, DC, police SWAT team. He had broken down countless doors, been shot in the line of duty, and had seen some of the worst humanity had to offer in hostage situations, drug raids, and murder scenes.

But then he'd been called to a small apartment building in the Southeast, the quadrant of DC known as the worst area in the city. He and his squad thought they were going to take down a crack house.

Instead, they found bodies. Nine of them. Someone had killed all the members of an extended family for a grudge or some deal gone wrong. Graham was the first one into the room. He saw a child curled into the arms of her mother, the same gunshot wound through both of their chests.

Graham could handle danger to himself. What he couldn't handle was the thought of being helpless to stop it from happening to someone else.

Since then, Graham had been on administrative leave. He'd lost weight. He didn't sleep. He drank too much.

After medication and regular therapy failed, he'd been sent to see Beck.

Everything in Beck's office was soft and beige, designed to soothe and calm, the visual equivalent of white noise. Beck's patients were people who'd had enough chaos in their lives already.

Beck was considered the counselor of last resort for people suffering from severe post-traumatic stress and burnout. His patients included paramedics who'd pulled charred corpses out of plane crashes; doctors who'd volunteered in war zones, patching up children dismembered by bombs; hospice workers who faced a 100 percent mortality rate in their patients; and Special Forces soldiers who spent months in combat, ruthlessly killing to keep the rest of the world safe.

Beck noticed that the one thing all these people had in common was they were used to saving the world, but they had a much harder time saving themselves.

Graham had spent most of their sessions just sitting on Beck's couch. Quiet. Staring. Today was no different.

"Do you want to talk?" Beck asked, after a long silence.

Graham shrugged. "What's the point?" he asked Beck. "What's the point of any of it?"

"You don't think there's any point to living?"

Graham shrugged again. He sat back, as he had in their other sessions, finished talking for the day. He seemed to think he could just wait Beck out.

Beck decided he was done waiting. He reached into a bag at the side of his chair and pulled out a Glock 9mm.

Graham was instantly alert.

Beck placed the pistol on the table between them.

"Okay," he said. "You really want to die? Pick up the gun. Get it over with."

Graham stared at him, wide-eyed. "You're crazy."

Beck shrugged. "I'm a licensed psychiatrist."

"You're still crazy."

Beck sighed deeply. "You don't want to do it yourself? Well. I'm here to help." Beck picked up the Glock and racked the slide back, jacking a shell into the chamber. He pointed it at Graham, his hand steady.

"Now. Do you want to die?" Beck asked, looking down the barrel at his patient.

Graham was out of his chair in a split second. He knocked the gun aside and landed on Beck with his full weight, toppling the chair over. He and Beck struggled for a moment as Graham tried to get his hands on the gun.

They rolled across the floor together. Graham came up on top, the Glock in one hand. He pointed it at Beck, kneeling on top of him.

For a second, they were frozen like that.

Then Beck looked up at Graham, bleeding from the corner of his mouth where a stray elbow had hit him.

And he smiled.

"You fought," he said, grinning.

Graham looked confused. Then angry. "Are you *crazy?*" he shouted. "Of course I fought you! You pointed a gun at me!"

He got off Beck and let him up, but didn't take the gun off him. Beck didn't seem at all worried.

"Dummy bullets," Beck said. "Wouldn't fire even if I pulled the trigger."

Graham eyed Beck suspiciously, then checked the Glock's clip. If anything, it made him even more angry. "I didn't know that!" he shouted.

Beck didn't stop smiling. "That's right. You didn't. And you fought me. For the first time since you walked into this office, you did something. You woke up," he said. "Looks like you're not quite ready to die after all."

Graham stared at him, shocked.

Beck stood up and straightened his clothes. He wiped the blood from his mouth with a tissue, and then took his chair again. He gestured to the couch. Slowly, Graham set the gun and the clip back on the table. Then he sat down, too.

"Excellent," Beck said. "Shall we get started, then?"

CHAPTER 2

"YOU PULLED A *gun* on him?"

Dr. Susan Carpenter was, like Beck, a psychiatrist. She was highly trained, widely respected, and thoroughly professional. She'd seen a wide range of patients with deeply disturbing problems, ranging from trauma to schizophrenia to complete psychotic breaks with reality. There were people who came to her convinced that space lizards were about to take over the planet, and others who were certain that the contestants on *Survivor* were plotting against them.

In other words, she'd heard a lot of crazy stuff without blinking. And still, she looked like she was on the verge of having Beck taken to a padded cell.

"Dummy bullets," Beck said. "I couldn't have hurt him if I wanted to."

"He didn't know that," Susan snapped at him.

"Of course not. It would have defeated the purpose. He had to find a reason to live. I gave him one."

Susan took a deep breath and got herself under control.

"Or you could have broken his trust completely. Or triggered a violent episode. Or convinced him that he really ought to commit suicide. Did you ever think of that?"

"Of course," Beck replied. "I decided to take the chance."

"You risked your patient's life."

"No. I judged him capable of pulling himself out of his depression, given the right motivation. I looked at his history. This is a cop who once charged a man armed with an AK-47 and took him down barehanded. He has been through the door on multiple drug raids. He needed a threat to bring him back to life."

"You could have done the same thing by talking to him. You could have reminded him of his experiences—"

"I don't have that kind of time."

Susan's expression softened. There it was. Sooner or later, their sessions always came back to this. It was inevitable.

Beck was dying.

"Do you think your condition is affecting your judgment?" she asked.

Beck made a rude noise. "*Condition*. Call it what it is. I've got a brain tumor. And yes, it's still killing me. No, it's not affecting my judgment. I haven't started drooling or playing with myself in public."

A month earlier, Beck had been walking to his car when the sidewalk suddenly came up out of nowhere and hit him in the face. He was knocked senseless, and someone passing by on the street called 911. The paramedics took him to the emergency room at Georgetown, where the attending physician knew Beck from several cases he'd consulted on.

Beck said he felt fine, he was just a little dizzy, but the doctor insisted on an MRI and a PET scan.

And that's when they found the tumor. It was a very rare type of glioblastoma that had clearly been growing for some time, undetected. It was nestled deep in Beck's brainstem, near the parts that regulated his heartbeat and breathing.

Beck saw several specialists. They all said the same thing. Chemo wouldn't work, because the drugs couldn't cross the blood–brain barrier. Radiation was too dangerous because the tumor was so close to the critical structures nearby. Which is also why there was no way to reach the tumor with surgery.

The tumor would go on growing, slowly but surely. He'd remain relatively healthy until he wasn't anymore. He might fall down, and he might have seizures. He might have severe personality changes, memory loss, or delusions. He might lose the ability to walk. Or he might not.

But eventually, the tumor would overwhelm his brain, crushing the parts of it that kept him alive, and he would die.

They had given him anywhere from three months to a year.

Friends suggested that he take a trip around the world, see lions on safari, or just drink margaritas on the beach until it was his time. Beck went back to work. He hated vacations. He didn't know what he'd do with himself if he wasn't in his office.

But the doctors were required to tell the medical board about his condition. The board said he had to get another psychiatrist to monitor him, just in case the tumor affected his mental state. It wouldn't be good to have a psychiatrist with access to patients and a prescription pad if he was losing his own marbles.

Susan seemed like the best person possible to keep tabs on him. They'd both been at the top of their class at Johns Hopkins and had been paired together for their residencies at Georgetown. Like Beck, she specialized in crisis psychiatry—taking the most severe cases she could find.

And she was more likely to put up with him than anyone else. Beck had a reputation as a loose cannon even before he discovered the tumor. He was impatient with theories and studies. He wanted to use whatever worked. It was one reason he was popular with his patients and unpopular with other doctors.

"How are you feeling?" Susan asked with genuine concern.

"I'm fine."

"Looks like he tagged you pretty hard."

Beck touched his lip. It was still swollen. "I'm a doctor, not a boxer."

She didn't smile. Beck suspected he was in for another version of the Talk.

"That's my point. You deliberately antagonized a man who gets into life-and-death situations all the time. It could have been much worse for you."

Yes, it was the Talk again. It usually went like this. She'd tell him he was being reckless. He would nod his head and listen. And then he'd go on doing what he'd always done before.

Today, however, Susan seemed to be out of patience.

"Maybe I should just tell the board to pull your license now," she said. "You don't listen. You don't want to change. And because of your condition—"

"Tumor."

"—your tumor, you've got no reason to change. Do you see that you're using it as an excuse?"

But Beck didn't have much patience today, either.

"Look," Beck said. "I help people. It's what I do. I don't have a lot of time left. And by the time these patients get to me, neither do they. They are at the end of their ropes, and they're thinking of tying a noose. I will do whatever it takes to help them."

"Because only you can save them? We've talked about your Superman complex before."

"That's Doctor Superman to you."

Still no smile. "Answer the question."

Beck shrugged. "Well. I don't see anyone else pulling on a cape to save the day."

Susan looked like she was going to keep arguing with him, but Beck's phone beeped with a reminder. He checked the screen. APPOINTMENT WITH KEVIN SCOTT—10 A.M.

"I've got to go," he said. "Seeing a new patient."

She frowned, but gestured for him to leave. "We're not done with this yet," she said. "Call me tomorrow to check in."

He saluted. "Sir, yes, sir, General, sir!"

She finally cracked a smile. "That's Doctor General to you."

"Yes, Doctor."

Beck went to the door, but Susan had one parting shot.

"So what happens when you're gone?" she asked. "Who's going to save your patients if you're not around, Doctor Superman?"

Beck shrugged. "I don't know," he said. "I'll be dead."

Then he walked out.

CHAPTER 3

KEVIN SCOTT SCOWLED like Beck owed him money.

Like a lot of Special Forces soldiers, he was compact and muscular. All gristle and sharp edges. He looked at the office with contempt. Too quiet, too beige, too soft.

Beck wasn't particularly surprised. Scott had been an Army Ranger for seven years. He'd endured grueling training just to have the chance to sleep on rocks in the desert while people shot at him. Guys like Scott were not usually into the touchy-feely crap. It was always the first hurdle he had to overcome.

Because as tough as he was, Scott was also coming apart, according to the reports in front of Beck. The local VA office had referred Scott for psychiatric treatment after he had been arrested in a bar fight. He'd nearly crippled three men after an argument about the Redskins devolved into a full-on brawl. Only the fact that they attacked him kept him out of jail.

So it was pretty clear Scott needed help. But Scott wasn't

an ordinary soldier. He was part of a unit that carried out top-secret missions for the Defense Intelligence Agency in Iraq, Afghanistan, and a few places that US soldiers weren't supposed to be. As a result, only a psychiatrist with a security clearance was allowed to talk to him. Beck was one of the few people on that list because of his experience in dealing with Special Forces veterans.

But it meant that Scott had been forced to wait for almost a month while the paperwork and red tape cleared.

Even though they'd never met, Beck had read Scott's file and it was obvious that he was getting worse. He was shifting in his seat, agitated, and kept checking over his shoulder, like he expected someone to come through the door.

Beck figured there was no time to waste—for either of them. "So," he said, "who do you want to kill?"

Scott nearly jumped in the couch. He looked at Beck like he was crazy. "What? Why would you say that?"

"Well, you put three guys in the hospital. You seem pretty pissed off at someone. Who do you want to kill?"

Scott made a face. "It was just a fight that got out of hand. I'm only here because the court said I had to get counseling. I'm fine."

"Right," Beck said. "You're fine. So breaking a guy's collarbone and another guy's arm in three places is just a fun night out for you? Maybe we should go to Vegas together. I can't wait to see what you do there."

Scott rolled his eyes at Beck. Nobody got his jokes. "I told you. It was a fight. They started it."

"And you finished it."

"That's what guys like me do," Scott said, looking him in the eyes for the first time. "We handle things other people can't. I know you get a lot of wackjobs in here. But I'm not one of them. Trust me. I'm fine."

He really sold it. It was almost convincing. Beck could see why people would follow him into combat. But Beck knew better.

"The thing is, Kevin, you don't seem fine. The VA's counselor talked to your wife."

"Jennifer?" Scott looked worried. "Why did they bother her?"

"She's concerned about you. She says you came home fine from your last tour. You were handling everything. You got a job, you were dealing with civilian life—and then, about three months ago now, you began to act differently. You began sleeping with a gun on the bedside table. You started drinking. You'd disappear at night and on weekends. And when she called your job, they wouldn't tell her where you were."

Scott was growing more anxious, picking at the fabric on the chair, shifting around. Beck thought he wanted to jump up and run out of the room.

"She called my work?"

"She cares about you. Maybe she thinks you're having an affair."

Whoops. That was the wrong thing to say. Scott stood up and pointed a finger in Beck's face. "Hey! I love my wife! You watch your damned mouth!"

Beck sat as calmly as he could with a trained killer in his face. "So you're not having an affair."

"That's right!" Scott snapped. "I'm not! And I keep telling you, I'm fine! So you sign whatever little piece of paper you have to, and you let me go back to my life and you leave my wife out of this!"

Beck looked up at him, waiting. Then he said, "No."

"No?" Scott loomed even closer.

"No," Beck said. He really wished he had a gun with real bullets. But he didn't look away.

For a long moment, Scott stood there. Then, Beck could tell, he started to feel stupid. He sat down again.

"Sorry," he said.

That clinched it for Beck. This guy was not mentally ill. He'd lost control, sure. But he got it back way too fast. He was angry and scared, but he was not suffering from PTSD. There was something else going on.

"I think there's something you're not telling me, Kevin," Beck said.

Scott looked back at him. There was something in his face. He opened his mouth, as if to start speaking. Beck could almost feel it. This was the moment where most of his patients began to open up—to reveal what brought them into the office in the first place.

"You ever done anything really bad, Dr. Beck?" Scott asked.

"Yeah. I have. What did you do, Kevin?"

Scott laughed, then almost choked.

"Nothing yet. But..."

"But what?"

Scott looked at Beck again. He suddenly stood up. "Forget it. Forget I was ever here."

He went to the door and flung it open.

Beck got up and went after him. He grabbed Scott by the arm. "Hey, wait a minute— " he said.

But he didn't get anything else out. Scott shoved him back, sending him flying.

"Leave it, Doc," he snarled. "You'll live longer." Scott stomped away.

It took Beck a minute to get to his feet. He was getting tired more easily these days, and his balance was off. Probably the tumor. But he was also angry. He never gave up on a patient, and he never backed down.

And if Scott beat the crap out of him, well, he was dying anyway.

Beck raced down the stairs of his building, breathing hard. He reached the lobby, but Scott wasn't there. He ran out the double doors to the street, where he saw Scott crossing the road to his car.

Beck was about to yell something at him.

Then a black SUV came screaming around the corner. It was on top of Scott in seconds. Scott turned and saw it, and started to run.

But he wasn't fast enough. The barrel of a gun emerged from the SUV's open window, and Beck watched helplessly as Scott was cut down by a hail of bullets.

CHAPTER 4

BECK SAT ON the edge of the sidewalk and looked at the blood on his hands.

It had been a long time since he'd had blood on his hands.

As a med student, still doing his rotations in surgery and emergency medicine, he'd been up to his elbows in it, all the time. He'd seen his share of gunshot wounds in those days.

So when he saw Scott hit the ground he knew two things:

Scott was probably dead already.

He had to try to save him anyway.

The black SUV had peeled away, tires smoking as it rounded the corner. For an instant as the car approached, Beck made eye contact with the shooter. He wore a black ski mask. His eyes, the only part of him that was visible, stared coldly back at Beck, and then Kevin Scott was down and the SUV was gone.

And then Beck was tearing open Scott's jacket and shirt, desperately trying to stop the bleeding.

But it was no good. Scott's chest looked like raw meat, with multiple bullet wounds opening holes in his chest so that the life poured right out of him. There was a flicker of life left in his eyes as he looked up at Beck, unseeing.

He said one word. It made no sense.

"Damocles," he gasped.

Then he choked and more blood poured from his mouth. The flicker in his eyes went out.

His chest stopped heaving.

Scott was dead.

The police and paramedics showed up fast. Beck's office was on a quiet, upscale block, not far from several embassies. It was not the kind of neighborhood that got a lot of drive-by shootings.

The cops pulled Beck away from Scott's body and sat him down. The paramedics took a look at Scott and didn't even go through the motions. They just covered him up.

The police took Beck's statement and asked him if he'd seen either the driver or the passenger. Beck told them about the ski mask.

But that was all he really knew. He was surprised at how useless he was as a witness. He shouldn't have been. He knew that severe stress—like seeing a man gunned down in the street—makes it hard to notice details.

Still, he couldn't remember if he'd seen a license plate, or what was on it. He didn't know what kind of SUV it was. He couldn't even remember the color of the gunman's eyes, and he'd been looking right into them.

The cops left him sitting on the sidewalk while they went

to look for other witnesses. And Beck looked at the blood on his hands.

He sat that way for what seemed like a long time. Trying to understand what happened. His mind kept racing. He didn't like where it was leading him.

In his office, Kevin Scott had been scared. Scott had been anxious. And Scott had been hiding something, even from his wife.

His wife. Jennifer. With a guilty start, Beck realized someone would have to tell her about her husband.

He looked up from his bloody hands, to find one of the cops, to tell them.

But instead, he saw two men in dark suits with serious faces walking toward him.

Federal agents. Beck had met enough of them to recognize the look. They wore earpieces and off-the-rack suits with the jackets big enough to hide their holsters. You saw them all the time in DC—at lunch, in line at Starbucks, standing outside one event or another.

These two, however, were here for him.

"Doctor Beck," the first one said, offering his hand. "I'm Agent Morrison. This is Agent Howard. We're with the Secret Service. We'd like to ask you a few questions."

Beck took his hand, and Morrison hauled him to his feet. He was about a head taller than Beck, who wasn't short, with cold blue eyes and blond hair spiked straight up. Howard, his partner, was darker and wider—he looked like he put in serious hours at the gym—with his black hair slicked back and frozen in place.

They waved their badges at him. He barely got a look. They both wore grim expressions without a trace of sympathy.

"How did you know the deceased?" Morrison demanded.

Beck tried to shake off his shock. "I told the other officers—"

"We're not the other officers," Howard snapped. "We want to hear it from you."

Beck started again. "He was my patient."

"You're a shrink? What was his problem?"

"I'm a psychiatrist, yes. And I can't say."

"Not much of a shrink, then, are you?" Howard said. Morrison smirked.

"No. I mean, I can't say. Doctor–patient communications are confidential. As I'm sure both of you already know."

Morrison and Howard exchanged a look. "Yeah. Thanks for reminding us, Doctor," Morrison said. "But the guy is dead, and he was walking out of your office. I think we need to know."

"And if I had any information that would help someone in immediate danger, I would be ethically bound to offer it. But I don't. Anything else is private. That's the law. Why is the Secret Service investigating this, anyway? Isn't this something for the police?"

"Are you a doctor or a lawyer?" Howard said, his tone sharp and mocking. "You're making this a lot more complicated than it needs to be."

"You don't have the expertise to know what's important and what isn't," Morrison added. "That's our job."

"Listen, I have a security clearance," Beck said.

"How special for you," Howard said.

"What I mean is, if you just call the coordinator at the Department of Defense—" Beck took out his phone to give them the number. Morrison and Howard reacted like he'd pulled a gun. They stepped back. With one swift move, Morrison snatched the phone from his hand and pocketed it.

"Hey. That's my phone."

"Doctor Beck, you're our sole witness," Morrison said. "Let's not get bogged down in technicalities. We need to know what he told you. And we need to know *now*."

Beck wondered where the hostility was coming from. He'd heard of good cop/bad cop, but this was more like bad cop/bad cop.

Then he recognized the technique. They were trying to put him off-balance. Make him more pliable, eager to please, by bullying him a little.

It only pissed Beck off.

"You want to know what we talked about? Try getting a subpoena. He was my patient. Even dead, he has rights."

Howard looked like he wanted to punch Beck. Morrison sighed and rubbed his face with his hands, then pulled Beck aside. He lowered his voice, as if someone might be listening.

"Look, Doctor. I didn't want to have to tell you this. We are in the middle of something big, and it involves your client. There is more going on than you know. You have to tell us what he told you. Lives are literally on the line here. I know you'll want to do the right thing."

This was even more transparent than the bullying. They were trying to make Beck feel like he was important—inside a big secret. He really didn't appreciate the manipulation, which wouldn't work on a first-year psych major.

And, for some reason, he just didn't trust these guys.

Beck lowered his voice, too, as if he were going to cooperate. "Can you tell me what this investigation is about?"

Morrison shook his head. "Sorry. Classified."

Beck went back to his regular voice, all pretense gone. "Yeah? Then so is what my patient told me. Sorry."

"All right then, Doctor. Have it your way." Morrison stepped back.

Beck thought that would be the end of it. He turned to walk away.

So he was surprised when Howard spun him back around, slammed him against a telephone pole, and slapped handcuffs on his wrists.

CHAPTER 5

THE POLICE DIDN'T object as the two agents marched Beck across the street and shoved him into the backseat of their SUV. They said they were taking him to their office for further questioning. The cops nodded. Not their problem anymore.

Beck realized they were really going to do this—just drag him off to jail, or some locked room, and interrogate him. Unbelievable.

"You can't be serious," he said. "This is basic doctor–patient confidentiality. Any judge is going to laugh you out of court."

"Shut up," Howard said as he dug around in Beck's jacket and removed his wallet. Then he slammed the door in Beck's face.

The window was still open, however. Beck looked at Morrison, who seemed slightly more reasonable.

"Look. If you're really going to take me away, someone needs to tell Scott's wife," Beck remembered. "Her name is

Jennifer Scott. Someone needs to tell her about her husband."

"Yeah, we'll take care of it," Morrison said. He nodded at Howard, who took out his own phone and dialed a number, then stepped away to talk.

Morrison got in on the driver's side and used the button there to roll up Beck's window. He looked at Beck across the backseat. "Now do as you're told: shut up."

Beck sat and stewed. This was really going to happen. He shook his head. *Well, at least I get to cross* being arrested *off the bucket list.* He wondered what would happen to his afternoon patients. He had no secretary who could call them to cancel. They would just show up at his office, and they'd wait. Some of them wouldn't handle it very well if he wasn't there.

It made Beck angrier. But there was nothing he could do about it now.

Howard got into the front passenger seat, and then, without a word, Morrison started the engine and drove away from the scene.

At first, Beck didn't pay attention to where they were going. He was too busy trying to think of an attorney he could call. He had a couple of acquaintances who were lawyers, but they did mostly lobbying and corporate work. . . .

Then Beck saw that they'd crossed the river and were headed into Southeast DC. Morrison turned off the main avenue and began going down side streets, deeper and deeper into some of the worst neighborhoods in the capital.

"Where are we going?" Beck asked.

Howard and Morrison ignored him. Morrison was driving too fast. He ran yellow lights and cut off other drivers. Both he and Howard sat in the same grim silence, eyes fixed ahead.

There was no partition between Beck and the two agents. He knew they could hear him.

"Where are we going?" Beck asked again, louder.

"We're taking you in for questioning," Morrison said, sounding bored.

"Then why are we driving away from H Street?" Beck asked. H Street was where the Secret Service's headquarters was located.

"Branch office," Howard said, still not looking at him.

The civilized part of Beck's mind told him that this could all be normal. That he should be polite, and wait to call a lawyer, and this whole mess would get straightened out. That was the part of him that had been a good boy his whole life, the part that told him, like his mother always did, to sit up straight and behave.

But there was another part of his brain talking to him as well—the part that seemed to have woken up since he was diagnosed with cancer. It was like some survival instinct had kicked in since finding out he was going to die.

And this part of his brain screamed at him that something was very wrong here.

Beck looked out the window. The streets were uglier. These were places Beck had only seen in the background on the TV news, usually with a reporter describing the latest gang killing or drug deal gone wrong.

"Where is this branch office?" Beck asked.

Morrison looked back at him in the rearview.

"Just relax, Doc. We'll be there before you know it."

And Beck suddenly knew he was in serious trouble.

Memory is a tricky thing, Beck knew. Stress affects the brain and interferes with the transfer of images from short-term to long-term memory. And then, sometimes, those same memories can return in an instant.

At that moment, Beck remembered the color of the gunman's eyes.

Because he was looking right into them again.

CHAPTER 6

BECK WAS HANDCUFFED and trapped in the car with Kevin Scott's killers.

He had no idea what to do.

He tried desperately to think. He looked out the window again. They seemed to be driving into the very worst section of town—probably so that when Beck's body turned up, it wouldn't be considered unusual. Maybe they'd say he was here to buy drugs. Or maybe they'd say he was shot trying to escape.

Beck knew Kevin Scott had been hiding something. But now he knew it was something worth killing for.

And these two federal agents—if they *were* federal agents at all—wanted to find out if Beck knew it, too.

Beck tried to measure his own pulse. His doctors had told him stress was bad for his condition. His body was working hard enough to regulate itself with the interference of his brain tumor. He could suffer dizzy spells or weakness or seizures if he pushed himself too hard, they'd told him.

And there was also the chance that he was suffering a paranoid delusion. It happened with his condition. People stopped thinking normally as the tumor increased pressure and swelling in sections of the brain. Was it possible that he was just imagining the danger he was in?

Beck didn't think so. He didn't feel crazy. He knew psychotic patients rarely did, but he was pretty sure he was still firing on all cylinders. Surprisingly, he felt almost calm. Even though these two men wanted to kill him, it didn't scare him as much as he thought it would. Beck already knew he was going to die—soon. He'd made his peace with that.

But these men were probably going to torture him as well. They wanted to know what was in his head, and what Kevin Scott had said in his last hour on earth. They would do whatever it took to get that information out of Beck, even though Scott had not told him anything but the word "Damocles."

Even if Beck told the agents that now, they wouldn't believe him. They'd hurt him until they were satisfied he wasn't lying.

Beck could handle the idea of dying. But these men were going to subject him to agonizing pain.

Was he going to let that happen?

Hell, no. If he had to die, it was going to be on his own terms.

That made his next decision easy.

Morrison was still driving too fast. Beck waited for the next yellow light. Predictably, Morrison gunned the engine to barrel through the intersection.

And then Beck flung himself into the front seats via the space between them, and landed on Morrison, knocking his arms away from the steering wheel. Beck began kicking and biting and flailing, his own hands still bound behind him.

Morrison shouted an obscenity. Howard began to scream something, then caught one of Beck's knees on his mouth.

Beck felt the steering wheel spin and the car tipped crazily.

There was a blaring horn, and then Beck was flying into the air as something hit the SUV like a fist.

Beck saw shattering glass. He felt the airbags explode all around him, burning him with white powder as they deployed. The SUV whirled like a top, and then came to an abrupt, crunching halt.

CHAPTER 7

BECK BLINKED AND sat up. His side hurt like hell. He shook a little bit and safety glass fell from his face, his clothes, his hair.

He was still in the front seat. The windshield and passenger windows were broken. Deflated airbags sagged from every surface along the dashboard and interior. Morrison groaned underneath him.

Howard was still in the passenger seat. Blood trickled from his forehead where he'd cracked his skull against the doorpost. He looked at Beck, momentarily dazed. His lip was split where Beck had kneed him before.

Howard's eyes snapped to focus on Beck. He didn't speak. He growled. And without hesitation, he went for his gun, which, lucky for Beck, he couldn't whip out with no trouble because Beck was half lying on top of him.

But Beck knew he'd get it sooner rather than later, and in the cramped space of the SUV's front seat, there was almost no way he could miss Beck if he fired.

If Beck was still being civilized, he might have been scared. But he was far beyond that by now.

And it's hard to scare a man who already knows he's dying.

What's he going to do? Beck thought. *Kill me?*

He reared his legs back and kicked as hard as he could. He caught Howard in the face. He heard a muffled snap and knew that he'd just shattered the man's nose.

Howard's head bounced against the doorpost again. Beck kicked him one more time for good measure.

Beck heard Howard's gun drop to the floor. He hadn't realized that the man had been able to get it so soon.

Morrison was thrashing around under Beck by now, pinned by Beck's weight. Beck struggled to get off him. He realized that Morrison was having trouble using one arm. Then he saw why.

The SUV had been knocked out of the intersection when it was hit. It had come to a halt against a streetlight, which smashed in the driver's-side door on impact. Morrison's left arm was trapped in the narrow space between the crumpled door and the steering wheel. It kept Morrison from grabbing Beck or holding him down. Or drawing his gun.

About time I got a little bit of luck, Beck thought. He struggled to sit up again. He had to get out.

Howard was blocking the passenger door, and that was crushed by the impact as well. But the windshield was gone. It was basically an open invitation for Beck.

He used his forehead to smash Morrison's head as hard as he dared, without giving himself a concussion, and when he saw Morrison's eyes roll back in his head, he kicked Howard one more time, then rolled across the dash, shedding more glass as he went, and then slid down the hood of the SUV.

He looked up and tried to get his bearings. There was a garbage truck in the middle of the intersection, its front smashed in where it had hit the SUV. The driver stood by, staring at the damage, looking stunned. Morrison, shaking off the hit to his head, was shouting something at Beck.

For a moment, Beck didn't know what to do.

Then a bullet hit the brick facade of a building, less than ten feet from his head, and he saw that Howard and Morrison had their guns out and were shooting at him.

With his hands still cuffed behind him, Beck began to run.

CHAPTER 8

BECK RAN, HIS head down, sprinting as fast as he could through the unfamiliar streets.

He had no phone, no wallet, no money, and there were two killers with badges right behind him. There was also the slight matter of him being handcuffed.

He had to get help. He had to get off the streets. Any moment now, a police car could stop him, or someone might see him, and then how would he explain this? He'd be on his way to jail, and probably right back into the custody of Morrison and Howard.

He didn't think anyone would believe him if he told them that the agents killed Kevin Scott. He barely believed it himself. But he knew what he saw. He just had no idea why.

Beck needed to find out the answers if he wanted to stay alive. He had to find out why Kevin Scott had been killed, and what those men wanted with him.

First, he had to get these damned cuffs off. He felt like a duck, waddling along with his hands locked behind him.

He turned down another corner blindly as he saw a car approaching. He was on a small, mostly residential street with a few businesses tucked in between the blank faces of apartment buildings and crumbling brick buildings. Then he saw exactly what he needed.

An auto repair shop. It was a small, independent operation, not a chain. An older African-American man in coveralls worked in the one-bay garage, spinning a tire off its wheel.

Beck ran across the asphalt to him.

"Hello," Beck said. And then realized he had no idea what to say next.

The man looked up from the tire at Beck, his expression blank. The name tag on his coveralls read LOUIS.

"Ah, listen," Beck said, thinking hard. "I'm having a bit of a problem."

Louis's mouth curled into a slow grin. "Yeah. I bet you are."

"I was wondering if you had any bolt cutters? Or anything like that?"

"I might," Louis said. "What exactly would you want with them?"

Beck wondered if Louis was screwing with him on purpose. Still, he was the only hope Beck had right now. Beck turned around and showed him the cuffs.

"Do you think you could cut these off?"

"I could," Louis said slowly. "But that's not exactly my line of work. And I'm not sure that whoever put you in those wouldn't come looking for me."

Beck turned back to him. He wanted to scream at the

man to *just cut the damn things off*. But he forced himself to calm down.

"Well, I could pay you." Damn it. No, he couldn't. No wallet. "Um. Eventually. I was sort of mugged."

"Sort of?"

"It's complicated. But if you can help me, I promise I'll pay you something later. I swear."

"I think I'm going to need a little more explanation than that," Louis said, his eyes serious despite the grin.

Beck thought fast. He imagined trying to tell this man that he was on the run from federal agents who were also murderers. He didn't think he'd get very far with that story.

He took another look at Louis. One advantage of being a shrink: he was used to reading people quickly. Louis seemed like a basically decent guy. Attentive to detail. A business owner. So, independent and self-contained. Which meant he was suspicious of outside authority. He trusted his own gut.

He'd help Beck, but only if he had a compelling story. A reason.

Beck looked for a wedding ring. Didn't see one. Looked for any religious paraphernalia—a cross, or a church calendar. Nothing like that on the walls of the shop.

It came to him in a flash.

Beck sighed and his shoulders sagged. He did his best to look embarrassed. It wasn't too hard.

"You ever have a fight with your girlfriend?" Beck asked.

Louis's grin got even wider. "No, not me. I do everything she tells me."

"Well. That's sort of how I got into the handcuffs," Beck said, and tried to laugh. "It was supposed to be a game."

"A game. Right."

"Yes. She said she wanted to try something a little, um, kinky."

"Kinky. And that sounded good to you."

"Well, you know. She made it sound better than it turned out."

"I'll bet. So how did you get here, looking like you've been beat up?"

"Well. She wasn't *exactly* my girlfriend."

Now Louis shook his head in mock sadness. "Oh, man. Let me guess. She was, uh, what do you want to say, a *professional.*"

Beck tried to look ashamed of himself. It was surprisingly easy.

"Yeah. And then her—well, I guess it was her pimp—"

"You got rolled."

"Yeah. Yeah, I did."

"Well, you should probably call the police. Those cuffs could be evidence."

Now Beck knew Louis was screwing with him. But he plunged ahead. "Ah, yeah, see, I would. But—"

"But you don't want your wife to find out," Louis said.

Beck nodded.

Louis laughed out loud for a good while. Beck looked down and waited it out. He felt like he deserved an Oscar for this.

When Louis finally stopped laughing, he said, "Stay right here."

Louis walked into the tiny office off the main garage bay. He was gone for a long time. Beck couldn't check his watch—because of the handcuffs, of course—but it felt like hours. Beck looked in through a grimy window in the door. Louis appeared to be checking the screen of his phone. What was he doing in there? Was he calling the police himself?

Beck felt sweat trickling down his sides and stinging a cut he didn't know he had on his forehead. He imagined Morrison and Howard driving up the street any second. The world seemed to spin for a moment. He took a deep breath and forced himself to remain calm.

Louis finally came back with his phone and a small, thin strip of metal. "Turn around," he said, and then Beck felt him tugging on the cuffs. Louis suddenly pushed one of the cuffs tighter. Beck felt the metal sink deeper into the skin of his wrist. "Hey!" he said.

"Just hold on, I won't hurt you any worse than your girlfriend," Louis said. And then Beck felt the cuff pop open.

A second later, Louis did the same thing on the other wrist, and Beck was free.

He turned around, and Louis was holding the cuffs and the metal strip and grinning. "All done," he said.

"How did you do that?" Beck asked, genuinely amazed.

"The shim undoes the ratcheting mechanism of the cuffs," Louis said. "Saw it on YouTube."

He put the cuffs and the strip of metal into Beck's hand.

"Here," he said. "You keep these as a souvenir. And you should probably watch the video yourself, in case you have any more problems with any other girlfriends."

"I owe you," Beck said as he pocketed the cuffs.

Louis grinned again. "No charge," he said. "It was worth it just to meet a man with worse luck with women than me. Now, I suppose you'll be wanting to use the phone?"

Beck took a moment to assess the situation. He was alone, with two killers after him. One man was already dead, and it was clear he was supposed to be next. He couldn't risk going to the police, who might hand him back over to the killers. He had no idea what he'd fallen into, and no idea how to get out of it.

But he knew who he could trust.

He took Louis's phone and dialed.

CHAPTER 9

SUSAN LOOKED AT him from the driver's seat. Her voice was full of concern when she spoke.

"Are you absolutely sure you're feeling all right?" she asked.

Beck restrained the urge to shout at her. He'd probably ask the same thing if one of his patients came to him with this story.

And she was the only person he could turn to right now.

She'd picked Beck up at Louis's shop after he'd called her. She looked over his injuries—a cut on the forehead, bruises, and scrapes—and put him into her car. All he'd told her over the phone was that he'd been in a car accident, and now he was stranded without his car or cash.

Louis hadn't said anything about the handcuffs, which were still in Beck's jacket pocket. He just muttered quietly to Beck, "Don't see why you're running around if you've got that at home." Then he grinned and waved as Beck and Susan pulled away in her Volvo.

Susan wanted to take him to the hospital, immediately. And so Beck told her what had happened.

She'd pulled to the side of the road and parked her car. Then she looked at him, and began speaking to him in the same tones that she'd use to talk a jumper off a ledge.

"I'm sure you believe this is what happened, Randall," is how she began.

He saw the sadness in her eyes. He knew what she was thinking. She believed that he'd finally begun to unravel, that the tumor was eating away at his ability to think, and he was suffering from delusions.

He was almost flattered that she seemed so moved. But the rest of him was angry and impatient. He didn't have time for her sympathy. He needed to find out why someone wanted him dead.

Beck wanted to have her drive back to where the SUV wrecked to see the damage, but he didn't want to take the chance that they were still there.

And after a few minutes, she lost her therapeutic voice and her temper, and they were both yelling at each other in the car.

"Just a minute," Susan said. She picked up her phone and tapped the screen. A news app brought up headlines for Washington, DC. "There's nothing here about a shooting anywhere near your office."

"Then they must have told the police to keep it quiet."

Susan gave him another skeptical look.

"I know how paranoid that sounds," Beck said. "But I know what happened."

"Do you?" she said. "Think of all the times you've had patients convinced that someone was out to get them. Think of how they acted. Do you see any resemblance?"

"Look, if I'm making this up, then where did I get these?" Beck snapped, and showed her the handcuffs.

"I'm not sure I want to know," Susan snapped back. Then she got her temper under control. She breathed deeply and started again. "Please. We should at least get your head looked at. An MRI or PET scan. Maybe the car accident shifted the tumor, or increased the pressure on your brain. You could have a blood clot. You might stroke out at any moment."

"I feel fine," Beck said, although he didn't. He felt tired and dizzy, but he wasn't about to tell Susan that. "Listen to me. My patient is dead. And they want to kill me, too. I know it sounds paranoid, but you know me. You know the difference between people who are crazy and people who are not. You've spent your whole life doing this. Look at me: am I crazy?"

Susan took a long look at him. "All right. Let's say this is true. Let's go to a lawyer. I have a friend, she's a former assistant US attorney, she could— "

"No," Beck said flatly. "No lawyers."

Susan threw up her hands. "You won't go to the police, you won't go to a lawyer, you won't go to the hospital. So what are we supposed to do, Randall? How are we going to find out what's happening to you?"

Good question, Beck had to admit. Then he remembered something that had been nagging at him since he got into the SUV with Morrison and Howard.

"Oh, my God."

Susan looked alarmed. "What? What is it?"

"Scott's wife. Jennifer."

"You think she can help you?"

"No," Beck said. "Think about it. If they are willing to kill me because I spent a few minutes with Kevin Scott, then what are they going to do about her?"

"Randall, for God's sake."

"Susan, think about it. If I'm wrong, I'll go with you to the hospital. Quietly. I'll get help. But if I'm right, then a woman's life is at stake, and we're the only people who can help her right now. They *will kill her,* Susan."

Susan thought about that for a moment. Then she cranked the engine back to life. "Do you have her address?" she asked. Beck didn't.

"Look it up on my phone," she said, tossing it to him, then pulled out into traffic. A horn blared as she cut another driver off. Susan ignored it as the phone began giving them directions to the house of Kevin and Jennifer Scott.

Susan's grip was tight on the wheel. For the first time, Beck thought, she looked like she believed him.

Because she looked scared.

CHAPTER 10

MORRISON AND HOWARD were in no mood for bullshit by the time they rolled up to the tiny auto repair shop.

The last hour had been the most humiliating of their careers.

First, the firefighters had to use pry bars to open their SUV and free Morrison. A paramedic put his arm in a sling. Then she plucked safety glass from an open wound on Howard's scalp and stuffed cotton up the other agent's nose before putting a brace over his face to keep the broken bones in place.

The agents had to call headquarters for another vehicle, which was delivered along with the tow truck that took away the SUV.

And while they waited, they had to call the Client and report what had happened.

There was disbelief and scorn in her voice. "A goddamn *psychiatrist* got away from you? Are you kidding me?"

They promised they would make it right.

"We'll handle it," Morrison said.

"He'd better be in a body bag before the end of the day," the Client said. "And anyone else he's talked to. Or I'll find someone who will put you in one."

She hung up. Morrison had winced. Even though their phones were encrypted, you never knew who could be listening.

Still, Morrison knew she wasn't threatening. She was promising. He'd worked for her long enough to know.

Morrison had called a contact at the National Security Agency. He had Beck's phone, which was as good as having the man's DNA and fingerprints. He explained that he needed to do a quick and dirty search for a high-value target, and had no time for a warrant or to jump through any other official hoops.

Morrison's friend at the NSA was happy to help. Morrison gave him the last phone number Beck had dialed—a person named Susan Carpenter. The NSA had back doors into every major telecommunications carrier in the world. A few keystrokes on a computer, and Morrison's contact had the data for Susan Carpenter's phone.

Sure enough, there was another call to her, right after the time of the wreck, from a mobile phone located a dozen blocks from the scene of the crash.

This was good news and bad news. It gave them a clue to where Beck was—but it meant he'd talked to someone new. Another loose end to snip.

The NSA guy said he could track Susan Carpenter's cell

phone for them, but that would likely draw the attention of his supervisor.

Morrison told him to forget it. They'd take it from there. But he did want the location of the phone Beck had used to call.

That was easy. The NSA's coordinates were exact. The phone Beck used had not moved since he called his girlfriend or whoever the hell she was.

So that was how Morrison and Howard ended up standing in front of Louis as he worked under the hood of an old Ford Taurus.

They showed him their badges. He didn't seem too impressed.

"What can I do for you gentlemen?" he asked, going back to work on the engine.

"We need to know if you've seen a man wearing handcuffs," Howard asked.

"You'd think I'd remember something like that," Louis said, calmly working his wrench into the guts of the car.

"So you didn't see him?" Morrison asked. Howard was ready to grab Louis's collar and pull him out from under the hood, but Morrison shook his head. Not yet.

"Not that I recall," Louis said. "What's he supposed to have done?"

"He's wanted in a murder investigation," Morrison said.

"Sounds like a bad guy. Wish I could help you."

Morrison sighed. Why did people always have to make things so difficult? He nodded at Howard.

Howard smiled and carefully moved the hood prop out

of place, then set it carefully into its clip, using his other hand to keep the hood up.

"What the hell do you think you're doing?" Louis asked.

Howard didn't answer. He grabbed Louis by the neck and kept him from moving back, slamming the hood down on his head.

Louis screamed. Howard lifted the hood back up, and Morrison hauled him out. He was bleeding freely from his head and cuts on his face where he'd been shoved into the engine block.

"You're lying to us," Morrison said.

"N-no," Louis stammered.

Morrison patted the man down, one-handed. He found his phone in the side pocket of his coveralls.

"We know he made a call from your phone," Morrison said.

Louis looked shocked for a split second—most people think the government is listening to their phone calls, but it's another thing to *know* it's really happened to you—and then shook his head.

"I—I leave the phone on my desk. Anyone could have used it. I swear!"

Morrison considered this. As excuses went, it was almost plausible. But it wasn't convincing. "Then how did it get in your pocket, if you leave it on your desk?"

Louis looked stunned, and didn't answer.

Morrison nodded at Howard, who shoved Louis down and slammed the hood again. Louis shrieked in pain. Howard smiled. He liked this part of the job. Morrison heard something crunch that time.

Howard pulled Louis back out from under the hood. He had several broken teeth, which explained the crunch. He was drooling blood.

"You sure you never saw anyone wearing handcuffs?"

Then it all came spilling out. "I shaw him, I shaw him," Louis said, his mouth full of mush.

"Where'd he go?"

"I doan know," Louis said, tears rolling down his cheeks now. "I doan *know!*"

"You're not lying to me again, are you?"

Louis shook his head violently, sending blood drops flying. Morrison flinched back with distaste. "I shwear to Gaa," Louis said.

Morrison believed him. He really sold it.

But it made no difference. He'd seen their faces, and knew they were asking about Beck. They couldn't take the chance. No loose ends. They'd promised.

Morrison nodded, and Howard pushed him back into the engine compartment. This time Louis was practically weeping, waiting for the metal to crack his skull one more time.

But Morrison wasn't cruel like Howard. He didn't let the other agent slam the hood down again.

He just took out his 9mm and put a bullet into the back of Louis's head.

They left the body in the garage. Howard stopped at the cash register, opened it, and took out the money inside. In this neighborhood, Metro PD wouldn't look any further for a motive than that. Case closed.

They walked back to the car.

"You should have let me talk to him some more," Howard said. "He could have told us where Beck went."

"He didn't know," Morrison replied. "He was telling the truth."

"So how are we going to find him?"

Morrison got behind the wheel. His arm still hurt like hell, but he had no intention of letting Howard drive. Guy was a maniac.

"Come on," Morrison said. "He's a *shrink*. How long before he goes running to the police? Where else is he going to go?"

CHAPTER 11

SUSAN PULLED UP to the Scotts' house. It was located in what an optimistic real-estate agent would call "a neighborhood in transition." There were some decent restaurants nearby mixed with cheap delivery joints and empty storefronts. Most of the windows still had bars on them.

"So what do we do?" Susan asked.

Beck sat in the car for a moment. Good question. They hadn't been able to call Jennifer Scott—her number was in Beck's notes, back in his office, and it was unlisted. So there was only one thing to do.

"Let's go up."

Susan hesitated. "You realize that if you're right, there could be someone waiting there already."

Beck had thought of that. But he didn't see any alternative. "Well," he said, opening the car door, "let's hope I really am delusional, then."

Beck got out of the car and walked up the sidewalk.

He started walking toward the Scotts' house, a crumbling, single-family home.

Then he had to stop as his head began spinning again. He was sweating. It was warm out, but not that warm. He'd pushed himself too hard today.

Susan noticed. "You need a minute? Or a doctor?"

Beck grimaced. "I've got you."

He expected a sarcastic comeback. Instead, she put her hand on his arm. "Yes," she said. "You do."

Beck caught his breath and touched her hand. His head was still pounding, but he felt better.

They walked to the Scotts' front door.

Beck knocked. The door creaked open at his touch. It was unlocked. It was barely even closed.

He looked at Susan. She shrugged. Quietly, they walked inside.

The door opened into a short hallway—only a couple of feet—before a living room and kitchen area. There was another short hallway branching off the living room, probably leading to a bedroom. Beck could see a door at the end of the short hall. It was closed.

On the inside, the house was tiny and cramped, but spotless. The thin gray carpet was peeling from the floor, but it had recently been vacuumed within an inch of its life. Bargain furniture was placed in front of a flatscreen on the wall, and a laptop computer sat open on a small dining table.

Beck walked over to the laptop. It was powered on and running a screen saver showing pictures from Kevin

Scott's photos. Beck watched the pictures dissolve, one into another, souvenirs from a life cut short just a couple of hours ago.

In one photo, Scott was grinning with a group of other men, all in camouflage, gathered for a group shot in the middle of some desert in the Middle East. They all looked young and healthy and unstoppable.

My patient is dead, Beck thought.

At that moment, he knew why he was doing this. Why he couldn't just give up. He hated to lose a patient. It always filled him with equal parts despair and rage. But to have a patient taken from him—that was unacceptable. Even if it was all in his head, Beck had to know why this had happened.

He tapped the space bar on the keyboard. The photos vanished, replaced by a log-in screen. There was Kevin Scott's name, followed by a space for a password.

Beck hit Return. The screen vibrated and reset itself. He'd hoped that Scott hadn't set a password. No luck. In fact, the screen told him he had only THREE ATTEMPTS REMAINING. Scott must have set a limit on attempts to log in, to keep people from breaking into his computer. Not surprising, considering he used to work top-secret missions.

Susan was searching the rest of the small room. She was thorough, but there wasn't much to see. She set down a pile of mail, putting it back in the neat stack on the kitchen counter.

"Anything?" she asked.

Beck shook his head. There was nothing here. Maybe he

really was losing it. Perhaps this was all in his head. Perhaps he was hallucinating. Perhaps he was becoming paranoid and losing his grip on reality.

He'd seen it before, in some patients. They were so convinced they were right, even as they babbled on about the shadow government and aliens and conspiracies.

Was he making all of this up? Did he injure two Secret Service agents just because of his brain tumor? He couldn't be that crazy, could he? Was that possible? Had his brain really turned on him like that?

Then he heard a noise from down the hall.

He looked at Susan. "You heard that, too, right?"

She nodded.

Beck went down the hall. Susan followed. He started to open the door, when it whipped open all by itself.

Beck found himself looking at a woman holding a gun.

Well. At least I'm not crazy, he thought.

CHAPTER 12

BECK WINCED, BUT no gunshot came.

Instead, the young woman just stood there.

She was blond and gym-toned, with sharp cheekbones and bright-blue eyes. And she looked terrified.

"Don't move," she said, her voice—and the gun—shaking.

"Don't worry," Beck said. Both he and Susan put up their hands. She quickly slammed the door behind her.

The woman gestured for them to back up. They did. She backed them down the hall, into the living room.

Then they stood there. No one seemed to be sure of the next move.

"Are you Jennifer?" Beck asked.

She blinked. "Who are you?"

"I'm Kevin's doctor," Beck said. "Dr. Randall Beck. Remember? I'm the one he went to see this morning. This is my colleague, Dr. Susan Carpenter."

She blinked again, holding back tears. "Is he—is he all

right?" She stopped and put a hand to her mouth and closed her eyes as she choked back a sob.

The gun remained up, however.

She doesn't know, Beck realized. But she was still armed. And afraid. Clearly something was going on here.

He decided not to tell her about Scott's death. Not while she was still so agitated and holding a gun, anyway.

Susan had clearly come to the same conclusion.

"Please," Susan said gently. "Put that down. We're here to help."

She stepped forward. Braver than Beck felt, the way that gun was waving around. But Jennifer Scott lowered the weapon, and then let Susan fold her into her arms.

She took a deep, shuddering breath, and then stood up straight, pushing Susan back.

"What happened to Kevin?" she said. "He went to see you this morning. He was ranting and crazy and paranoid. I thought he might—might actually *hurt* me. So I was hiding in the bedroom with his gun. Just in case. And then you two show up. What are you doing here? Is he all right?"

Beck had delivered bad news to relatives before, both as a med student and when his patients decided they couldn't take the pain anymore. There was no good way to say it, ever. So he always thought it was best to just say it.

"He's dead, Jennifer. I'm so sorry."

For a second, her face showed nothing. "What?"

"He was shot outside my office. We don't know why. I thought the police would have told you—"

Then the news seemed to hit her all at once, and she turned away quickly.

Susan reached out to her again, but she pulled away. "Please. I need a minute," she said, and hurried down the hall and into the bedroom. The door slammed again.

Beck let out a long deep breath. None of this made any sense. Where were the police? Why hadn't they come to see her?

And something about Jennifer's story nagged at him, too. Kevin Scott had been angry, but not violent when he arrived at Beck's office that morning. He didn't seem like a man who'd just threatened his wife. In fact, the only time he did get angry was when Beck suggested he was having an affair.

That didn't necessarily mean anything, of course. Beck had seen domestic abusers who were as cool as ice outside of the home. But it was just one more thing that didn't add up.

Plus, there was just something *off* about her. He'd seen many people grieve—too many. He knew everyone reacted differently. But there was always a feeling of depth to it—he could always see the impact of the loss, how it almost echoed inside them, like a stone dropped in a well. Jennifer Scott had seemed like she was holding back a sneeze, not like someone holding back tears.

He said to Susan, "Did it seem like she—"

Susan interrupted. "Randall," she said.

"What?"

She pointed at the laptop. The screen saver had activated again. It was going through family photos of Kevin Scott. There was a series of pictures from his wedding.

And the woman in the pictures had dark-brown hair.

She was not the woman who said she was Jennifer Scott.

CHAPTER 13

THE WOMAN'S REAL name was Natalie Mullen. She made sure that Jennifer Scott's body was stashed completely behind the bed. She hadn't had much time to hide it before.

Killing Jennifer Scott was easy. Mullen had knocked and said a big friendly hello when Jennifer had opened the door earlier—no one ever suspected that a woman might be dangerous, especially not another woman. It was a real asset in her line of work.

Then before Jennifer could say anything else, Mullen used the butt of her pistol to hit her in the face, knocking her back into the house.

They'd struggled. Jennifer was badly hurt, but still managed to fight back, which shouldn't have been too surprising since she was a soldier's wife.

Mullen had hit her with the pistol again. She collapsed on the floor. Mullen dragged her to the bedroom and shot her in the face.

Then she'd heard someone out in the living room.

She worked herself up into some tears, took the suppressor off her pistol, and then came out of the bedroom crying and shaking.

Of course they fell for it.

But now she needed to know what to do about them. She pressed a button on her prepaid burner phone and waited. The Client picked up immediately.

Mullen started to explain, but when she said the name "Beck," the Client cut her off.

"He's there? Morrison and Howard were supposed to bring him in. They lost him."

"I've got him right here. He doesn't suspect a thing. He thinks I'm the target's wife."

"We need him," the Client said. "I want to know what Scott told him and who else he's talked to."

"I'll bring him in," Mullen said. "He's with another woman. A doctor. What about her?"

"We don't need her," the Client said, and hung up.

Mullen put her phone away. Fine by her. That just made her job easier.

She went to the door and put on her best sad face. This was going to be a cakewalk. Beck and his girlfriend still thought she was the grieving widow. They'd stand there flat-footed and she could do whatever she wanted. Two in the face of the woman, and Beck would wet his pants in terror. He'd do whatever she told him after that.

They'd never see it coming. Nobody ever saw her coming.

Mullen opened the door, tears in her eyes, gun in her hand.

But the living room was empty.

Beck and the woman were gone.

CHAPTER 14

THE WOMAN CAME out of the bedroom. Beck couldn't see her. But he could hear her.

He'd heard the door open, but the woman didn't come out right away. Then she did and he heard the door close, quietly. He heard the woman's soft footsteps on the carpet in the hallway, then the living room. He was certain he even heard the woman's sharp intake of breath a moment later.

Then he heard the woman call for him. "Dr. Beck?"

He'd stopped thinking of her as Jennifer Scott. Because whoever she was, she was not the woman in Kevin Scott's wedding pictures. Now she was just the woman who happened to be in their house. With a gun.

As soon as he'd seen that picture, he'd grabbed Susan and prepared to run out the front door. But the bedroom door began to open, and Beck didn't think they could make it in time.

So he'd turned the other way and pulled Susan with him into the kitchen. They crouched behind the tiny island in the tiny space, their backs to the counter and the living room.

Now they were frozen, like children with their heads under the covers, hiding from some nightmare.

Beck had to remind himself: it was possible he was wrong. His brain was, by definition, not working properly these days. But it didn't *feel* like he was wrong. And Susan seemed just as scared as he felt. She huddled next to him on the cheap tile floor of the kitchen. She took short, shallow breaths. As if she was afraid the woman would hear her breathing.

The woman moved carefully. Slowly. She didn't act like a woman in her own house. She acted like a hunter, stalking prey.

Beck searched frantically for a weapon. There was a good set of knives in a butcher block on the island over their heads, but if he reached up for them, she'd see him.

He was facing the sink and the lower kitchen cabinets. They were right in front of him. The toes of his shoes were almost touching them. He'd have to find something in there.

He reached carefully. He opened the kitchen cabinet. There was a set of high-end cookware inside—probably bought on sale a long time ago. What was he supposed to do with that?

He heard the front door close, and then lock with an ominous click. They were stuck in here with her now. The woman moved toward them. Susan clutched his arm and huddled into him, as if she was cold and looking for warmth.

Beck pulled out a heavy, cast-iron frying pan and felt faintly ridiculous, like a character in some old sitcom.

He tried to shut the cabinet door quietly, but it slipped from his fingers and closed with a solid *clunk*.

Beck felt rather than heard the woman turn toward the kitchen. He could almost see her, like a hunting dog going on point.

"Dr. Beck? Dr. Carpenter? Are you in here? You're really starting to worry me. . . ."

Beck needed something else. He needed a miracle. He opened the cabinet under the sink.

There was a creak as she crossed from the living room into the kitchen. Susan's grip grew tighter on his arm.

It would only take another step and she'd be able to see Beck and Susan crouched behind the little island.

It was still possible he was wrong. That his brain was simply playing tricks on him.

But he thought of Susan. He had dragged her into this. He couldn't let anything happen to her. He couldn't let anyone hurt her.

He had to make a decision, and he had to make it now. He had to do something.

"Dr. Beck," the woman said, and there was the edge of a cruel laugh in her voice. "You're a little old to be playing hide-and-seek."

He heard her take that next step. She was right on top of them.

He looked at Susan, and silently mouthed, *Stay down.*

Then he sprang up and faced the woman.

She had the gun they'd seen her holding before. Only this time, it was pointed right at Beck's face.

CHAPTER 15

BECK DIDN'T HESITATE. He put his arm forward and pressed the nozzle of the can of oven cleaner he'd found under the sink, and sprayed it directly in the eyes of the woman with the gun.

The woman shrank back and shrieked in pain as the chemicals hit her in the face. She waved the gun around wildly, bringing it back in Beck's direction.

Beck swung the frying pan, with all his might.

He heard a *clang* and a gunshot, almost on top of each other. He felt something connect with the frying pan at the end of his arm, and lost his grip on it. It went tumbling to the floor. He went deaf in one ear and his vision went blank from a bright flare, and he realized that was the muzzle flash of the gun being fired. For a moment, he wondered if he'd been shot.

But he didn't let it stop him. He leaped blindly over the kitchen island and slammed into the woman with all his weight.

They went down in a tangle of arms and legs. The woman was still screaming, but now in rage mixed with pain. They collapsed on the floor.

Beck somehow got on top of her. He blinked his vision clear and saw the woman he'd thought was Jennifer Scott underneath him. The oven-cleaner foam still clung to her face in places. The chemicals had scorched her skin, leaving vivid red burns. She was bleeding from burst capillaries in her eyes, and she stared up at him blankly, unseeing. She was blind. Probably for life.

For a split second, the doctor in Beck wanted to help her, even though he'd caused her injuries. He hesitated for just a moment, unsure of what to do. She had to be in tremendous pain.

But it didn't even slow her down. She reached up, found Beck's face with her hands, and immediately landed two hard punches to his head.

Beck tried to grab her, to stop her, but her fists were as fast as a boxer's. She hit him again. And again.

It suddenly became painfully clear that this woman had killed Jennifer Scott. She had been trained, and probably knew a dozen ways to kill him with her bare hands, even as injured as she was.

She hit him again. Then her hands found his throat. She dug her thumbs into his Adam's apple and started to squeeze.

He had to get up, get away from her.

With everything he had, Beck knocked her hands away from his neck, and staggered backward.

He fell on his ass and bounced into the kitchen island. He felt it come loose, pulling away from the floor.

Beck became aware of Susan, suddenly jumping into the fight. He wanted to shout at her to stay back, but he could barely breathe, let alone speak. Susan was already on the woman. She was trying to rescue him.

The woman couldn't see Susan, but it didn't matter. As soon as Susan landed on her, the woman punched her hard and fast in the chest, stomach, and throat. Susan recoiled in pain, and the woman kicked up with both legs and sent Susan flying.

She hit the kitchen island and knocked it completely away from the floor. Beck heard wood splinter as Susan fell back and hit her head on the refrigerator door.

She slumped to the floor and didn't move.

Beck saw her fall and felt rage hit him like a tidal wave. It swamped all his thoughts. All he wanted to do was hurt the woman. He scrambled toward her on the floor, ready to beat her, to strangle her with his bare hands—

Only she'd found the gun again.

The woman turned and aimed it in Beck's direction. Blindly. But she was close enough. She could not miss at this range.

Beck was dead.

CHAPTER 16

BECK DIDN'T EVEN have time to close his eyes. He knew that she was going to pull the trigger and kill him, and there was nothing he could do.

Then Beck noticed something. The barrel of the gun was bent slightly where he'd hit it with the frying pan.

He wondered, stupidly, what that would do to the gun.

He found out a split second later as the blind assassin pulled the trigger—and the gun exploded in her hand.

Beck went completely deaf in that one ear again, but he could still hear the woman's wail of pain as she pulled back her mangled hand. The bullet had caught in the chamber and backfired. She screamed louder and louder, clutching her bloodied fist to her chest.

Beck tried, again, to attack. He was clumsy and off-balance, but he knew this was the best chance he had to stop her, to subdue her before she could recover.

But she'd been trained, and he had not.

She intercepted him as he tried to tackle her, rolled

with his momentum, and threw him painfully through the kitchen doorway into the living room.

Beck hit the floor hard, feeling the concrete under the thin carpet. He realized she was still screaming, an unholy wail of pain and rage. He tried to stand, and she was immediately on top of him again. She was like some demon dragging him down. They both landed on the floor.

She scrambled over his body, searching with her undamaged hand, looking for any vulnerable spot. He tried to kick her away. She landed another punch, this one deep in his stomach, and for a second, all the air left his lungs. A second later, her right foot swung around and clobbered Beck in the head.

He saw stars. His limbs stopped working for a moment. When he got control of his body again, she'd already put her feet on either side of his neck. Then she had a leglock around his throat, just like he'd seen in some mixed-martial-arts bout on TV once.

Except this was really happening to him. And he couldn't pull her away. Couldn't get her off. He tried to get to his knees, and she yanked him back down again.

She would not stop screaming.

Beck's vision started to go dim around the edges. He couldn't sit up anymore. She somehow managed to ratchet her lock even tighter on his neck. He felt like bones were about to break. Oxygen came into his lungs in a thin trickle.

He was going to die. The tumor wasn't going to get him after all.

And the woman's scream sounded like a cry of triumph now. She sounded almost happy.

Beck couldn't breathe at all. He couldn't even see anymore. He started to go limp. . . .

And then abruptly, the screaming stopped as Beck heard a hollow thud. It sounded like a pumpkin being dropped on concrete.

The pressure on his neck vanished. Air streamed back into his lungs and the feeling returned to his arms and legs. He choked and coughed, and rolled over and looked up again.

Susan stood there with the frying pan. She'd knocked the blind assassin out cold with it. She was battered and bruised, but on her feet.

"Come on," she said, reaching down and hauling Beck off the floor. "We have to get out of here."

She helped him toward the front door. Then he stopped and staggered back toward the kitchen.

"What are you doing?" Susan demanded.

Beck couldn't talk yet. His throat was still on fire. He wondered if he'd ever talk again.

But he managed to stumble into the living room and picked up the laptop.

Whatever was inside it, the woman had wanted it. And that meant Beck wanted it, too.

Then Beck went back to the assassin, lying on the floor.

"You're not really going to *help* her, are you?" Susan asked him.

No. Beck was not going to help her. He'd just decided the Hippocratic Oath didn't apply to anyone trying to kill him.

He searched her pockets, clumsily. He found a wallet, a convenience-store cell phone, and a car key.

He took it all.

Beck carried the laptop. Susan carried him. The woman was still on the floor. Maybe not even breathing now. Beck couldn't tell.

They left as fast as they could.

CHAPTER 17

THE ASSASSIN'S CAR key was for a Dodge. Beck and Susan didn't have to search far to find it. They walked around the block, pressing the Alarm button over and over until a plain sedan—the kind federal agencies bought and used—began honking and flashing its lights.

Beck clicked off the alarm and unlocked the car. He opened the driver's-side door and began searching.

Susan opened the passenger door and sat down next to him. "I still think we should get you to the hospital. And then call the police."

Beck checked behind the sun shades and inside the glove compartment. Nothing. "The police let those agents take me before. I'm not going to trust them again," he said.

"That's a little paranoid, Randall."

"You saw what just happened. It's not paranoia if they're really trying to kill you."

"Then we should at least get you to a hospital."

"I don't need one. I feel fine."

Surprisingly, he was telling the truth. He felt better than he had in weeks. His strength seemed to have come back, despite all the punishment he'd taken and the stress he was putting on his body.

Beck realized he wanted to solve this, to find a solution to the problem. He was charged full of adrenaline, and it was fueling him, pushing him past his limits.

He felt more alive than he had since he'd been diagnosed.

Another minute of searching confirmed what was obvious. The car was empty. There were no clues. No paperwork, no registration. Nothing but that new-car smell.

Beck sat in the driver's seat, stumped for a moment.

Susan looked at him. "Then what do you want to do?"

Beck could only think of one other move now.

He took out the assassin's phone. He pressed the Redial button.

The phone rang twice. Then someone picked up.

A woman said, "Is it done?"

"Not quite," Beck answered.

He was speaking to the person who wanted him dead.

CHAPTER 18

"YOU MUST BE Dr. Beck," the woman said. "I'm surprised to hear from you."

Her voice was muffled and difficult to make out. Beck thought it sounded slightly familiar, but he wouldn't have been able to swear to it. He wasn't even sure he'd be able to identify it if he heard it in person.

He looked at Susan, who looked back, bewildered. What exactly were you supposed to say to the person who was trying to kill you? They didn't teach this in any of their psychology courses.

But therapy is mainly talking: asking questions, and getting answers out of people, even when they don't want to face them. Beck figured he could come up with something.

"Yes," Beck said, "I imagine you are. Why are you doing this? Why are you trying to kill me?"

Beck didn't think he'd get a real answer. But he definitely wasn't expecting the burst of laughter, either.

"Oh, God, you really are a shrink, aren't you? You don't

ask me who I am. No, you want to know *why*. It makes me so glad I quit going to therapy."

"You probably should have stuck with it," Beck said. "You don't strike me as the sanest person I've ever met."

There was a pause on the other end of the line. "I don't think you're taking this seriously enough, Doctor."

Beck wasn't sure he was, either. It probably wasn't a good idea to insult an obvious sociopath. But on the other hand, what did he have to lose? He was already dying, and there was clearly no way he could talk her out of whatever she had planned for him. He wasn't going to make any mental-health breakthrough with her.

So he might as well be honest.

"You've tried to kill me twice. And I'm still here. I don't think you're taking *me* seriously enough. You've sent a couple of mouth breathers and an incompetent killer after me. Whatever your master plan is, I'm not too worried. You can't threaten me, you idiot. You've already done your worst."

Susan stared at him, wide-eyed. *What are you doing?* she mouthed.

Beck tried not to grin. Not real smart, he had to admit. But it felt good.

Then the woman on the other end of the line said something that put a halt to his little victory dance.

"How's Susan?"

Beck felt himself go cold.

"Nothing to say, Doctor?" the woman asked, her tone mocking now. "I know you're already dying, Dr. Beck. I've seen your medical records. You're right. I can't threaten you. But I can make Dr. Carpenter's life much more unpleasant—at least, for as long as it lasts."

Beck found his voice again. "If you try to hurt her, if you even come anywhere *close* to her—"

"Don't be pathetic. You can't threaten me, either, Dr. Beck. So we have a standoff. Here's what I'm offering you. Stay quiet. Go hide somewhere. Don't go to the police, or the media, or anyone else. And if you're a good little boy for the next twelve hours, then your friend Susan won't get hurt."

"And if I'm not?"

"Then she pays for your mistakes. I'm sure you can imagine what that will be like. You're such a smart guy, after all."

Beck's mind raced. He needed to talk to her; he could find a way out of this, if he just had more information. "Listen—"

"No," she said. "This is not a negotiation. Do as you're told. Or Susan dies."

She hung up. Beck looked at the phone, and then at Susan.

She looked back, worried. But not about herself. She'd only caught his side of the conversation. She looked concerned because she was worried about him.

She cared about him, and he hadn't thought of her for a second. Of course they knew she was with him. They'd known everything else so far.

He'd screwed up. He'd been stupid.

And now Susan was in danger—even more danger than he was—because of him.

Beck dropped the phone. It was useless now.

He got out of the car, feeling dizzy. He heard Susan get out of the other side. She said his name. "Randall?"

But it seemed to be coming from very far away. He was having trouble breathing. His pulse hammered behind his ears.

He hit the ground hard as his legs went weak.

And all he could think was that he'd put a target on Susan's head. It was all his fault.

CHAPTER 19

SUSAN DRAGGED HIM to his feet. He managed to walk almost a block toward her car before he nearly fell again. Fortunately, there was a bus shelter nearby. Susan set him on the bench.

Beck breathed deeply and closed his eyes. He taught his patients relaxation techniques for moments like this.

Funny how useless they seemed to him now.

But after a moment, his pulse returned to normal. The world stopped spinning. He'd screwed up. That was done. The question now was how to fix it.

"Susan," he said, opening his eyes. "You have to get away from me. Find a place to hide. I will deal with this on my own. But you have to go. Now."

She stared at him for a moment. Then swore, quietly, under her breath. Then she asked, "Are you completely out of your mind?"

"It's not safe to be around me—"

"Shut up," she said, her voice like a door being slammed.

"Do you really expect me to run away just because you tell me to? You think I didn't know this was dangerous? I am trying to keep you alive. I will not let you run off and commit suicide now."

"I am dying anyway—"

"So you're just going to give up? Really? You? You never give up. *Never*. Remember? Not on your patients. Not when you think you're right. So don't ask me to do it, either."

Beck shrugged. He was too tired to argue with her. And it didn't help that she was right. "Fine," he said. "What do you suggest?"

"I know you're frightened. But I really believe our best chance is to go to the police. Whoever is behind this, they cannot control everything. That's the problem with conspiracy theories. No one has that much power. There are still people we can trust. They cannot possibly control all the cops—"

The sound of sirens and screeching tires drowned out whatever Susan was going to say next.

They both looked up the street and saw several squad cars barreling around the corner, lights flashing, zeroing in on the bus shelter.

Beck watched, helplessly. He should have known. The woman kept him on the phone to trace his location. It was so obvious.

Now the police were headed right for them.

CHAPTER 20

THE METRO PD'S squad cars raced toward them on the street. Beck hunched back inside the bus shelter, as if that would protect them.

Then the cars skidded to a halt a block away.

They surrounded the assassin's car.

Where Beck had dropped the phone.

The cops were out of their cars, guns up, almost before their tires had stopped spinning. One officer grabbed his mike from the dashboard and began shouting into it.

"You! In the car! Come out with your hands up! Now!"

Beck realized they couldn't see inside the car. The windows were tinted, and the glare from the sun made it impossible.

"I said, come out now or we—"

Whatever the officer said was lost in a sudden hail of gunfire.

Someone decided not to wait for the order to fire, and the rear windshield exploded. The other cops, afraid that someone inside the car was shooting at them, unloaded their weapons as well. The entire street echoed with staccato pops and cracks as the bullets slammed into the car. The windows disintegrated first. The door panels deformed and crumpled as they were hit by ammo from both the pistols and shotguns of the police.

It seemed to take forever before the shooting stopped, as the officer in charge bellowed, "Cease fire! Cease fire!" over and over through his car's PA system.

A moment later, the car sat in the street like a wounded, dying animal. It had been torn apart by the shots.

It was clear that if anyone had been inside the vehicle, they would have been dead many times over.

A police officer carefully moved toward the shot-up car. He swung the passenger door open. Then he looked at the other cops. He shook his head.

The officer in charge dropped his mike and yelled at the other cops. "All right! Who shot first? I want to know! Who shot first?!"

No one spoke up.

Beck and Susan sat in the bus shelter, hardly breathing. No one had seen them. No one had even glanced in their direction.

The police were arguing among themselves now. Beck, carefully and quietly, stood up, and Susan followed.

They walked away.

The entire time, Beck felt an itching between his shoulder blades, just waiting for someone to shout for him to stop.

Or a bullet.

But they made it around the corner to Susan's car and got inside without getting caught or shot.

Beck collapsed into the passenger seat and sighed deeply.

Susan did the same. "They knew where we were," she said numbly. "It's like they were tracking down terrorists or something."

"For all we know, that's what they were told," Beck said.

"I take back anything I told you about being paranoid."

Beck chuckled a little at that. Then he sat straight up as he remembered.

"The laptop!" he said.

Susan put a hand on his arm. She opened her bag. The laptop was inside.

Beck sighed again, in relief. She'd remembered it. Thank God.

"I can't believe I forgot it."

"You've got a few other things on your mind," Susan said.

"Including a tumor," he muttered. He took the laptop from her bag and opened it. Maybe there were some answers in here. If he could only get to them.

There was the log-in screen. Beck thought hard. What would Kevin Scott use as a password? What mattered to him?

He'd barely met the man. But he was an Army Ranger. He valued duty. Loyalty. Honor.

Beck entered the Latin motto of the Rangers: *Sua Sponte,* which meant "Of Their Own Accord." It symbolized the Rangers' willingness to volunteer for the toughest missions.

And it didn't work. The screen blurred and shook, and then reset itself.

TWO ATTEMPTS REMAINING.

"Still looking for clues?" Susan asked.

"I'm out of ideas."

The screen saver kicked in again. Kevin Scott's photos began to roll across the laptop once more.

Beck was only halfway paying attention. Then he saw something that made him stare.

He looked at the picture on the screen. It showed Kevin Scott with a bunch of other men and women, all in business attire, in front of a big corporate logo. Beck remembered that from the case history. Scott had been working as a contractor with a private security firm, like a lot of ex–Special Forces who'd come back home. The pay was decent, and it was usually nothing more strenuous than looking after a CEO or billionaire with delusions of importance.

The case history didn't include the name of his employer. It wasn't relevant to Scott's problems.

Except that it was.

Beck looked at the logo on the screen. It was a sword hanging over a stylized graphic of the globe. And across the globe was the name of the company:

THE DAMOCLES GROUP

"Randall?" Susan said. "Randall, are you all right?"

Beck didn't seem to hear her. He looked at the picture and the logo.

Then he nodded, making a decision.

"I think you're right," he said. "We should go to the police."

Not for the first time that day, Susan looked at him like he was insane.

CHAPTER 21

SERGEANT TODD GRAHAM of the Metro PD wasn't expecting to see his psychiatrist show up at his home. That much was obvious from the look on his face when he opened the door.

But Graham didn't hesitate. He grabbed Beck and Susan and hustled them inside. "Get in here, for Christ's sake," he said, "before someone sees you."

It confirmed Beck's intuition about Graham: he was a good cop, and he could be trusted.

It also confirmed something else: Beck was a wanted man.

But Graham was still willing to help him.

Graham slammed the door behind them, then turned and faced Beck and Susan. "What are you doing here? Do you have any idea the shitstorm you could bring down on my head?"

Beck decided to be honest. "No," he said. "I'm hoping you can tell me."

For a moment, Graham looked like he was going to hit Beck. Then he shook it off. "You really don't know?"

"All I know is that people are out to kill me. And I need help. That's why I came to you."

Graham scowled and crossed his arms. He turned away from Beck, clearly thinking. He knew what his duty was, but he was obviously conflicted.

Susan chose that moment to speak up.

"I'm Susan," she said. "We haven't met."

It was just the right oasis of normalcy in the desert of insanity all around them. Graham was forced to turn to her and acknowledge her. It took some of the anger out of him.

"Yeah. I know. You're on the warrant, too."

"What warrant?" Beck asked.

"The arrest warrant. The one issued by the Secret Service." Graham smiled, as if he were joking, but there was no real humor in it.

"Congratulations, Dr. Beck. Apparently you're plotting to kill the president of the United States."

CHAPTER 22

"THAT'S CRAZY," SUSAN said. Shock was etched on her face.

"I know," Graham replied. "You think I'd even be talking to you if I believed it?" He looked back at Beck. "You're crazy, but you're not that crazy. Nobody who'd work that hard with me would do something like that. I know."

Beck stayed quiet. For the first time, he was beginning to figure out what was going on. Things were starting to come together. He just had to think.

"What are they saying?" Susan asked.

"I don't have a lot of detail, but there's an APB out for you both. The Service says you've been implicated in a home-grown terrorist plot to kill President Martin. You're the highest priority in the Washington, DC, area. They thought they had you in a car an hour ago, but that turned out to be a false alarm. They're keeping it quiet for now, but if they don't find you soon, they're going to go public. You'll be the most wanted people in America."

"That's insane," Susan said. "We've done nothing wrong. People have tried to kill us, and we have no idea why. And now you tell us we're supposed to be assassins? It's unbelievable!"

But Beck shook his head. "No," he said. "It makes sense."

That stopped both Susan and Graham in their tracks. "You're going to have to explain that," Graham finally said, his voice very serious.

"Sorry," Beck said, dragging himself back from his thoughts. He could see it very clearly, like a chain, one link after another. But he needed some confirmation. "I mean, I think I have an idea of what's going on. Can we please sit down and I'll explain?"

Graham made a face, but he led them further inside his house to a breakfast nook that he'd also set up as a workspace. Beck took Scott's laptop from Susan's bag and opened it, showing the display to Graham.

The screen saver kicked on again. "Look," Beck said.

Graham watched the pictures of Kevin Scott scroll past. "Who's that?"

"That's the man who was killed in front of my office today."

Graham grunted. "Yeah. I heard something about that. That's supposed to be what tipped the feds off to you."

You ever done anything really bad, Dr. Beck? Kevin Scott had asked him.

"No," Beck said. "He was killed by the people working with him. They were afraid he'd had a change of heart, or a guilty conscience. They murdered him. But they were too late to stop him from talking to me, and they wanted to know what he'd said. So they arrested me."

"Who? Who are you talking about?" Graham demanded.

The group photo came up on the screen saver again. Kevin Scott with his coworkers.

"Them," Beck said. "That was all he said to me. He said the word, 'Damocles.' I didn't know what it meant. But now I do. He was naming his killers."

"Damocles?" Graham said. "Dr. Beck, do you know who you're dealing with here?"

"I do," Susan said. "They're a security company."

Graham snorted. "The guy who installs your burglar alarm is a security company. This isn't some rent-a-cop operation. Damocles is one of the biggest private military contractors in the world. They do billions of dollars' worth of business with the government. They're basically a small army."

Susan reached over to Graham's computer and typed the name "Damocles" into a search engine. A list of articles popped up.

"And they're in trouble," she said. "I was listening to this on NPR just the other day. The Senate is investigating them for cost overruns, corruption, and even torture and murder. They've got a lot of friends in high places, but they've been getting hammered in the hearings. Do you really not know this, Randall?"

"If these are the people after you, then you picked a hell of a fight here, Dr. Beck," Graham said.

Beck looked at some of the headlines. Susan was right: he hadn't been paying attention to any of this.

"I've had other things on my mind," he said. But he wasn't completely oblivious.

There it was. There was the connection he was looking for.

He pointed at one of the articles on the screen.

The headline read:

SENATOR ELIZABETH PIERCE DEMANDS ANSWERS FROM DAMOCLES

"That's who's leading the hearings," he said.

Senator Elizabeth Pierce. Ranking member of the Senate Committee on Intelligence. And currently, the leading challenger in the upcoming election against the president of the United States.

Twelve hours.

The woman's voice on the phone. She'd told Beck to be quiet for twelve hours.

What's happening in twelve hours?

Then Beck remembered. At Georgetown tonight. He wasn't as out-of-touch as Susan thought.

"The presidential debate," he said.

"What?" Graham asked.

"The presidential debate. That's why she told me to stay out of the way for twelve hours. Senator Pierce is debating the president tonight. She's beating Martin in the primaries. And if she wins, Damocles could lose billions of dollars when they lose their military contracts."

It all made sense to Beck now.

"There's an assassination plot," Beck said. "But it's against her. Damocles is going to kill Senator Pierce."

CHAPTER 23

"YOU'D BETTER BE damn sure about this, Dr. Beck," Graham said for what seemed like the tenth time. Beck had lost count.

They were in Graham's unmarked sedan, driving through the thick downtown traffic, heading toward Senator Pierce's campaign headquarters.

Beck had explained it to Graham and Susan several times. Susan believed it made sense. Graham took more time to convince.

"You know what this means, don't you?" Graham asked Beck. "You're accusing President Sharon Martin of plotting to kill her opponent in the primary elections. Because there is no way that the Secret Service cooperates with Damocles without her knowing about it."

"I don't know," Beck admitted. "Maybe. Probably. I don't know where the president fits in. All I know is that these people are killers, and we have to stop them."

Beck knew this was probably an abuse of the doctor–

patient relationship. Graham never would have bought this story if it was coming from some perp he'd arrested on the street. But Graham decided to put aside his skepticism and believe in Beck mainly because Beck had believed in *him*. Beck had refused to give up on *him* when he was at his lowest point. And that got Beck a lot of credit with the cop.

So Graham made a few calls to some friends on the force, who'd given him the names of some people he could trust inside the Secret Service. Good people, he promised Beck.

Beck was nervous about that, but Susan had taken him aside and whispered to him, "He trusted you. It's time for you to trust him."

So Beck did.

After an excruciating hour of waiting and muttered conversations on the phone, Graham had put on a suit jacket and tie and put his Glock 19 into his shoulder holster.

They were going straight to Senator Pierce. With any luck, they would get to her in time.

"Are you sure this is a good idea?" Beck asked.

Graham, next to him in the driver's seat, honked his horn impatiently and squawked his siren at a driver who was too slow to move at a green light. "I'm sure," he said. "Even if the Service is corrupt, the men and women next to the senator—the ones on her personal detail—they will not be in on this. You have to agree to take a bullet for the people you protect. You don't betray that on a whim. Trust me. I know some of these guys. They become like family. There's a real loyalty there."

"I hope you're right," Susan said from the backseat. She

was looking at the laptop again, staring hard at the log-in screen, as if she could see inside the machine's circuits to unlock the password.

"Susan, we're not going to figure it out," Beck told her, again. "Scott was in covert ops. It's probably a string of random characters."

"You're probably right," Susan said, but she kept staring at the laptop, ignoring the traffic around them.

Beck sagged in the front seat. He checked his own pulse. Neither Graham nor Susan noticed. It was thready. He closed his eyes and took a deep breath and tried to force himself to be calm.

Just let me live long enough to do this, he thought. He wasn't sure whom the thought was directed to, really. But he thought it again anyway. *Just let me live long enough.*

The car slammed to a halt. Beck opened his eyes. They were outside the offices of Senator Pierce. The front of the building was covered with her campaign logo, and posters of her face smiled from every window.

Graham hopped out. "Come on," he said. "Let's go ride to the rescue."

Beck looked back at Susan, who nodded, and they both got out of the car.

Let me live long enough to do this, Beck thought again, then followed the cop inside.

CHAPTER 24

SENATOR PIERCE'S CAMPAIGN headquarters was controlled chaos. Every manner of electronic device was beeping and pinging, demanding attention. Multiple screens showed every news channel, each one with a constantly scrolling stream of information. Volunteers ran from one cubicle to the next, as a dozen other people talked urgently into their phones. Dozens of pizza boxes layered a long table, and empty coffee cups overflowed the wastebaskets.

They were united in a cause. Beck could almost see the excitement and purpose binding them all together, like a warm glow in the air despite the cheap fluorescent lighting.

Then someone shouted, "QUIET!" as the latest poll numbers hit the screens. A blond, tanned anchorwoman on CNN announced, "And the latest polls show upstart challenger Senator Elizabeth Pierce within striking distance of President Sharon Martin, with just a few days to go before the crucial Super Tuesday primaries. . . ."

The cheers drowned out the rest of her words. People were hugging and high-fiving, before returning to their work with renewed purpose.

Beck overheard someone say, in a tone of disbelief, "Holy crap, man, we could actually win this thing!"

Only if the candidate survives, Beck thought bitterly. He once believed that assassination plots and conspiracy theories were just for his patients and bad TV. That was this morning.

Now he knew better.

Graham pulled him through the packed room.

"The senator and her detail are willing to meet with you," he said, keeping his voice low. Beck had to strain to hear. They stopped in front of an office. Graham turned to Susan, looking slightly sheepish. "Sorry, can you wait in here? The agents are a little nervous about too many strangers getting close to the senator right now."

Beck began to protest, but Susan cut him off. "I don't blame them," she said. "It's fine. I'll wait."

"You sure?" Beck asked. He would not have made it this far without her. It seemed somehow ungrateful to put her in a waiting room right now.

"Randall, I am ready to be done with this," Susan said. "I promise. Do what you have to do. Go."

Graham nodded, grateful, and pointed her to a chair in the room. Susan sat down. She opened her bag and took out the laptop and offered it to Beck. "You'll need this," she said.

Beck hesitated. Some instinct told him not to take it. *After all,* he thought, *it's not paranoia if they really are out to get you. . . .*

"You hold on to it," Beck said.

"Hey, they need that," Graham said.

"Probably," Beck agreed. "But I'll feel better if Susan holds on to it."

Graham scowled but didn't argue.

"Fine. Whatever. Just don't try to open it again," he said. "The Secret Service has people that can crack it. They'll take care of it."

If Susan resented being talked down to, she didn't show it. "I understand," she said. "Don't worry."

She slid Scott's laptop back into her bag.

Graham turned and led Beck out of the office again, closing the door behind him.

He went down the hall to a solid-steel door at the end of the corridor. Beck followed. A plainclothes Secret Service agent—dark suit, earpiece—stood on guard.

Graham flipped his badge. "Todd Graham, MPD. They're expecting us."

The agent nodded. Beck watched him carefully. He would never really trust people in dark suits again. Probably not for the rest of his life.

Of course, that's not going to be very long, he thought.

The agent rapped on the door. A heavy bolt clunked and the door swung inward.

Almost over now, Beck thought. He was glad. Susan was right. It was time for the professionals to handle this. It was time for this to become someone else's problem.

CHAPTER 25

SUSAN WATCHED BECK follow the cop out of the room, and immediately took out the laptop again.

Randall was safe. They were both safe. She finally had a moment to think, without guns going off or someone trying to kill her. Now she could actually solve this.

She cared about Randall Beck a great deal. If one of her friends took her out for drinks, off the record, she would admit that she probably cared about him more than was strictly professional. She thought he was one of the smartest people she'd ever met. She knew he cared about people, and had constructed his impatient manner to hide just how vulnerable that made him. And she knew he was like a pit bull clamped on to a steak when it came to figuring out a problem.

But he had blind spots a mile wide.

That was the thing about being a therapist. She could see his blind spots, even when the patient—even though he was also a psychiatrist—couldn't.

Randall, for instance, had almost nothing in his life except his work. The same applied to most of his patients. They believed in duty, in a higher calling.

So of course he thought that Scott's password would be the Ranger motto. It was the only possibility in Randall's mind. He believed that Kevin Scott was like all his other patients, focused more on saving the world than anything else.

It was a noble way to look at the world, but it left a few things out.

Like family. Friends. Love.

But Kevin Scott wasn't like Randall's other patients. Susan could see it from the pictures that were now scrolling across the laptop screen again. Sure, there was the one picture of him at work, and a couple of him in the field in Afghanistan and Iraq—but these were not pictures of him doing a job. They were pictures of him with his friends.

Most of the rest of the pictures were with his wife, Jennifer. (Susan did not want to think about what must have happened to her. Poor woman.) In each picture, Kevin Scott looked at her like she was the center of the universe.

Randall also thought the password would be some high-security code. Susan knew most people didn't think like that. Even the ones who have been in top-secret jobs. Especially those people. At home, they just want to be normal.

And normal people don't put a lot of effort into the passwords on their laptops.

Susan typed the name JENNIFER into the password space.

The computer immediately opened to the desktop.

Scott hadn't gone to any trouble to hide what she was looking for.

There was only one file folder on the screen, marked DAMOCLES.

Susan opened it and began reading the first document she found.

Within moments, she knew they'd made a terrible mistake.

But she would have known that anyway when the door opened, and a man with a gun walked in on her.

CHAPTER 26

GRAHAM WENT THROUGH the door into Senator Pierce's inner office, and Beck followed.

Two things happened, so fast that Beck would swear they were simultaneous.

First, the door swung shut, the heavy bolt locking again.

Then Agent Howard stepped forward, his face masked behind bandages and a splint for his nose. He was smiling like he'd just heard the funniest joke in the world.

He hit Beck across the face with the barrel of his gun.

Beck reeled from the blow.

He looked up at Graham. He'd trusted the cop. He couldn't believe he'd been so wrong.

But Graham looked just as surprised. He was clearly taken off guard, just like Beck was.

That moment of disbelief cost him his life.

He was still reaching for his Glock in its holster when Agent Howard shot him in the face.

Graham's body dropped to the floor, landing right next to Beck.

Beck had a moment of pure horror as he saw the wet, red wound in the middle of Graham's forehead, the cop's eyes already empty and staring.

Then he felt nothing but rage.

He prepared himself to leap at Howard, but the agent was ready. He hit Beck with the barrel of the pistol again—Beck realized it was longer than it should have been, a suppressor attached to the end—and spots danced before Beck's eyes as his body failed underneath him.

It took him a long moment just to keep from vomiting.

When he was finally breathing normally, he looked up.

Agent Morrison stood above him now, with his right hand on his gun and his left hand holding Susan by the arm. Agent Howard was still grinning at him.

"I know you don't care if you live or die," Howard said. "But I bet you feel differently about her."

Beck wanted nothing more than to wipe that smirk from Howard's face. "I swear to God—" he began.

A woman's voice cut him off before he could say anything more. It was the voice of the woman on the phone.

"Oh, please, Dr. Beck, don't say anything stupid."

Beck turned and saw Senator Elizabeth Pierce standing beside a heavy, slab-like desk. Sergeant Graham's dead body lay on the floor less than five feet from her brand-new Ferragamo pumps.

"I think we've had enough empty threats and promises, don't you?" she said. "Now it's time to get down to business."

CHAPTER 27

BECK DIDN'T THINK that the bad guys really explained their plans to their victims. Not in real life. He thought he'd get a bullet in the head, just like Graham did.

But as it turned out, Senator Pierce needed him to understand.

Howard pulled Beck up from the floor, then sat him down in a chair next to Susan so the senator would have an audience. He bound their hands and feet with zip-ties, and then dragged Graham's body into another room while the senator waited patiently.

She looked at them for a moment.

"Scott didn't have a chance to tell you anything, did he?" she said.

"He told me enough," Beck said. He decided to try to bluff his way out of this. It had to be worth a shot. "And we told Graham. His superiors know he was coming here. The police will be here any moment—"

"No, they won't," Pierce said. "Really, Dr. Beck. We know

they're still looking for you. Your friend was willing to hide you, to try to keep you safe. And look what you did to him in return. You got his brains blown out the back of his skull. Now. Can we please try again?"

Beck shut up. Bluffing didn't work. There didn't seem to be any point in pretending he knew what was going on anymore. So he asked an honest question.

"Why are you working with Damocles? Why are you doing any of this?"

Pierce looked at him like he was an idiot. "Because I want to be the president, of course."

Susan couldn't restrain herself, either, apparently. "But you're winning," she said.

Pierce smiled. "No," she said. "At the moment, I'm the distraction. I'm the challenger who's interesting. Who brings up some issues, and makes the race competitive. I make the ratings go up, and I give the TV people something new to talk about. But none of the big donors have broken my way. The overall machinery is still firmly on Martin's side. And when I'm not fresh or entertaining, I'll be written out of the script. It happens almost every election. It's just my turn."

Beck was starting to put it together now. "And Damocles came to you with a proposal."

Pierce snorted. "No. I had to go to them. Repeatedly. For a company that kills people on a daily basis, they were surprisingly squeamish about getting their hands dirty. But after I pressured them a bit with those hearings, they came around. You'd be surprised how many former Damocles employees there are in the Secret Service."

Beck couldn't help looking up at Morrison when she said that. Morrison caught his eye and shrugged, as if to say, *Hey, it's a job*.

"Kevin Scott was supposed to be the distraction tonight. He was going to trigger an explosion. And while everyone panicked, a sniper would open fire on the debate stage, wounding both of us." Pierce allowed herself a smile. "Tragically, only one of us would survive."

"And you'd ride that wave of sympathy right into the White House," Beck said.

Pierce nodded. "We'll blame some Middle Eastern country, and Damocles will have a new war to fight. Everybody wins."

"But Scott wouldn't go along with it," Beck said.

Morrison spoke up. "He had an attack of conscience," the agent said. "He wanted his wife to be proud of him." His tone was scornful.

"And you were worried he'd told me about the whole thing."

"You know, if you'd just cooperated with my agents and told them that Scott didn't say anything to you, none of this would have happened. You could be at home, waiting for that tumor to kill you. That's right—I know you're dying. I know everything about you. You might have helped a few more patients."

Beck had to admit, she had a point.

"So you lost your bomber," Beck said. "And you had me running around loose."

"It could have gotten really ugly," Pierce said. "Fortunately, you showed up just in time. You really thought you were going to protect me, didn't you?"

Beck shrugged. He wasn't usually this wrong about people. He wondered, if he'd had a chance to meet Pierce in person before this, would he have known she was a sociopath?

"Well, you can still help me, Dr. Beck," she said. "And you can help Dr. Carpenter as well. Even if it is the last thing you'll ever do."

That was why she'd explained everything to him. And that was why Morrison and Howard strapped a vest with twenty small bricks of C-4 to his chest.

Because he was a part of the plan now. Now he was one of the bad guys, too.

CHAPTER 28

BECK WAITED IN line and wondered if he had the guts to sentence Susan to death.

He was outside the auditorium on the Georgetown campus, along with a few hundred other people waiting to go through the metal detectors at the entrance. Like everything else in the contest between the president and Senator Pierce, the location of the debate had been argued back and forth for weeks. Pierce's people wanted it in New York or Miami, one of the bigger media markets with more primary votes. President Martin's people had argued that the president was too busy actually running the country to make the trip—and they didn't want to raise Pierce's profile any more than necessary. They both backed out of the debate several times before finally agreeing on Georgetown. It was a small space, which limited the candidates' exposure to the public. Tickets were given to only select lucky citizens, including Beck.

Beck had seen the bickering in the media. He never thought it would mean anything in his life.

Now it looked like they were choosing the place he was going to die.

The question was, how many people was he willing to take with him?

A small radio inside Beck's ear—almost invisible to anyone else—began speaking to him. "You're doing fine, Doc," Agent Howard said. "Remember, we can see everything you're doing. Just stay calm, and it will be over before you know it."

Beck wondered where the cameras were, or if Morrison and Howard had agents following him. Probably both. He had no doubt they could see him.

Back at campaign headquarters, they'd cleaned him up as best they could before they sent him out. They gave him a fresh shirt out of a box kept inside one of the staffer's desks. They put his suit jacket back on him, over the suicide vest. To cover the bulk, they wrapped him in one of the special oversize raincoats that the Secret Service used while they were carrying shotguns and automatic weapons in public. It made him look normal, at least at first glance.

Then they clipped an all-access pass to his coat. It had the senator's campaign credentials stamped on it, along with a photo they'd snapped of him and printed onto the badge.

He had a trigger for the vest inside the pocket of his suit, but Howard had disconnected it—it was just a piece of plastic now. The real trigger was a code that could be sent at any time from Morrison's or Howard's phone.

And for leverage, they had Susan.

"Remember, Doc," Howard told him in the car as he was dropped off. "You deviate from our instructions in any way—talk to anyone, try to warn the president, go anywhere near a cop—and you will end your girlfriend's life, as well as your own. It will be quick for you, but not for her. Understand?"

Beck understood. He just had to decide if he could do it anyway.

He saw uniformed security at the metal detectors. They were checking everyone. Campaign staffers had to surrender their phones. Big-name donors had to put their $20,000 Rolexes and Fendi purses into little buckets and send them through the X-ray machine. Beck even saw the secretary of state being patted down. As usual, they were taking no chances when it came to the safety of the candidates.

Beck knew he could stop the plan right there. He could tell the nearest security man he had a bomb, and they would immediately take him down. With luck, it would start a panic and people would scramble to get away from him. Even if Howard detonated the vest remotely, fewer people would die out here than inside the auditorium.

And Damocles's sniper would never have a chance to kill the president. Pierce's twisted scheme would fail. On balance, more lives would be saved than lost.

But it would mean Susan died. Probably in the most horrible way possible. Beck didn't fool himself about Howard or Morrison. They would do their worst, if only for revenge against him, even if he were dead.

Beck was willing to die. But he wasn't sure he could live with sentencing Susan to torture and slow death.

The line moved forward, one agonizingly slow step at a time. The people around him were smiling like they were heading into a football game. This was the playoffs for political junkies. Pierce had been right about that, at least. She'd made the race more exciting.

Beck had to decide. Who was going to live, and who was going to die?

No one should have to make this choice, he thought desperately.

But here he was.

He was two places away from the metal detector now. He wondered if it would pick up on the wiring in the vest. Maybe he wouldn't have to make a choice at all. If they pulled him out of the line and patted him down, would Howard trigger the bomb just to keep him from talking?

"You're looking a little nervous there, Doc," Howard said. "Just take a deep breath and try to enjoy it." There was a chuckle in Beck's ear as the agent laughed at his own little joke. Beck truly loathed the man.

Then Beck was at the metal detector.

He made his choice.

Susan, forgive me, he thought.

He turned to the man in the uniform and opened his mouth to speak.

CHAPTER 29

AT THAT MOMENT, Susan was looking at Agent Howard's gun.

She and the agent were parked in the alleyway behind the university's performing arts center, which was where the debate was being held. Morrison had gone off with Pierce back at campaign headquarters, while Howard had taken Beck and Susan. He didn't even have to threaten them with the gun—one look at the vest strapped to Beck had been enough to keep them compliant.

Howard had bundled her inside the car with Beck, and then kept her as a hostage after dropping him off at the front of the building. Since then, he had been running the operation from the rear of the car.

The interior of the limo was outfitted like the cockpit of a high-tech fighter jet: screens showed multiple angles from security cameras inside and outside the auditorium. Howard's microphone connected to radios carried by a half-dozen Damocles operatives who were involved in the plot—Susan had heard him giving orders over a secure channel—and he also monitored the Secret Service and police frequencies as well.

The limo itself was bombproof and bulletproof. Heavy ceramic armor plates were concealed under its panels, and it had a specially designed chassis that could shrug off anything short of a rocket launcher. It was one of the alternate limos used to carry the president and other high-ranking dignitaries. Howard had bragged about it when he put Beck and Susan inside. Like he was a tour guide.

Now Howard's gun rested within easy reach of his right hand, on a small tray-table next to the command console.

Susan stared at it for what felt like a long time. She wondered if she'd be able to shoot him if she had the chance.

When she looked up, she saw Howard grinning at her, his eyes and nose swollen behind the bandages.

"Try it," he said. "It's been a long day, and I'd love to have an excuse."

Susan lifted her hands, and sat back in her seat in the limo as far away from him as she could. She knew better than to antagonize a psychopath. Howard would act on impulse and worry about the consequences later.

Howard grunted. "Smart. A lot smarter than your boyfriend. Now just sit there and stay quiet."

He turned his attention back to the tiny screens. She could see Beck at an odd angle, looking down on his head from above. Susan realized that she must be seeing him through a security camera at the entrance. He looked tense and nervous, but nobody else would really notice. You'd have to know him to realize that expression on his face wasn't his usual way of looking at the world.

So Beck was going to make it inside the debate, unless he did something to change that.

He would try something, however. He wouldn't take this quietly, and he would not allow anyone to use him as a weapon. Part of it was his need to do the right thing—that Superman complex she was always telling him about—and part of it was just his innate stubbornness. Randall was a fighter. He had to do something, even if it got them both killed.

She looked at Howard's briefcase, sitting by his feet. That was where the agent had stashed the laptop after Morrison took it from her, and he'd brought it with them in the limo. She supposed they still wanted to know what was on the hard drive and make sure it was disposed of properly.

It was dangerous to them. They were afraid of it.

So Susan made sure she kept her eye on it.

When Beck made his move, she would make hers.

They might both get killed, but at least they weren't going to surrender.

CHAPTER 30

BECK PREPARED TO tell the security guard at the gate about the bomb under his jacket. He took a deep breath, and wondered if there was going to be time for pain, or if it would all happen too fast to feel anything.

Then he saw the logo on the man's uniform.

It was the globe and sword of Damocles.

The man smiled at Beck and waved him through the metal detector.

Beck didn't move.

The man's smile froze into something more like a grimace. He stepped forward and put his hand on Beck's shoulder.

"Come on now, *Doctor,*" he said quietly. "You're holding things up."

He guided Beck forward and pushed him through the metal detector with a not-so-gentle shove.

Beck braced himself for a buzzing noise, for people to notice him, for the code that would blow him—and all these people around him—into pieces.

The metal detector didn't make a sound.

A second later, Beck was through, and in the lobby outside the auditorium before he knew it.

Damocles had a man at the door. *Of course* they did. They were an elite security outfit, just the type of company contracted for events like this.

"See, Doc?" said Howard's voice. "Told you we'd handle everything. Now all you have to do is wait."

Howard was right. They were handling everything. He was surrounded by dignitaries and party officials and young campaign staffers. Not one of them expected to die tonight.

Beck would have to think harder. He would have to find a better way.

The doors opened behind him, and Senator Elizabeth Pierce entered the lobby, flanked by her Secret Service detail and her campaign staff.

Some of the people in the lobby broke out into applause and cheers.

"You can do it, Liz!" one of them shouted.

"You're going to win!"

"Take her down, Senator!"

There was laughter and more clapping at that.

Beck barely heard it.

It was too late now. He had no more time to think. No more plans. No more last-minute, buzzer-beating, Hail Mary plays.

Any minute now, the president would arrive as well, and Morrison would trigger the bomb.

Beck was out of time.

CHAPTER 31

AGENT MORRISON TOOK his position in the catwalk above the seats and the control booth of the auditorium. The Secret Service had already blocked off access to this section of the building.

It was, after all, the perfect spot for an assassin.

Morrison carried an H&K MP5 machine pistol. With its extendable stock, and set to single-shot fire, he could easily put a bullet into the head of President Sharon Martin. He was less than a hundred feet from her podium on the stage, standing above the seats, and backlit by all the lights.

No one would see him.

He'd wait until the candidates were both on the stage, and then he'd hit the button on his phone that would trigger Beck's vest.

People would be distracted, looking back at the lobby. That's when he'd kill the president.

Then he would fire another burst along the floor of the stage. Senator Pierce might get hit, or she might not. At that point, his colleagues—some of them people he'd known for years—would already be pulling both the women offstage and to the ambulances waiting in the back.

They'd also be shooting at him, but he was prepared for that. He would fire randomly into the crowd. He had a description all ready of a man of Middle Eastern descent as the shooter. Everyone would start looking for the suspect.

And no one would seriously believe Morrison had been involved. He was, after all, a Secret Service agent.

He and Howard had already picked out a patsy, a local college student who spent too much time on jihadi websites in between playing video games. They would hide the H&K in his dorm room and send in an anonymous tip to the police.

If the kid got killed while resisting arrest—well, so much the better. Damocles had friends in the FBI and the police department as well.

Morrison had been worried for a while today. First Scott had his attack of conscience, and then it looked like that smartass Beck was going to cause some real problems.

But it all worked out. And he was about to have a multibillion-dollar defense contractor and the future president of the United States deeply in his debt.

Howard's voice suddenly began speaking through his radio earpiece.

"Morrison. The senator just entered the building. You good?"

Morrison smiled.

"Yeah," he said. "I'm perfect."

CHAPTER 32

IN THE LIMO, Susan watched Howard carefully.

The agent pressed a button on his console and spoke into his mike. "Morrison. The senator just entered the building. You good?"

"Yeah," came the reply. "I'm perfect."

"All right," Howard said. "We're almost there. Just a couple more minutes."

He looked at a digital clock in the console. The debate was due to start at 9:00 p.m. The clock read 8:56.

Howard pressed another button on the console and switched channels again. Now the feed from the Secret Service's radios came over the limo's speakers.

"This is Howard," he said. "Senator Pierce is in the lobby, on her way to the stage. We're cutting it a little close. Do we have an ETA on Minerva?"

Minerva. Like most people in DC, Susan knew that President Martin's Secret Service code-name was Minerva, after the ancient goddess of wisdom—the *Washington Post* had done a whole feature on it.

Howard was checking to see when she would arrive. Susan realized that he and Morrison and all the other Damocles operatives would all know, down to the second, where to find their target.

"Minerva is two minutes out," an agent replied over the radio. "Onstage in five."

"Roger that," Howard said.

Howard watched the screens carefully, then glanced over at Susan.

"Might want to stick your fingers in your ears, sweetheart," he said. "We're about to have a very big bang."

CHAPTER 33

SENATOR PIERCE MADE her way across the crowded lobby, smiling and shaking hands. Beck watched her carefully.

No one paid any attention to him. Their eyes were all on the senator.

Beck didn't know what to do. He was completely out of ideas.

And he was sweating, and his head was killing him.

Senator Pierce moved forward, her protective detail clearing the way respectfully and carefully. It was more stagecraft. Nobody here would do anything against her. They were all vetted beforehand to get a seat at the debate.

Beck was the only truly dangerous man in the room.

Pierce drew even with Beck in the crowd now. She turned and saw him. They locked eyes. And Pierce gave him a radiant politician's smile. She looked happy.

Because she was going to get away with it. Beck could see that, almost written on her face.

She was barely five feet away from him. If the trigger in his pocket actually worked, he'd be tempted to squeeze it.

He reached into his pocket, and found not the trigger, but the handcuffs that Howard had used on him that morning. It seemed a million years ago to him now.

Useless. Just like him.

Beck was still sweating. His head throbbed, and his pulse pounded behind his ears.

He took a deep breath. This would be the absolute worst time for one of his episodes. But all this stress, the sudden spike in his blood pressure, the adrenaline. All of that, on top of his exhaustion and the punishment he'd already taken today…it would make sense if his body couldn't take any more, if the pressure inside his skull was too great.

It would make sense.

Beck began gasping for air.

The people closest to him in the crowd looked at him.

"You okay?" a young man who looked barely out of high school asked him. He looked like a kid wearing his dad's jacket and tie.

"I'm fine," Beck choked out, and bent over, hyperventilating now.

Other people began to notice. Including Howard, who spoke through the radio.

"What's going on, Beck?" he said, a warning in his tone. "You'd better pull it together."

Beck didn't answer, just kept breathing hard.

"Sir, are you all right?" someone else asked. "Do you need help?"

"Someone get a doctor. Is anyone here a doctor?"

Beck would have laughed at that if he could.

"I'm fine," he said again. It came out in a wheeze. Beck sounded weak even to his own ears.

Howard's voice spoke in the radio again. "What the *hell* are you doing?"

"Can't breathe," he said. He stumbled to one side and bumped into several people. "My *head*—"

Now people were beginning to grab for him, trying to keep him upright. Pierce was stuck in the crowd as everyone froze in place, wondering what was going on.

Now Pierce's protective detail was moving away from her, and toward Beck.

"We need a doctor over here!" someone shouted. "Call 911!"

"Get yourself together, Beck," Howard snapped. "Do I have to remind you—"

Whatever he was going to say next was lost in the shouts of the crowd as Beck fell forward and lay facedown on the carpet.

CHAPTER 34

"GET UP, BECK! *Get up!*" Howard screamed into his mike.

"That won't work," Susan told him. "You can't bully a cancer patient into getting up. He needs medical attention."

Howard turned to her and snarled, "Shut up or I will shut you up."

He turned back to the console, his eyes searching the screens, listening to the multiple radio channels, where chaos reigned.

But for all that data, he still had no idea what was happening right in front of his eyes.

"What's going on?" the driver asked from the front seat. "Should I call Morrison?"

"Shut the hell up and let me think!" Howard shouted back. He was unraveling right in front of Susan's eyes.

The sound of a 911 dispatcher suddenly broke through one of the speakers: "We've got a call for a paramedic at the Georgetown University debate. Is the Secret Service aware of the problem? Do they require assistance?"

Howard pressed a button on his console and switched channels. Then, in a surprisingly calm voice, he said, "Metro Dispatch, this is Secret Service. We are aware of the problem and have a medical unit onsite. We have no need for assistance."

"Are you sure?" the dispatcher asked. "We have a unit on the way."

In a slightly tighter voice, Howard answered, "We have it under control, Metro Dispatch. Please let us do our job, and you do yours."

There was a pause. Then: "Copy that, Secret Service. Call if you need help."

The dispatcher broke the connection.

"You have to get him help," Susan said. "He needs an ambulance. He could be bleeding into his brain, he could be going into cardiac arrest—"

Howard pointed his gun at her and cocked the hammer back.

"Not. Another. Word," he said, biting off every syllable. Then he switched the channel on his console again.

An urgent voice broke through all the other chatter. It was the same Secret Service agent that Howard had spoken to before about President Martin. "Base, what's going on? You have a man down? Should Minerva abort?"

Susan understood immediately that the president's Secret Service agents were asking if it was safe for her to come to the debate.

Howard clicked onto that channel and answered in the calmest voice possible. "No need for that," he said. "It looks like a medical issue. All clear here. Minerva is okay to proceed."

"Copy that, base. See you in one minute."

"See you here," Howard said. Then he switched back to his other radio channels, stabbing the buttons frantically.

"Dammit, is there anyone who's got eyes on Beck?" he barked into his mike.

"I'm at the door," a voice said through the speaker. "I can get to him, but it will mean leaving my post—"

"Then leave your damned post!" Howard shouted. "Move it!"

Susan knew that if Beck had collapsed, he might well be dying on the floor. Or maybe even already dead. She had no idea how his body was holding up after everything they had been through today. He could already be gone.

The thought nearly broke her heart. If she stopped to think about it, she knew it would paralyze her.

So she pushed it aside.

Randall would want her to live. And more importantly, he would want her to beat these bastards.

Howard was distracted. He was staring at the screens, watching a uniformed Damocles guard shove his way through the crowd around Beck.

She leaned all her weight back in her seat in the limo and pulled her knees to her chin.

Howard caught the movement from the corner of his eye and turned to face her.

"What do you think you're—"

Susan snapped her legs straight in a double-footed kick

that caught him full in the face, bouncing his skull off the roof of the limo.

He screamed in pain and dropped the gun. He used both hands to clutch at his broken nose, now gushing blood again.

Susan thought for a second that her Krav Maga instructor would be proud.

She snatched the case from the floor of the limo and popped open her door, and ran as fast as she could as soon as her feet touched the ground. She heard the driver's door open behind her, heard him yelling at her to stop. She risked a look back and saw him draw his gun, but she knew he wouldn't start shooting out here with so many non-compromised cops and Secret Service agents. She sprinted away to find somewhere to hide and think.

Randall, forgive me, she thought. *But you're on your own.*

CHAPTER 35

THE DAMOCLES GUARD—his name was David Cook—shoved and bullied his way from the metal detectors and the screening station to the center of the lobby. He knew the other guards—the ones who weren't in on the plot, and who weren't on the secure channel—were probably wondering why he'd abandoned his post, but screw them. The only instructions he cared about now were from Howard. He had to get to Beck. If anyone else should reach him first, they might open his shirt and jacket and see the vest. And then the whole plan would be ruined. There was no way the presidential detail would allow the president anywhere near the building if there was a bomb inside.

One of Pierce's Secret Service agents—not a Damocles plant, unfortunately—was almost to Beck.

Cook yelled at him, "Protect the senator! I've got this!"

The woman nodded and stepped back to flank the senator again.

Cook grabbed and pulled the idiots surrounding Beck out of his way. "Move!" he yelled. "Come on, move it!"

Beck was on the floor, looking like he was hours away from his own autopsy.

Damn it, Cook thought. *We've come so far, we can't have it all go to pieces now.*

He just had to get Beck on his feet. That was all. Then he had to get out of the lobby himself before the bomb was triggered. It could all still work. The plan could be salvaged.

Cook pulled on Beck's shoulder and rolled him onto his back. Beck's face was pale. Cook couldn't tell if he was breathing.

Cook leaned down and brought his face close to Beck's. He felt around the man's neck for a pulse.

He was surprised to find that Beck's pulse was strong and steady and fast.

Then he was even more surprised to feel Beck's hand at his belt as the doctor grabbed Cook's gun and yanked it from his holster.

Cook looked into Beck's eyes, which were wide open now.

"Change in plans," Beck said.

Then he put the gun against Cook's chest and pulled the trigger.

CHAPTER 36

THE SOUND OF the gunshot worked like a starter pistol. Everyone began running, even if they had no idea where to go.

Beck knew he only had a few seconds before he would lose the element of surprise. He'd managed to fake a seizure and fool everyone, but he didn't think their shock at seeing him rise from the dead would last long.

He was right. Pierce's Secret Service detail was already moving between him and the senator, trying to block him as he stepped toward her.

But he was too close, and he already had a gun drawn. They were hampered by the panicking crowd, and they were really not expecting any trouble. The best they could do was shield her.

Which was precisely what Beck expected them to do.

He stepped up to each of the agents guarding Pierce, who was looking at him with shock and horror as—too late, they scrambled to draw their guns.

Beck fired the gun three more times, putting a bullet each into the body armor that the agents wore on their chests.

He looked over to the Damocles guard he'd shot first, who was yelling and cursing on the ground, clutching his chest.

Even with a bulletproof Kevlar vest, a point-blank round to the chest could break ribs. More importantly, it really, really hurt.

Beck had learned that from listening to his patients' stories in therapy. He was happy to see that it worked in practice, too.

The Secret Service agents were now all on the ground, the breath knocked out of their lungs. Only Pierce was left standing. She turned to run from him.

But there was nowhere to go.

Beck could have shot her. He could have ended her life right there.

But he was not, despite everything that had happened today, a killer. He could not make himself cross that line.

And he wanted the world to see her for what she really was. He didn't want revenge.

He wanted the truth. For Kevin Scott. For Susan. For Todd Graham. For Jennifer Scott, who he now assumed had been murdered by the woman in her house. And even for Louis, who Beck had a terrible gut feeling had also felt the wrath of Damocles. And for himself, too.

So he grabbed her by the wrist and yanked her close. He jabbed the gun in her side.

Then he used his free hand to snap the handcuff around her left wrist.

The other cuff was already locked around his right wrist.

Pierce tried to pull away from him. Couldn't. "What did you just do?" she shrieked.

Beck ignored her.

He pointed the gun at the ceiling and fired a round into the air.

The crowd moved like it had a single mind, everyone trying to get away from the madman with the gun. Beck found himself at the center of the lobby with no one but Pierce by his side.

She tried to pull away again. Beck tugged her back, the metal of the cuffs biting into both their wrists. He thought they wouldn't risk taking a shot at him, for fear they would miss and explode the vest, killing Pierce. But he also knew, as long as he didn't come anywhere close to President Martin, they wouldn't detonate the vest remotely.

Pierce wasn't going anywhere. They were locked together. Their fates were now inextricable.

CHAPTER 37

SUSAN DECIDED TO risk it. She snuck out from between the two news vans where she'd been hiding, and forced herself to walk slowly, to try to look normal, like she was supposed to be there, the laptop tucked under one arm.

She had no idea where she was going. She was behind the performing arts center, trapped inside the security cordon for the event. There were temporary barriers and police tape strung all around the building. The street was blocked by heavy, military-style Humvees. And every few feet, there were police and Secret Service and private security all wearing the Damocles uniform and logo.

Any one of these people could be an enemy; any one of them might grab her or shoot her or turn her back over to Howard.

Susan wasn't sure what to do. The only person she could trust was wearing a suicide vest and was stuck inside the center. She had to figure this out on her own.

If she went to the police barriers, she was going to have

to face the Secret Service and the Damocles guards. They might be in on the plot, or they might not. She was already getting suspicious looks.

But she had to do something fast. She heard a bellow of anger a block behind her. "Somebody stop that woman!"

She turned in time to see Agent Howard stumbling from the limo, clutching at his face with one hand, blood spilling down his shirt. She took satisfaction in that. She'd hurt him. Good.

Unfortunately, now people were *really* gawking at her. A pair of police officers moved away from their posts at the barriers. One began walking toward her; another toward Howard.

"Get her!" Howard screamed, his voice clogged like someone suffering a bad cold.

Susan turned and walked away, as calmly as she could. The media had been set up in their own holding pen, TV news vans and mobile satellite trucks, all parked together. The reporters clustered together near the front of the pen. They all seemed agitated about something.

If Susan could just reach them, forty feet away, she might be able to blend into the crowd.

"Excuse me, miss? Miss?" It was the police officer behind her. He was polite. Still confused, still unsure of what was going on. Which meant he wasn't a part of the plot. But he would detain her, still ask questions. And there was no way he would take her word over Howard's. In his mind, she'd just be some crazy person who had assaulted a Secret Service agent.

She kept walking, forcing herself to go at a normal pace, as if she hadn't heard. Just another reporter, just another random woman in the crowd.

"Miss, please *stop right there,*" the cop said, and his voice was louder and harder now. Not being polite anymore.

She kept walking. He wouldn't shoot her in the back.

Would he?

She was almost at the media pen. None of the reporters or technicians were looking at her. Their eyes were all glued to the front doors of the building.

She sprinted through the crowd of reporters, then ducked the police barrier, and—she hoped—blended into the crowd there. She didn't risk a look back to see if the cop was able to stay on her tail.

The big black car known as the Beast—the presidential limo—glided to a halt at the front steps.

Secret Service agents jumped from their cars to open the door for the president.

Susan realized that the president was about to walk right into the lobby, and within range of the bomb strapped to Randall.

They would kill her. They'd trigger the bomb and kill her, and Randall, and everyone close to him.

They were all about to die, and there was nothing she could do about it.

Then Susan heard someone say, "What the hell is going on in there?"

Susan finally risked a look over her shoulder. She saw Howard half-running, half-staggering toward her. The police officer spotted her when she turned around and began running toward her, his hand on his holster.

She turned away quickly and picked up the pace.

She pushed her way through the huge crowd that had shown up to try to glimpse the president, or to just cheer her on or boo her.

Susan had almost made it. They wouldn't try anything in front of so many witnesses.

Would they?

Then she heard gunshots, and flinched, expecting to feel a bullet between her shoulder blades.

But the shots came from inside the building.

And then she and the crowd and the reporters and the cops were engulfed in a flood of people running from the exits of the building, all of them fleeing in panic. It was chaos, like opposing tidal waves crashing into each other.

She heard someone shout, "Run! He's got a gun!"

Everyone was now trying to get away from the building.

But not Susan. She pushed her way closer, fighting against the tide.

Randall, she thought. *Whatever you're pulling, I hope it works.*

CHAPTER 38

"WOULD SOMEONE PLEASE just *shoot* this man?" Senator Pierce screamed as Beck yanked her closer. She kept trying to pull away, and it caused the metal cuff to dig even deeper into his flesh.

They were surrounded by a circle of Secret Service agents, police officers, and Damocles guards. A half-dozen laser sights danced over Beck's face and body as they searched for an angle that would not also harm the senator, or explode the bomb. Beck looped his non-handcuffed arm through her free arm, so that they were back to back. He started turning them in circles, at different rates of speed and changing direction without notice. Getting a clean shot at him in this position and with this movement would be nearly impossible.

A few yards away, Beck could see the people he had already shot, still writhing on the ground in agony. They were all going to be very sore, and as furious as he was at them for what they were, and for putting him in this situation, he was glad they weren't dead.

Which was more than Beck could expect when this was over. He and Susan would probably be killed.

Pierce tried to pull away. Beck tightened his grip, using her as a shield. He kept his gun pointed out toward the officers and Secret Service men surrounding him. He wasn't sure he could hit anyone, shooting from this angle and being jostled by Pierce, but he tried to look confident and hoped the threat would be enough.

"Shoot him!" she screamed again. She sounded more outraged than scared, as if some barista at the coffee shop had just given her the wrong flavor of latte.

Beck jabbed her with his elbow. She squawked in pain and shut up.

Beck looked around frantically. He just had to stall them for long enough. The president had to get away. That was the best he could hope for.

Through the big glass panels of the lobby, he noticed the big limousine. The Beast. It slowed down, rolling to a stop. A Secret Service agent went to the back door, ready to open it—

No, Beck thought.

And then, suddenly, the limo picked up speed again. The agent was left standing as the Beast accelerated, and made a smoking-tire exit from the front of the building, out of Beck's view.

Beck almost couldn't believe it. The president was safe now. He'd actually done it.

Despite everything, he allowed himself a small moment of satisfaction.

"Looks like the debate is canceled, Senator," he said, over his shoulder.

"You idiot," she hissed back. "You are never going to get out of here alive."

Sadly, Beck knew she was right. He'd managed to save the president, but this was as far as he'd gotten in his master plan.

Now he was out of ideas, and he was just waiting for someone to shoot him.

For the first time, he noticed the big screens on the walls of the lobby, all tuned to CNN. They were supposed to show the debate to the overflow crowd, Beck supposed. Now, they showed the panicked crowds outside the center with the chyron scrolling across the bottom of the screens:

BREAKING NEWS . . . TERRORIST HAS TAKEN SENATOR PIERCE HOSTAGE . . .

Beck had seen headlines like this before. He knew how these stories always ended.

It looked like the cancer wasn't going to kill him after all.

CHAPTER 39

ON THE CATWALK, Morrison heard the gunshots from the lobby. Then the screams. He spoke quietly into his throat mike. "Howard. What's going on?"

No response.

He tried again. "Howard. Do you hear me?"

Nothing.

Damn it, he knew he shouldn't have let Howard run things from the limo. That idiot couldn't pour piss out of a boot if the instructions were written on the heel.

But they'd needed thugs to pull this off, and Howard loved to hurt people. Unfortunately, most thugs weren't that bright. Howard would have been bounced out of the Service long ago if Morrison hadn't found him useful.

Morrison got out of his sniper position and began to crawl. He needed to get to higher ground, where he could scope out the entire situation.

His arm hurt and the H&K rifle jabbed him painfully in the ribs when he began climbing a ladder upward at the back of the auditorium.

Morrison was already planning on killing at least one more person today. Not like he'd been looking forward to it or anything. He wasn't a psychopath like Howard. It was a part of the job, that was all.

But if Randall Beck had somehow managed to screw them, then it was going to be a pleasure to put a bullet through his brain.

CHAPTER 40

BECK USED TO have a patient named Gregory Lucas who was an FBI hostage negotiator. The stress was eating him alive by the time he came to Beck for treatment. Together, they worked through his anxiety—though it's tough to tell someone to relax when lives are literally at stake every time he goes to work.

However, Beck taught him to live with the fact that he couldn't control everything.

And in the process, he taught Beck all about how hostage negotiation worked.

Which came in handy for Beck right about now.

"All right, back off," Beck shouted. "Put those guns away!"

The agents didn't move. They kept their guns trained on him, their faces grim and frozen.

Which was keeping with what Lucas had told him. *You never walk away from a live situation,* he said. *Never put down your guns unless you absolutely have to.*

Beck figured it was time to put all his cards on the table.

"I've got a bomb!" he shouted, using his gun hand to open the raincoat and his jacket as best he could.

Now everyone could see the vest with its wires and plastic explosives.

Again, the agents did not move back. But Beck could see their faces grow even more tense.

"You shoot me, and the bomb goes off!" he shouted.

This was not precisely true, of course, unless the bullet hit the explosives. He had no control over the bomb. He wondered why it hadn't been detonated already. Howard's voice had stopped yammering in his ear a few moments earlier, and he didn't miss it.

Beck knew that this bought him just a little time. Eventually, someone was going to take a shot.

That would kill everyone in the room. Beck decided to remind the agents of that fact. "If anyone takes a shot, this bomb will explode!" he shouted. "Put away your guns or I'll detonate!"

Now he had some leverage. He could see it in their eyes.

At first, Lucas had told Beck, *you have to agree to everything. Never say no. We do whatever the wackjob wants until we can get control of the situation. A plane to Cuba? No problem. Luxury box at the Redskins game? You got it. Pizza with anchovies? It's on its way. Whatever you want.*

So Beck was not surprised—relieved, but not surprised—as one by one, the laser-sights dotting his chest winked off, and the armed men and women surrounding agreed with his wish and put away their guns.

Senator Pierce, however, was shocked. And not at all happy about it.

"What are you doing, you idiots?" she shrieked. "Shoot him!"

"They can't risk it," Beck said to her, over his shoulder. "A stray bullet might trigger the bomb. Wouldn't look good on the news if they accidentally blew up a presidential candidate because of an itchy trigger finger."

Pierce didn't say anything. Good. At least she'd be quiet for a while.

Then Beck noticed something. He got a weird sense of seeing a mirror in the corner of his eye. He looked up at the big TV screens again, and there he was. Holding a gun on the senator with a bomb strapped to his chest. Bruised and hollow-eyed. He looked very much like the stereotypical lone gunman. For a brief, idiotic moment, he noticed his hair looked terrible.

The footage was going out live over the networks.

He scanned the room and saw that one of the TV news crews covering the debate had not fled with all the other people in the lobby. They'd stuck around to get the story of the year.

The Secret Service noticed at just about the same time. "Get those people out of here," one of the agents snarled.

That wouldn't help Beck at all. He needed as many witnesses as possible.

"Wait!" he shouted. "I want them to stay!"

The more people watching, the less likely it was that he'd be shot. He knew Morrison and Howard and Pierce—and whoever else Damocles had here—wanted him dead. But they'd think twice before executing him live on TV.

The agents hesitated. They seemed to be trying to judge how serious Beck was. He decided to amp up the crazy for a moment.

"I mean it!" he yelled. "They can transmit my demands to the American people! I want the truth to come out! Or I pull the trigger!" He shoved his handcuffed hand in his pocket and came out with the useless plastic trigger, still connected to the vest via several wires.

"No way!" shouted one of the Damocles personnel. But two of the Secret Service agents—a man and a woman—exchanged a glance. Beck realized they must be the senior agents on the scene. They were the ones really in charge.

So he held the trigger up as high as its tether would allow, as close to Pierce's head as possible. "You've got five seconds to decide!"

Again, he was following Lucas's advice. *We always try to slow things down whenever possible,* Lucas had told Beck. *Drag it out. Suck the momentum out of the room. If they start pushing us to do things quickly, make snap decisions, we've lost control.*

The Secret Service agents nodded. "All right," the woman said. "They can stay. Now just tell us what you want. Nobody else has to get hurt. What do you want?"

Good question. Beck wanted to get this bomb off him. He wanted a cure for cancer. World peace. Maybe a pony.

He wanted Susan to be safe.

In other words, nothing the agents could supply.

But then, he finally had an idea.

"I want a limo!" he shouted.

Pierce twisted in his grip. "What?" she said.

Nobody else heard her. "We can do that," the lead agent said, her hands up, her voice soothing.

Beck had to keep them off-balance. "Not just any limo! Senator Pierce's limo! Bring it out front! Right now!"

The female agent made a face. She was confused. "Okay, we can certainly look into that—"

Beck couldn't let her waste any time. He had to keep things moving. Keep Damocles—and everyone else—guessing.

"Now!" he said. "Right now!"

"All right, all right," she said, trying to placate Beck again. "We can do that."

She spoke rapidly into her radio.

Beck waited. Pierce hissed at him, "What do you think you're doing?"

He ignored her. He felt the sweat slide down his ribs, under the suicide vest. He could feel his heart beating under the C-4. It could go off at any second.

There was nothing he could do but wait.

Another few minutes ticked by like an eternity.

Then he saw the limo crawl slowly to the front steps, visible through the lobby windows. Just like the president's car.

"Let me see inside that car!" Beck demanded. "Open all those doors!"

The agent frowned, but she spoke into her radio again.

Outside, Beck saw an agent get out of the driver's seat, and then open all the limo doors. Another agent reluctantly got out of the back. Beck could see the whole interior now.

There were all the screens and radios that Howard had been using. It was the same car.

But no sign of him, or Susan.

Where were they?

CHAPTER 41

SUSAN WAS TRAPPED in the mob. She couldn't move. The crowd of people trying to escape from the performing arts center had come up against the people from the media trying to get in for a better look and the other cops, causing the mass of bodies to become grid-locked.

The police and security were doing their best to manage the mess, but they weren't helped by the sudden cry of alarm from someone near the front door: "He's got a bomb! Run!"

Susan was jostled back and forth as the panicked crowd surged for the security barriers. The media still wasn't moving, despite the shouts and threats of the authorities.

The only good news in all of this was that she hadn't seen Howard or Morrison. At least, not yet. But she felt exposed, like she had a target on her head for a high-flying drone strike.

She didn't know what Randall was doing in there, but

she had to find a way to help him. He was alone, and risking his life. So she'd have to figure out a way to help save them both.

She had the laptop. It could prove everything. But there was no way to get it to the right people, not right now—

Then Susan wanted to hit herself in the forehead. She was surrounded by the right people. They were pushing her from every direction.

Susan looked around for the closest person with a video camera.

While she was scanning the crowd, she saw two eyes burning behind a mask of bandages, a scowling face painted with drying blood.

Howard.

He locked eyes with her at the same moment, and began shoving his way through the mass of people, holding his badge over his head. "Secret Service," he bellowed, loud enough for her to hear despite the distance and the noise of the mob.

She started moving in the other direction, sliding between people as best she could.

Then she couldn't move any farther. She was pinned against a news van.

She looked over her shoulder and saw Howard coming for her, moving through the crowd like a shark through the water, eyes fixed on her.

She tried the van's door handle and pulled.

It opened.

A woman wearing heavy makeup turned and stared at

her. So did a man with a scruffy beard, and a producer sitting in front of a board of equipment.

The woman spoke first. "What the hell are you doing?"

Susan stepped up into the news van, and slammed the door behind her.

She recognized the woman. Danielle Crain, one of the field reporters for CNN. She smiled a lot more on TV. Right now, she was glaring at Susan.

"The guy in there with a bomb?" Susan said. "I know him. And I can tell you everything about him."

Danielle was suddenly all smiles. "Sit down," she said. "Start talking."

CHAPTER 42

BECK DECIDED HE didn't have time to worry about where Susan and Howard were now. He had to move. Keep the momentum going. Keep anyone else from stopping him.

He rushed out the door, pushing Pierce ahead of him. He had her arm pinned behind her like a perp, his gun aimed at her head. He tried to stay crouched behind her, walking as low as he could, continuing to use her as a shield.

Then he pushed her into the limo.

From the backseat, he slammed all the rear doors and pressed the button to close the screen between them and the front seat.

Then he sat back in the plush leather.

For a second, he simply took in a deep breath.

Pierce stared at him.

"Now what?" she asked. She sounded truly baffled. "Do you think you're going to drive out of here?"

"I don't think we're going anywhere," Beck replied.

"There's nothing here that can help you, Beck! The whole world saw you! They think you're a terrorist! The whole world saw you take me hostage and bring me into this car—"

"That's right," Beck said, cutting her off. "Into this car. This car that your friend Howard was so proud of. Just like the president's, he said. Bulletproof. And bombproof. If your men trigger the bomb now, the explosion will be contained in here."

Pierce looked at him with wide eyes. "But we'll both still die!"

"I'm dying anyway, Senator," Beck said. "Remember?"

She glared at him with pure hate. "You're crazy," she said.

For some reason, that just made Beck grin.

"Yeah," he replied. "I get that a lot."

CHAPTER 43

"THAT'S THE MOST insane story I've ever heard," Danielle told Susan. "You sound more like a mental patient than a doctor."

Susan had only had time to give Danielle Crain, her producer, and her cameraman the highlights of everything that had happened today. She knew Howard was outside the news van, and the clock was ticking on Randall's life.

From inside the van, they'd all watched on one of the small TV monitors as Randall forced the senator out of the lobby and down the steps into the waiting limo.

And then they had waited, along with everyone else in America, glued to their screens.

Nothing was happening right now. The police were trying to get the crowd and the news media away from the building. Nobody wanted to move. Nobody wanted to miss it when the crazy man was finally killed.

Every camera was locked on to the limo, waiting for the

moment they could broadcast Randall's messy death to millions of viewers. The chyron at the bottom of the screen read:

LIVE FROM THE PRESIDENTIAL DEBATE—
ARMED MAN HAS TAKEN SENATOR PIERCE
HOSTAGE.

That left Danielle Crain outside and off the air during the biggest story of the year. She was annoyed, Susan could tell. Susan had to give her a way to get back into the action.

All she had to do was convince her.

Susan opened the laptop and quickly typed in Kevin Scott's password. The Damocles e-mails and documents popped up immediately, still onscreen from when Susan had found them before.

"Look," Susan said. "Look at all of this. It will show you that I'm telling the truth. Randall is telling the truth. This is all part of an attempt to kill President Martin."

She turned the screen toward Danielle. There were e-mails laying out the plot in meticulous detail. There were schedules and maps and step-by-step instructions for assembling the bomb. Damocles, like so many other corporations, believed in proper paperwork. And any conspiracy is a complicated machine—it requires a lot of planning to pull off properly.

Scott had documented all of it. There was even a video Scott had recorded using a hidden camera. It showed him meeting with Pierce and Morrison and Howard.

But before the newswoman could go through the evidence, there was a heavy pounding on the door of the van.

"Open up!" a clogged, nasal voice demanded. "This is the Secret Service! You've got a wanted criminal in there!"

Danielle looked at Susan. "That's you, I guess?"

"Don't open that door," Susan said desperately. "Do not listen to him. He's got a badge, but he's a murderer. I swear, he will kill me if you open that door—"

Danielle made a face. She reached past Susan, grabbed the handle, and yanked open the door of the van.

Howard stood there, shocked for a moment.

Then he saw Susan and smiled.

CHAPTER 44

BECK STRUGGLED TO get out of the suicide vest. He knew it didn't really change anything. If Morrison triggered the bomb, he'd still die. But at least he wouldn't actually be wearing the thing.

But it wasn't as easy as just taking it off. He was still locked to Pierce, and he had to get his arm out of the raincoat and his jacket.

Pierce wasn't exactly being cooperative, either.

She pulled against him, reaching for the door handle, as if she could drag him outside of the limo.

He engaged in a useless tug-of-war with her for a few moments before Beck remembered he had a gun. He showed it to her. She stopped struggling.

They both sat back in the limo's seat, staring daggers at each other.

Then Beck remembered something.

He reached into his pocket. There it was.

The shim, the metal strip that Louis had given him when he'd opened the cuffs before.

It seemed like a lifetime ago. He hadn't seen the YouTube video that Louis mentioned. But Louis had told him how it worked. He tried to remember the mechanic's instructions. *Louis.* He was sure now that they had killed him. He just knew it. And it was all Beck's fault.

He put the strip of metal into the ratcheting mechanism of the cuffs. Then tightened. It hurt his wrist.

And then, the cuffs slipped on the metal and popped open. Just like magic.

Even Pierce looked impressed.

"What did you just do?" she said.

"Quiet," Beck snapped. Now for the really tricky part. Taking off the vest.

"Did they booby-trap this?" he asked Pierce.

She just looked at him coldly.

"If they did, you're going to be the second person who hears the bang," he reminded her.

"I don't know," she spat. "I left the details to them."

"Right," Beck said, suddenly even more disgusted. "You don't get your hands dirty. You let other people do that. You just step over the bodies when they're done."

She shrugged. "Sometimes sacrifices have to be made."

"And people like Kevin Scott and Todd Graham are the ones who make them," Beck snapped. "And Jennifer Scott and Louis. They were good people."

Pierce smirked at him. "No such thing, Doctor."

She didn't deny that they had killed Jennifer and Louis.

So it was true. Beck was suddenly enraged again. He didn't care what happened next. He just wanted to wipe that smirk off her face.

He tore open the Velcro straps of the vest.

Both he and Pierce froze, waiting for the explosion.

CHAPTER 45

SUSAN COULDN'T MOVE. Looking like something from a horror movie, Howard began to reach inside the van for her.

No. Not for her. For the laptop.

But before he could put his hands on it, Danielle grabbed it and pulled it back.

Howard wasn't pleased. "You're interfering with a federal investigation," he growled.

"And you're interfering with my interview," Danielle shot back.

Howard looked like he'd been slapped. "That woman is a fugitive from justice—" he began.

But Danielle cut him off. "Really? On what charge?"

"That's classified," Howard said.

Suddenly he winced and stepped back out of the van as lights blazed in his face. Danielle's cameraman had turned on his camera, and the light was pointed right at Howard.

"Classified?" Danielle said with a snort of contempt.

"Secret charges? Really?" She was thrusting a microphone at him. "That's even crazier than what she was telling me. Do you want to try again for the viewers at home, sir? What is your name? Who is your superior? Do you have a warrant?"

Howard stepped back, looking like each question was another blow to the head. His hand began to drift toward his holster.

Susan froze. She'd seen Howard kill. She knew he would do it again.

But Danielle had not. She was behind the camera, and she thought it made her invulnerable.

"Why won't you answer these questions, sir? May I see your badge?"

Howard took another step back. His hand was under his jacket now.

Susan held her breath.

"Again, sir, who are you, and what do you want with this woman? Is it related to the hostage situation inside? You're live, sir. Please speak up."

Howard glared at the newswoman, then dropped his hand from under his jacket. He turned, and walked back into the crowd.

Susan let out a deep sigh of relief. Apparently not even Howard was crazy enough to shoot a reporter live on camera.

Danielle leaned forward and slammed the van's door again, shutting out the noise of the crowd. "Asshole," she said, not even remotely aware of how close she had just come to getting shot.

She turned back to Susan. “All right,” she said. “That was interesting. Let’s get you on the air.”

Susan thought, for a moment, she hadn’t heard the other woman properly. “You believe me?” she asked.

“Oh, God, who knows?” Danielle said. “But you’ve got a hell of a story, and that’s enough for me.”

CHAPTER 46

INSIDE THE LIMO, nothing happened.

The bomb did not go off.

Beck and Pierce both let out a huge sigh of relief.

Beck stashed the vest behind the front seats, as far away as he could manage. Again, it wouldn't make a difference. But it made him feel better.

Small comforts. Like a kid hiding under a blanket to get away from the monsters. Even psychiatrists aren't immune from that kind of thinking, Beck realized.

He began to put his jacket and the raincoat back on. He wasn't sure what he was going to do next, but it would probably be smart if people outside the limo thought he was still wired to explode.

But he wasn't paying attention to Pierce. He turned his head for a moment, and heard the clunk of the limo's door opening.

He'd forgotten they were no longer cuffed together. She was trying to get away.

She was his only shield. Without her in the car, Morrison or Howard would be happy to activate the bomb.

Beck couldn't let that happen.

Pierce was almost out the door when he grabbed her. He got a handful of her suit jacket. His fingers slipped. He snagged her foot. She kicked him, losing one of her expensive shoes.

But she tripped and fell.

Beck scrambled after her. She kicked him again, in the face. It hurt.

They were both wedged in the car door when he got his arm around her throat again. He hauled her to her feet and put the gun at her head once more. She elbowed him viciously in the ribs once, but he managed to hold on.

When he looked up, once again, he was facing a firing squad. And this time, they had reinforcements.

It seemed like an entire army battalion had surrounded the limo while he was inside.

Beck looked around wildly. He saw the same federal agent who'd spoken to him before. She'd apparently taken charge of the whole situation. Again, she looked at him from behind a gun.

"Let her go!" she screamed.

Beck shook his head. He needed the truth to come out.

"I want to talk!" he shouted. "To the president!"

The agent scowled back at him.

"That's going to take a little time. She's on her way to a secure location now because of this little stunt you pulled."

Good, Beck thought. *Maybe that will keep her safe from*

Damocles. But he had to get the whole truth out. That was the only way to make sure this ended.

Then he realized he was speaking live to an audience of millions. He looked at the cameras, just beyond the police barriers.

He could tell the whole world what was really happening right here and right now.

"I want to talk to her on the phone!" Beck shouted. "She needs to know that Senator Pierce and Damocles—"

That's when Pierce began shrieking at the top of her lungs, drowning him out.

"Oh, God, oh, God, don't let him kill me, please! You have to do something!" She kept screaming as loud as she could.

Beck tried to bellow to be heard above her, but it was no use.

No one could hear a thing he said.

Beck wanted to scream in frustration. He knew he was much more vulnerable. Any second, a sniper could shoot him.

He was out in the open now.

An easy target.

CHAPTER 47

MORRISON TURNED ON his laser sight. Ordinarily he never needed the damned thing, but this would be a tricky shot even for him.

He looked over the edge of the roof at the back of Beck's head.

He'd found the entrance to the roof and got here as quickly as he could, once he'd heard over the radio that Beck demanded a limo.

Now he was half-hidden by the air-conditioning unit, his rifle propped on the roof's edge, trying to get a clear angle on Beck without also killing his boss. With all the chaos down on the street, no one was even looking up at the roof.

Beck kept bobbing in and out of his line of sight, however.

It would help a lot if Pierce would just stop screaming, too. Morrison understood that it was meant to keep anyone from hearing Beck. But it was giving him a migraine.

He tried to focus down the barrel. Pierce kept screaming.

Beck kept moving. And there were a half-dozen other armed men and women who might open fire at any moment.

He reached for his phone in his jacket pocket. All it would take was the tap of a few numbers on the screen. Then the bomb would go off.

The problem was, that would kill Pierce, too. And he was pretty sure that would mean the end of his meal ticket.

Morrison clicked his radio back to the secure channel.

He needed some backup. And Howard was in just as deep as he was, which made him almost trustworthy.

"Howard."

Nothing.

"Howard, come on, are you there?"

Still nothing.

"Dammit, Howard, I know you can hear me—"

Finally, with a small snap of static, Howard's voice returned through his earpiece. "Shut up."

"What? I'm in position. I need to know—"

"Shut up, Morrison," Howard said. "It's over. Believe me."

What? That couldn't be right. Howard was like a pit bull chomping on a bone. He never gave up.

"What are you talking about?"

"The woman. Carpenter. She's with a reporter now. I'm out."

Morrison was not a coward. He'd fought in Iraq. Walked into rooms where people were waiting to kill him. Stood next to presidents and presidential candidates in the middle of thousands of people, knowing that any one of them could be aiming a gun at his head.

But now he felt his stomach clench and his head spin. Somehow Susan Carpenter had made it to the media.

They were screwed. Even if no one believed her. Even if she was completely discredited, he was going to be investigated. The clues would start to add up.

It didn't take him long to do that math. He was about to become a liability to Damocles. And he knew what the company did with liabilities. He'd done some of that wet work himself.

"Jesus," he said quietly. "Howard, what are we going to do?"

"What's this 'we' shit, Morrison?" came the reply. It sounded like Howard was laughing now. "You never thought I was that bright, but I know when it's time to cut my losses. Good luck, pal."

The channel went dead.

Morrison was on his own. Even if he got out of here and started running, his life expectancy could be measured in days now. Weeks at the outside.

Unless he could somehow prove his loyalty. Show the company that he would not talk. No matter what. If he could show them that he still had value.

He still had his rifle. He could do Damocles a big favor right now by removing the main witness against the company.

Beck had given him a death sentence.

Morrison put his eye back to the sight and squinted.

Maybe he could return the favor.

CHAPTER 48

BECK KNEW THAT Pierce was a politician, and that politicians were nothing if not long-winded. But he still couldn't believe how long she could go on screaming.

She had been yowling at the top of her lungs nonstop, making it impossible for him to say a single thing. The FBI, the police, even some of the Damocles guards had all tried to speak above her. They were trying to open negotiations, to get Beck to let her go.

She wouldn't let them. She was using the last tactic she had left. She wouldn't allow anyone to talk to Beck, for fear of what he might say.

But sooner or later, it had to end. Beck hoped he could wait it out. Unfortunately, he really was at the end of his endurance. His head felt like someone was crushing it in a vise, and the pressure only kept ratcheting up. His vision would go blank for seconds at a time, and despite all the guns pointed at him, his attention kept wandering. His body felt like it belonged to someone else. He almost felt like he was floating in the ocean.

A calm, clinical part of his mind made the diagnosis. Detachment. Exhaustion. Fatigue. Drowsiness. Altered perception.

Any first-year med student would be able to recognize the signs. He was going to lose consciousness soon. He wondered if they'd still shoot him.

Or if Morrison or Howard would take the opportunity to trigger the bomb.

His whole life, he'd believed he could control everything. That if he just worked hard enough, thought quickly enough, he could save people from the demons inside their heads.

Now he had to face it. This was all out of his control. And he couldn't save himself.

Something was different. It took Beck a full second to realize what it was.

The reporters, the media—there was something different going on behind their lines.

Most of the cameras were still pointed in his direction. But some had turned. Some were clustered around a reporter at the back of the mob.

Their lights shone down, and the crowd parted, and he saw her.

Susan.

Despite everything she'd been through since this morning, she looked magnificent. She was talking to a reporter, and there were a dozen other microphones shoved toward her face.

Senator Pierce stopped screaming. Beck realized she could see the whole scene unfolding right in front of them, too.

She was watching all her lies unravel, right before her eyes.

In the sudden silence, Beck could hear Susan clearly. She was in the middle of a sentence. "Yes, *I am* saying I watched them kill a police officer—"

Beck could just imagine what was scrolling on CNN right now:

SENATOR ACCUSED OF MURDER AND COVER-UP
BY MAN HOLDING HER HOSTAGE.

Beck realized it didn't matter what happened to him anymore. Susan was safe. It was out of his hands now.

So he dropped the gun. Raised his hands, as high as he could.

"I surrender," he said as loud as he could.

Pierce looked at him, trying to comprehend what had just happened, the horror only growing on her face. Beck smiled at her.

"I surrender," Beck said again. "I will tell you whatever you want to know."

The police and the other gunmen began moving forward, cautiously. Beck had put the jacket back on so that they would think he was still wearing the vest. He hoped his ploy was going to work.

Then Pierce screamed again. But now it was a completely different message coming from her mouth.

"It wasn't me!" she said. "It wasn't me! It was Damocles! They forced me to—"

Beck was distracted from what she said next. A red dot struck him in the eye, and he blinked and staggered back.

He realized that it was a laser sight. Someone had just turned him into a target again.

A microsecond later, he heard the gunshot.

CHAPTER 49

MORRISON HAD BECK lined up perfectly. The senator was clear. One squeeze of his finger, and Beck was going to disappear in a puff of red mist. That would show Damocles. That would prove Morrison was still loyal.

Then he heard what was coming out of Pierce's mouth.

She was spilling everything. The word "Damocles" over and over. All on live, national TV.

Morrison sighed. He knew, in the back of his head, that Howard had done the right thing. Morrison should have run while he had the chance. There was no way anything he did now would make a difference.

But it was still worth a shot.

He pulled the trigger.

CHAPTER 50

BECK FELT BLOOD hit his face.

But he didn't fall.

Pierce did.

She looked stunned. Her mouth was still open, even though blood was pouring out of it now, as she tried to draw breath into lungs that had just been punctured by a bullet.

People screamed. The police shouted at Beck. Confusion reigned. Nobody knew where the bullet came from.

Then the red dot struck Beck in the eye again.

Susan was telling her story again, as clearly as she could with all the interruptions—and then every head in the crowd turned.

They all heard the gunshot. First from the limo, and then, after a microsecond delay, from their screens that were carrying the live feed.

For a second, Susan thought her heart would stop.

"Holy shit," someone said. "They just shot the senator."

Relief flooded into Susan. Her legs went weak. Surely that would be the end of it. Surely this was where the insanity had to stop.

Then they heard the next shot.

Morrison looked at Beck, standing like an idiot as Pierce lay there, blood already pooling on the asphalt.

It didn't seem right that he should get out of this. That he should be the one to walk away, after screwing up all their plans.

Morrison thought about waking up in prison every day. Eating that industrial slop. Sleeping on a cot in a concrete room. Watching for the knife in his back.

Knowing that Beck won.

Revenge was all Morrison had left, really.

Might as well take it.

He pulled the trigger.

Beck knew what the red dot meant. He thought about running, but he knew he wouldn't have made it two steps.

And he was tired. The pain in his head was the only thing he felt anymore. His legs were already failing him. His vision had narrowed to a black tunnel.

He said, "Susan."

He didn't hear the second gunshot.

Didn't feel his body hit the ground.

CHAPTER 51

MORRISON SMILED TO himself as he went down the stairs from the roof.

Everything around him was pure pandemonium. His badge got him past the cops in the lobby with little more than a glance.

A dozen yards away, there were paramedics clustered around two bodies. Beck and Pierce. The paramedics had put them on stretchers. A bomb squad tech was standing by. Every eye, every camera, was focused on the drama as the emergency crews worked desperately to save them.

There was Beck's girlfriend, held back by a Secret Service agent, sobbing.

And there was the limo, completely forgotten. Totally unattended.

Morrison got into the driver's seat.

The crowds had cleared, clustered around the latest spectacle, leaving the road open to the exit.

He started the engine. Pulled forward so quietly he could hear the crunching of gravel under the tires.

One of the cops gave him a look, but Morrison just flipped his credentials and his badge out the window, and the cop moved on. More important things than a Secret Service agent moving a car out of the way.

He hit the road. It was empty. All traffic was blocked coming into the university. But not going out.

Morrison started grinning. He could barely believe it. He was not only going to get away, he was going to do it in style.

Maybe he wouldn't get paid, but at least he wasn't going to die in prison. That would have to be enough.

There was just one last thing.

He needed to cover his tracks completely. He needed one last big distraction.

And if there was any chance that Beck or his girlfriend was going to live—well, Morrison needed to take care of that, too.

He took out his phone. He entered the code for the vest, and paused before he hit the Send button.

Morrison wondered, for a moment, if he'd hear the explosion.

He hit Send.

He heard a beep from the seat right behind him.

And then nothing else, ever again.

SIX MONTHS LATER

CHAPTER 52

BECK OPENED HIS EYES.

The room was dark. He didn't bother to check the clock. He'd been waking at 3:00 a.m. for a month now. Sometimes he would look at the ceiling until his alarm went off.

But usually, he got out of bed, like he did now. He'd been on his back long enough in the hospital, after the surgery to remove the bullet that struck him in the upper chest when Morrison shot him.

Either Morrison was a lousy shot, or Beck slipping into unconsciousness and falling backward the moment the trigger was pulled had caused Morrison to miss. He certainly would have been aiming at his head.

Beck had been arrested in the ICU. He woke up to find that someone had put another pair of handcuffs on him, locking him to the bed.

Eventually, however, the police sorted it out. He was hailed as a national hero. Or an assassin who'd gotten away with it, depending on which cable news channel you watched.

Beck looked out the window of his new condo. Bulletproof glass. One of the upgrades he'd installed when they moved.

The information on Kevin Scott's laptop had led to the first indictments within a couple of weeks, and now, the fallout was still coming down all over Washington, DC. At first, it seemed as if the damage would be contained to just Pierce and Morrison—whatever they'd managed to scrape off the sidewalk—and Howard, and a few of their fellow conspirators. Damocles issued a statement that blamed everything on a small number of rogue employees, and then the board and executives hid behind their lawyers.

But it's never a good idea to take a shot at the president and miss. Damocles was now the subject of no less than five congressional inquiries, not to mention the FBI investigation, the Department of Defense probe, and the ongoing housecleaning in the Secret Service. All the company's contracts had been suspended. There were new arrests almost daily. High-ranking officials were cutting deals.

President Martin was grateful, at least. She'd arranged for Beck to be bumped to the head of the line of an FDA trial for a new cancer-fighting treatment. It used genetically altered cells to target inoperable tumors.

It seemed to be working. His cancer, miraculously, was in remission. His fingers no longer went numb. He was hitting the gym every day to rebuild muscle that had atrophied during his recovery. He had an MRI every week, and his tumor just kept shrinking.

It looked like he was going to live.

At least until he testified.

The first trial, of the former Secret Service agent Howard—he'd been captured before he boarded a flight to Rio—began in a few weeks. Then Beck would appear before a joint House–Senate commission. And he would also go on TV, and tell his story as many times as it took.

He was putting a target on his head again.

Beck heard something behind him, and turned to see Susan sitting up, the sheet pulled around her waist.

"Come back to bed," she said. "You can't keep brooding about it."

She always seemed to know what he was thinking. It made sense. She'd been his shrink, after all.

"They're not going to let me testify," he said. "Damocles. They'll try again. At me. And you."

"Maybe," she said. "But we survived before. And we will again."

Beck smiled at that. "What makes you so sure?"

"Experience. Six months ago, you were a terminal case."

Beck shrugged. "We're all terminal cases. Everybody dies eventually."

"But not yet," she reminded him.

"No," he had to admit. "Not yet."

"Then come back to bed." She threw the sheet back.

Beck went to her. As usual, she was right.

He wasn't dead yet.

So there was nothing else to do but go on living. As long as he could.

KILL AND TELL

JAMES PATTERSON

WITH SCOTT SLAVEN

CHAPTER 1

Wayne Tennet

I ALMOST CHOKED on my sip of whiskey when I read the text from my agent.

Your stepdaughter has accused u of sexual abuse.

I was in first class on Air Australia, relaxing for the first time in weeks. My film shoot was almost over. It had been grueling, but I felt good about what I had in the can. In half an hour I'd be back in LA, back to my regular life, not having to say "G'day."

My hands were shaking as I clutched the phone. Bewilderment and concern ricocheted in my head. *How* could she say this? *What* was happening?

I'd known my eighteen-year-old stepdaughter Breelyn since she was five. Back then, she was the greatest kid in the world. But as a teenager, she went Hollywood on me, big time. Sullen, snobby, obsessed with her looks, hounding me for parts in my films. And now this. How the hell could I ever face my colleagues again?

I must have been breathing heavily, because the pretty redhead next to me looked over with alarm.

"Anything wrong, Mr. Tennet?" she politely asked.

Was her name Sharon? Shannon? I'd been flirting with her since we took off from Perth. She was so impressed to be seated next to Wayne Tennet, above-the-title film director.

"Ah – no, I'm great," I said, smiling broadly through a wave of dizziness. "Nice of you to ask, though."

How long before she heard about these charges? I wondered. *Please, not before we landed.* Hopefully she hadn't paid for Wi-Fi. I wished I hadn't, either.

Goddamnit!

Of course, I knew who was behind this: my wife, Valentina. I clenched my armrests till I thought my fingers would snap, wishing they were around her throat. Before I could stop myself, I slammed a fist into the wall partition in front of me.

Shannon looked at me in horror. I had to pull myself together.

"So sorry," I said, trying to sound normal. "Just when I think I've gotten over my fear of flying, it rears up. Feel free to pelt me with mini-bottles if I act up again."

She gave a wary little laugh and went back to her *Us Weekly* magazine.

I itched to make about thirty calls at once, all screamed at the top of my lungs. No, no, *no!* Damnit, I couldn't give in to my insane temper. I had to handle this with a cool head.

As soon as we landed, I'd put in a call to Melanie Levitz – head of distribution at the studio. She'd get her best public relations contact on this, Sydney Paige – slick, savvy guy. This was right in his wheelhouse. And I'd ask for that hotshot kid he had on his team – Eric something. Eric Logan.

I'd give them twenty minutes from the time I made the call to meet me at Customs. And I'd need to hear exactly how they were going to make this go away – including every word, every *syllable* of Breelyn's public accusation.

CHAPTER 2

Eric Logan

GET TO LAX. Wayne Tennet coming off Air Australia flight. Requests u.

Taking this courtesy lunch with a new CAA agent at Shutters on the Beach – ten minutes from the airport – might be the luckiest break of my career. I jumped up from the table with barely a "Later!" I didn't even stop for the hot hostess's number.

As I drove to LAX, I speculated that Tennet must have first asked for my boss, Sydney Paige. But Sydney was eight thousand miles away, downing mai tais on a beach in Thailand. After three years of junior-league status, I was finally getting an opportunity to fly solo.

And I knew exactly what I was heading into. The news on the radio was all about Breelyn Doyle's allegations, and it was dead certain that there would be a mob of press at the gate. As I pulled into the parking garage, I got a text from Tennet:

I'm here.

How was I supposed to sneak an instantly recognizable

star director past thirty industry reporters? And then I had it. *Damn, I'm good.* Cocky self-talk is mandatory when you're a twenty-seven-year-old PR rep.

I shot off a text to Tennet:

Get oversized jersey and baseball hat at gift shop. You're my dad.

I opened my car trunk and pulled off my Hugo Boss suit and tie. Good thing I always keep a stash of gym clothes in the car.

In sneakers, a ratty tee with cut-off sleeves, and nylon shorts, I messed up my $150 haircut and looked the part of a bro from the suburbs. When I got to the international arrivals gate, passengers were exiting, weaving around the news cameras and reporters that were scanning every face.

Toward the back of the crowd I spotted a tall guy moving slowly, wearing an LA Dodgers jersey and a loose baseball cap pulled down low on his face. As he neared the entrance, I made my way forward and began jumping up and down.

"Dad! Hey, Pop! Over here! *Dad!*"

Everyone turned and stared, even the reporters. I looked and sounded like an asshole, which is just what I wanted.

I rushed at Tennet and into his arms. I whispered, "*Hug me – HARD! Give me tears!*" For a hotshot filmmaker, Tennet took direction surprisingly well. He got me in a bear hug and let out a big sob. Without letting go of each other, we moved through the crowd. The only looks we got from the reporters were out of irritation for blocking their view.

I hustled Tennet out the terminal doors and he started to pull away, but I didn't let him – I couldn't be sure someone wasn't giving our showy performance a second look. I patted his back, laughed uproariously at something he hadn't said, and whispered, "Keep it up till we get to my car."

Inside the parking garage, Tennet shrugged me off and let out a huge sigh of relief. He took a few deep breaths and seemed to be trying to get a grip.

"Thanks, my friend," he said, giving me a fist bump.

We'd only met in a few large meetings, and he'd never said more than two words to me. He was a good-looking guy – a long face with a strong nose and piercing blue eyes. His hair was almost all gray but full and bushy. He looked like an English actor in a period rom-com.

"So, what the hell is going on?" he asked. "Where's your boss?"

I could see he was seriously freaking, but I wanted to hold off on talking until we were safely in my car.

"Sydney's on vacation," I said quietly as I tried to guide him forward. "We'll try to call him as soon as we get in the car."

"And Breelyn? Please tell me this is some kind of joke – just a misguided Facebook post, right? I'll give you the lead in my next movie if you'll just tell me that."

It couldn't be avoided. "Your wife filed a complaint on your stepdaughter's behalf with the county sheriff this morning."

He went ballistic. "*I knew it was her!* But why would anyone listen to Valentina? What proof did she give? Has anyone talked to my lawyer?"

I tried to take his arm, but he kept pacing back and forth. I knew his temper was legendary.

"Look, I'll drive you to the office, we'll get your lawyer, and we'll start to develop our plan," I said. "But we gotta keep you out of sight until we know what we're going to say."

"But why isn't there *already* a plan? I thought you guys were the best in the business!"

"We're going to take care of you, Mr. Tennet," I said. "But we have to phrase our response in just the right way. Especially if –" I cut myself short, but it was too late. Bad, horrible, *catastrophic* slip of the tongue, Logan.

Tennet got right up in my face.

"Especially if *what?*" he said, his face red and his eyes bulging scarily. "If there is any *truth* to it?"

Before I could answer, he was on me. All his anger and frustration came at me in a blow that I wouldn't have thought a pampered fifty-year-old director had in him. I dodged as best I could, realizing that I was going to end up in the ER if I didn't fight back. I got in a punch to his gut, which he responded to by heaving his whole body on me. Down we went onto the oily concrete floor, rolling and punching and grunting.

It was maybe the third *click* that registered. We both froze and looked up. A white Prius was sitting ten feet away with the window down. And the person inside was snapping away like crazy with a professional-looking camera. Then the vehicle sped off.

CHAPTER 3

Kayla Ross

SCORE, KAYLA, SCORE!

I hit the gas. I know the LAX short-term parking garage backward and forward, but I'd never tried to exit it at 40 mph before. I reached over and felt around the mess on the passenger seat for my ticket. All I found was an empty Starbucks cup, so I glanced down for one split second – and that's when he jumped in front of my Prius.

I slammed on my brakes about a centimeter away from impact, shaken by how close I'd come to hitting him. I threw my car into Reverse and started to back up, but he kept moving fast to the driver's-side door and grabbed the frame through my open window.

"*Wait!* Hold on a sec!" he panted. He had big green eyes and a Henry Cavill cleft chin. I had to admit he was a seriously hot guy. Of course, I'd spotted him right away in the international terminal. Eric – Eric *Logan*. The first time I'd seen him was working the Emmy Awards red carpet, and I remembered wondering why he hadn't gone into acting instead of PR.

"You cannot sell those photos," Logan said. I guessed he was going for a mix of charming and threatening.

"Sure, I can," I replied. "It's called fair use. Photographing people in public is absolutely legal."

"Don't give me a journalism lesson," he said, "and I won't give you an ethics lesson on the sleazy way you make your living."

Asshole. "Yep, it sucks," I retorted. "But student loans gotta be repaid."

I gave him a shrug and stepped on the gas again. He jogged after me.

"Come on," he pleaded. "What you saw was a misunderstanding. My client just flew over fourteen hours through hell and got the worst news of his life!"

"Yeah? What about his *stepdaughter's* life?" I snapped. He flinched a bit but then regained his Chill Dude attitude.

"Fair enough. But we really don't know anything about her allegations at this point, so –"

"Oh, so you think she's lying?" I asked. If he wanted to offer a tone-deaf statement we could tease on social media, even better. I looked over at Tennet. He was a few yards away, sitting on the hood of a car with his face in his hands.

"Hey, my ass is *totally* on the line here," Logan said. "What's your name?"

"Kayla Ross. Sorry, but I'm just doing my job. Oscar-nominated director with a rep for a horrible temper gets accused of sexual abuse by a minor. Then the first thing he does is assault his PR rep! That's news."

"No, it isn't. It's dirt," he said as he looked me over. I could tell he was sizing me up, wondering which move might work on me. "Look, if you don't want to be doing this kind of work, why don't you let me help you? I know a lot of producers."

If I was tougher and just a little less green, I would put pedal to the metal right then and there.

He was so obviously a Hollywood player. But against my better judgment, and betraying my Omaha roots, I felt for this guy – disheveled after the tackle by a washed-up Hollywood perv. Unless Logan's dad owned the PR firm, it was a sure bet he'd lose his job over this skirmish.

And he would blame me.

"That's nice of you, but –"

"Just think about it. Please," he said as he pulled out his business card. "Let me take you to dinner tonight. If it turns out that I can help you, great – a win-win for both of us. If not, you can always sell those pics tomorrow. A few hours won't make any difference."

It was tempting. On the one hand, these photos were the first exclusive I'd scored in a year of doing this – it was going to be my best paycheck ever. On the other, I was sick of ambushing drunk and/or medicated celebrities. My college dreams of a reporter gig at CNN were beginning to seem way out of reach. And this guy *did* work for a very high-end firm.

I took his card. "I'm not promising anything."

Before he could respond, I bolted. Driving out of the garage, I asked myself if I'd even be considering his offer if he wasn't drop-dead gorgeous. On cue, my cell rang. It was my roommate, Zoe – best bud since seventh grade and the only person I would choose to make a go of it with in Los Angeles.

"Hey, girl!" she screamed. I could hear clanging dishware in the background, so I knew she was at work, waiting tables at a hip but dirt-cheap Hollywood diner. "Bad news: our evil landlord is filing eviction papers if we don't pay the last two months' rent by tomorrow. I've made thirteen dollars and eighty-three cents so far today. Any ideas?"

I glanced at the business card that I still held in my hand. Sorry, Eric Logan. Our friendship was nice while it lasted.

CHAPTER 4

Wayne Tennet

"I DIDN'T DO IT!"

The whole place went silent for about a millisecond, and then it was chaos. The judge slammed his gavel four or five times. Before the arraignment began, he'd already threatened to clear the courtroom of the media; obviously this wasn't a guy angling for a shot at his own syndicated judge show.

My lawyer, Aaron Parker, clamped his hand on my forearm and hissed, "Jesus, Wayne. The one thing I asked you to do was to *keep your mouth shut!*"

"Sorry," I said through gritted teeth. "Hearing all those charges out loud – *statutory rape and worse!* – just set me off. Aaron, this whole thing is outrageous!"

The judge barked out over the commotion for Parker and the DA to approach the bench. The DA was a tough-looking woman who could barely contain a smile of delight at the publicity she was getting from this case. My hands were shaking – I couldn't tell if it was because I was angry or scared, or because I'd gone cold turkey since getting off the plane forty-eight hours ago. Drinking was the source of a lot of my troubles, but damn if it wasn't hard to get by without it.

I snuck a glance back into the crowded gallery behind me where my wife, Valentina, was sitting with her and – I assumed – Breelyn's lawyer. Val was definitely ready for her close-up. Auburn hair upswept, subdued gray suit, face immobile as a mask – whether that indicated calm or her overreliance on Botox, I couldn't say. She never once looked my way.

I entered a not-guilty plea and bail was set. I also had to turn over my passport, which was somehow the most humiliating aspect of the proceeding. I say "somehow" because getting arrested last night and marched into the precinct, my photo snapped by hundreds of paparazzi and the media, was pretty humiliating.

Thankfully, the judge granted bail, which I put up in cash. When it was all over, Parker turned to me. "Well, that could have been worse. I think –"

"How could it have been worse?" I asked. "Even if I'm cleared of this, aren't people always going to wonder if I'm some kind of pervert for the *rest of my life?*"

I again looked over at Valentina as she was making her exit. For a moment I didn't care if I did life or got the chair, I just wanted to shake the hell out of her. But when I started toward her, the kid, Logan, stepped in front of me and put up a hand.

"Careful, Mr. Tennet," he said. "There are about a hundred reporters outside."

Parker took my arm, and though I was rigid with anger, the two men managed to steer me backward into an adjoining chamber. A lone security guard was waiting inside, and he led us through a back hall to a restricted elevator used by the court staff. I saw Logan pass him a c-note. Though something about this kid bugged me, I had to admit he got things done.

We hurried across the plaza and got into the Town Car just as the press spotted us. They swarmed the car, but the driver plowed right through them. Despite my pledge of sobriety, I found myself looking around the inside for a mini-bar.

"So, now what?" I asked with a sigh, not really wanting to know.

"Now we begin our defense," Parker said tersely. "But there's not much point unless you get that temper of yours under control, Wayne. You didn't sound outraged and innocent in there – you sounded angry and violent."

That I already knew. I looked at Logan.

"Is there any good news? What's the press like on this?"

He looked surprised. "You haven't read anything?"

"Haven't so much as clicked on a headline."

Logan glanced at Parker, who shrugged helplessly.

"It's pretty bad," Logan said matter-of-factly. "You've made some enemies, Mr. Tennet, and more than a few are glad to see you get a kick in the balls. Now, to counteract, we need to find –"

"Where's Sydney?" I interrupted. "The amount of money I pay that guy and he's not even here?"

"He's on his way back from Thailand. He'll be in tonight and will take over."

We drove in silence for a moment. I finally had to ask, "And the studio? Have they made any kind of statement on this?"

Logan again looked at Parker as though waiting for permission to speak. Parker just frowned.

"They've replaced you on the film," Logan said simply. "Morals clause in your contract."

I'm sure they were both surprised that I didn't explode or start screaming or bash out a car window. I just sat there quietly for a few minutes. The trial hadn't even started and I'd already received a death sentence.

"Well," I said wearily, "I think that calls for a drink."

The car came to a stoplight on Pico Boulevard. I opened the door and stepped out. I walked right through the moving traffic as Parker and Logan called after me. We were in Koreatown, where there was a bar on almost every corner. I walked into the nearest one – a dark and dingy place with a television on over the bar.

"Whiskey, neat."

As the bored bartender poured, I glanced up at the television – just in time to see the images of my parking garage fight with Logan splash across the screen.

"Make it a double," I said. "Scratch that – a triple."

He followed my eyes and looked up at the TV.

"And pour one for yourself," I said as I raised my glass. "After today, you're probably the last person in Hollywood who'll have a drink with me."

CHAPTER 5

Wayne Tennet

THERE WAS SO MUCH yelling and so many flashbulbs exploding in my face that, through my drunken haze, I almost thought I was at a film premiere. For just a moment, I let myself imagine I was at the most exciting event of my career – the culmination of twenty years of both crazy dreams and dogged hard work. But deep down, I knew that my premiere days were over. From now on, I was an industry scandal. A pariah. A punch line.

"Wayne! Have you always been into young girls?"

Logan had warned me that there would be a swarm of reporters outside my house, and he wasn't kidding. There was even a helicopter hovering.

"Did you beat your stepdaughter as well as molest her?"

I lived in Nichols Canyon above Franklin Boulevard, where the streets get narrower, twisty, and more vertical the farther up the canyon you go. Even locals sometimes get lost. But the press clearly had no problem finding my house, an early thirties Spanish style that Valentina had covered in pink and white bougainvillea when we were first married.

"Is it true that you gave Breelyn crystal meth?"

They screamed their questions one after another. Even if I wanted to respond to them, they couldn't have heard me. So I just pushed and shoved my way through the mob to my front door. One squat guy in a suit clutching a microphone got in my face as I fumbled with the electric lock. As I shoved him out of the way, flashbulbs blinded me.

Then suddenly I was inside my house. It seemed eerily dark and quiet despite the muffled voices outside. It was almost peaceful. It didn't last.

As I headed toward my bar, I heard the familiar click of high heels coming down the hall. Valentina was here. She had the nerve to be here, after what she was putting me through. I should call the cops on *her!*

She strode into the room wheeling a suitcase behind her, then stopped and stared at the bottle in my hand.

"Don't mind me, pour away," she said contemptuously.

I did just that.

"Why are you in here?" I asked. "The cameras are all outside."

She pursed her artificially plumped lips and glared at me. "*That's* what you have to say to me after what you've done to my daughter?"

It took every ounce of restraint I had not to fly across the room and strangle her.

"I have never *touched* Breelyn," I seethed. "And you know it."

"I know what Breelyn told me," she spat out.

I could feel my self-control slipping, but I did my best to keep it together. I moved to the other side of the room to maintain distance from her and took another gulp of my drink. My head was spinning.

"Val, I don't know why she's said what she did," I told her in the calmest manner I could manage, "but I swear I have never, *ever* done anything inappropriate to our daughter!"

"She isn't *yours* – thank God. At least you haven't committed incest," she said. "At least I don't have the shame of people throwing *that* at me."

"And that's what this is really all about, isn't it? *YOU!*" I shouted. "Valentina Doyle gives the performance of her career – outraged mother and wronged wife! The best role she's had in years. Just think what all this attention could lead to. I'm sure it's *never* crossed your mind!"

She gave me a look I had never seen before, though I had studied her face many times over the years as a lover, a husband, and a director. It was hard and calculating, and incredibly, it was as if some part of her was actually *enjoying* this scene we were playing. Whatever she was up to, I had to hand it to her – she kept her cool a lot better than I did. But then again, I was the one with everything to lose.

As she started toward the door, all restraint left me and I flew across the room. I grabbed her arm and spun her around.

"Val, this isn't a game!" I pleaded. "My *life* is being destroyed! Everything is being taken from me – my film, my reputation. After all our time together, can't you give me the benefit of the doubt? Help me find out why Breelyn would say this. One word from you could make a huge difference!"

She looked daggers at me. "Don't you dare put this on *me*. Everyone who has ever been around you for more than five minutes knows that you're angry, controlling, violent. It's not my fault or Breelyn's that it all finally caught up with you. Whatever you think you've lost, Wayne, has really just been thrown away – by *you*."

I'm not a stupid man, so I have to assume at some level I knew what I was doing. I knew there was a throng of reporters outside the door. I knew what little support I had was shaky at best. Worst of all, I knew Valentina was right.

And yet I still did it. I opened the front door and, grabbing my wife by the neck, shoved her forward. I'm ashamed to say I felt the muscles of her neck spasm in my hand. She flew out the door and across our short front porch. But she didn't land face-first on the elegant imported tiles or among the crowd of reporters. Instead, she fell up against someone who had just been stepping forward.

Together, they ended up on the front pathway in a tangled heap. There was a gasp throughout the crowd and then silence for a moment. It lasted until the other person got up.

My stepdaughter. Breelyn. I wasn't supposed to be

within fifty feet of her, per the judge's instructions, and here we were, a few feet apart, as the paparazzi got it all on film.

She'd hit a step and had a horrific gash across her forehead that all at once erupted in a flow of blood down her beautiful face. It was, by far, the worst image I've ever seen.

Thank God, the flashbulbs once again blinded me.

CHAPTER 6

Eric Logan

I WAS JUST GETTING to the office when I got a text from a number I didn't recognize:

Hey, it's Kayla Ross. Sorry about the pics. Can I make it up to you? Drinks?

Kayla. I'd been wondering if I would hear from her. She was a cute kid, obviously new to all of this. She followed up with another:

Also, I have Tennet info you need to know.

Of course, in her position, I would've sold those photos in a heartbeat. I understood. Plus, she wasn't bad to look at; her jet-black, almond-shaped eyes were sexy as hell.

Intrigued. Sky Bar in 30 mins.

I'd stayed away from the office till the end of the day hoping that my boss would have had time to cool down. But from the way the receptionist, Michelle, pointed at Sydney's office, I figured I'd probably be filing for unemployment before the day was out. I paused at the TV in the lobby, where it took about six seconds for the shots of

Breelyn Doyle's injured face to flash up on the screen – probably for the hundredth time that day.

Sydney was on the phone trying to muscle someone out of running a story on Tennet. Sydney Paige was a silver-haired, classy guy; before he started the firm, he'd been a model. He gave me a slow-burn glare, pointed at me, then cut his finger across his neck. Yep, I was screwed.

He finally slammed down the phone, then picked it up again and mock-threw it at me.

"A *brawl* in a *parking* garage?" he yelled. "*Really?* God-damnit, Logan! Were you as drunk as he was?"

"No one is ever as drunk as I am," someone said behind me.

I whipped around as Tennet entered the office. He looked like the walking dead. Pasty skin, sunken and red-rimmed eyes – he clearly hadn't slept in days. He just stood there for a moment, then went over to Sydney's couch and collapsed on it, face-down. Sydney looked thrown and carefully approached him.

"Sorry to see you again under these circumstances, Wayne," Sydney said awkwardly. He may as well have been addressing a corpse on his couch. "I have a press strategy to review with you but . . . well, the first order of business is, to be absolutely frank, finding a rehab facility for you."

Tennet flopped his hands helplessly and talked into the couch pillows. "A funeral parlor would be more to the point."

Sydney frowned and paced back and forth. Finally he

shot me an irritated glance. "Is there a reason you aren't clearing out your desk, Logan?"

"Wait," Tennet said as he rolled himself over, rubbed his eyes, and sat up. "It's not the kid's fault, Sydney. Don't fire him because of me. Let me have one small thing off my conscience."

Sydney scowled at me, then shrugged. "All right. Not even sure I meant it. But we need to get ahead of this – way ahead. Wayne, is there *anything* else out there that I should know about?"

I thought about Kayla's cryptic message. More media fuel was in the pipeline. I glanced at my watch. I was due to meet her in ten minutes.

"Thanks, Mr. Tennet," I said, prepping for my departure.

"You may as well call me Wayne," he said ruefully. "At this point, you outrank me on the Industry Respect Scale."

He hung his head in his hands.

Sydney came over to me and whispered, "Stay with him while I try to put out a few fires. At the very least, I want to get a doctor in to look him over."

I nodded as Sydney went into his side office. As I reached for my phone to text Kayla, Tennet suddenly broke into choking sobs. I didn't know what to do – ignoring him seemed rude, texting even worse.

"Sorry, Logan," he sputtered as he tried to pull it together. "But I guess you're used to this from me, huh?"

His body shook. Everything seemed to be pouring out of him. I paused, then took a seat on the couch next to him. What the hell was I supposed to do? Hug him? Give him a pep talk?

It turned out all I had to do was listen. For the next forty-five minutes Tennet unloaded – everything from his messed-up marriage to a fading actress, to his temper issues, to his fears of failure. I thought it sad that a junior PR rep was the only person Tennet had to talk to, and he was on the clock.

And the whole time I kept getting text alerts from the cell phone buried inside my blazer. I imagined Kayla sitting alone at the bar as ten minutes passed, then twenty, then thirty. Finally, my phone went silent.

Sydney eventually stuck his head in the door and signaled for me, then turned back to his secretary.

"Michelle, make a reservation for him at the Hotel Palomar in Beverly Hills," he told her sternly. "It's the first thing you should have done with him, Logan. From now on, I don't want Tennet in front of any cameras unless we control them."

I sucked it up. It was important for Sydney to know he was The Man and called the shots. I could see that he was starting to get a sense that he had this in hand. Still, I had the feeling that a shit storm was growing out there – one that I wanted to be in front of.

So I was not encouraged by the last text I got from Kayla:

I tried. Think we're even now.

CHAPTER 7

Eric Logan

I DUMPED TENNET'S LIFELESS body on the bed and stared at it. I hoped he was dead.

But it looked like he was only dead drunk.

"One last round of drinks before I give it up for life."

That's what he'd said when he insisted on taking me out for dinner and drinks as a thank you for listening to his sob story. Which, of course, just meant three more hours of the same, topped off by his demand to sleep not in the hotel room but in his own bed. Not a great night for me, but it was hard to be too pissed at the guy when he beat himself up so brutally.

I pulled off his shoes and rolled him over onto his back so he wouldn't suffocate. Tennet's bedroom was a shambles – his wife had left a mess when she packed up and stormed out in a rush, the cops had trashed the place when they'd searched it, and he'd told me over dinner that this morning he'd fired the housekeeper when he spotted her talking to the press. As if she could avoid it – they were camped out in front 24/7. And they'd gotten some choice photos tonight of me dragging him in from the car. Sydney was going to have a stroke.

I went to shut off the light but paused for a moment. This seemed a good opportunity to do some snooping. If I was going to stay on top of or, better yet, in *front of* developments, I needed to get the full picture. I dug around through the piles of clothes, under the bed, and felt around between the mattresses. The rest of the house had clearly been searched, but it wasn't quite as trashed in the living room, and when I sat down to think, I felt something in my back. I turned and reached behind the pillow, and there was a laptop that the cops had somehow missed? Or Wayne had drunkenly left there? *No way the cops would have left this behind,* I thought, and figured there was no better place to start than there. I went back and checked in on Tennet; he was clearly out for the night, so I went back to the living room with the laptop.

I tried a few obvious password choices like "valentina," "wayne," and "wtennet" but didn't get anywhere. I thought for a moment, then entered the name of his first film, "conflictofinterest." Bingo. His computer desktop was a mess – so many photos and documents littered the screen you could barely make out the background image. I started separating the program icons from one another and then saw something buried beneath a jpeg – a folder called "bdoyle_pool."

I clicked on the folder and it opened to reveal a list of at least twenty images. I tapped the first one. And couldn't believe what I was looking at.

It was an outdoor photograph of his stepdaughter, Breelyn Doyle.

And she was topless.

She was getting out of a pool, smiling, but with an uncertain look on her face – as though she wasn't sure she was doing exactly what the photographer wanted.

God, she really *was* stunningly beautiful. Tawny hair, big hazel eyes, slim but not eating-disorder skinny like so many LA chicks.

I opened another image. More of the same. I opened one after another. They got progressively more explicit.

I tried to imagine how these had come about. And what they meant. This was literally the A-bomb for Tennet – anyone with even a shred of doubt about his guilt would cave if these ever saw the light of day.

I thought for a long time about what I should do.

Finally, I took out the thumb drive I always carry and transferred the folder onto it. As I dragged the folder on Tennet's desktop to the trash bin and emptied it, I noticed that my hand was shaking.

So I helped myself to some of Wayne's top-shelf whiskey. I swore to myself that I wouldn't make a habit of it. Then I got a rag and wiped my fingerprints off the laptop. Just in case.

CHAPTER 8

Eric Logan

"BY SAYING THAT YOU'VE never touched your stepdaughter inappropriately," the woman with the stiff hair said, leaning in, "you are, after all, calling her a *liar.*"

Tennet took a moment to reply. I could almost see him counting "one thousand one, one thousand two, one thousand three" as I'd advised.

"Breelyn is not a liar," he said calmly. "She is an eighteen-year-old girl who is as impressionable as any child that age. I think she's just confused and scared and has been influenced by someone –"

"Meaning your wife, Valentina Doyle!" she interjected. Jacky Tokiwa was the go-to interviewer for all celebrities that needed a high-profile platform for whatever message they were trying to either get out or control.

Again, Tennet took it slow. "I didn't say that, Jacky. I haven't talked to Breelyn, not since I got back from location shooting in Perth. I don't know who has been in her life or what has been –"

"So, your relationship is distant, and not just geographically."

I saw his brow furrow just a bit. Sydney worriedly gripped my arm. We were watching from a booth in the news studio on the Fox lot as the interview was taped.

"He's got it, we prepped for this over and over," I whispered to Sydney, though in reality, I was saying a *very* desperate Hail Mary.

"Breelyn and I had Skype chats twice a week," Tennet said. "I never missed one. And neither did she – despite the twenty-one-hour time difference. Do you have any idea how hard it is to get a teenager to follow that kind of schedule?"

He asked it with a nice bit of warmth. Jacky almost smiled. He'd nailed it.

I'd spent most of the last forty-eight hours coaching Tennet on how to present himself: what to say, what *not* to say, how to check his temper, how to deflect, how to subtly suggest that Valentina Doyle was bipolar without coming out and saying it. I'd been impressed at how cooperative and determined he was – not to mention that he'd stuck to his vow to stop drinking. He'd been stone cold sober the entire time.

"You are legendary for having one of the worst tempers in the film business." Jacky craftily made it a statement, not a question.

Tennet nodded. "My reputation is horrible, and I am ashamed to admit that it is completely just. I do have serious anger issues, and I have no one to blame but myself for the trouble they have caused me. I'm finally getting help, and I just pray that it's not too late. I owe a lot of apologies to a lot of people. But my stepdaughter is not one of them."

Forthright, humble, yet strong. I wanted to scream, "*Cut, print it!*" Sydney was grinning from ear to ear.

"Slam dunk!" he cried out as he gave me five. The booth technicians glanced back at us. We'd have to limit our enthusiasm about our client possibly dodging child abuse charges.

On the set, Tennet and Jacky were making nice now that the interview was over. She'd asked tough questions, and he'd addressed them openly and directly. It was a win-win for both. Ratings were sure to be sky high.

Totally stoked, I turned to Sydney, who suddenly had gone stone-faced. He was staring at one of the monitors that showed what the competition was airing.

On the screen, a good-looking kid – brawny, with hipster facial hair – was being interviewed. The graphic below him said "Omar Sabat, boyfriend of Breelyn Doyle." He was nodding his head and earnestly saying something. Sydney leaned forward and turned up the volume.

"– I don't know exactly when it started. Bree never said anything about it to me until – well, I saw what I saw," Sabat stammered.

"And what did you see?" a female interviewer probed gently, off screen.

Sabat looked troubled and hesitated before answering.

"I came over one night without calling – though I knew it wasn't cool," he said. "Bree hadn't answered her cell in, like, two hours, so I was getting worried. I went around to the back of the house. And then I saw them. They were together in the pool. And he was behind her, pressing up against her. Her father was. And they were . . . naked."

As he continued with even more graphic descriptions, the camera cut to the interviewer, a pretty, surprisingly young woman with dark eyes and thick black hair: Kayla Ross.

CHAPTER 9

Kayla Ross

"I SERIOUSLY CANNOT *BELIEVE* we are here! You and me – total *nobodies!*"

After a year in Los Angeles, Zoe *still* hadn't learned to chill. Everything excited her, and when it came to celebrity sightings, there was a good chance she'd pass out. We were going to SoHo House, the most exclusive spot in the city – ground zero for movie stars. She'd been talking about it since before we'd even moved here, and I'd promised that if I ever became a legitimate news reporter it would be the first place we'd go.

On the elevator up to the penthouse suite, I looked at the two women riding with us: effortlessly thin and dressed elegantly in simple cocktail dresses. Right away I saw that Zoe and I had gotten too done up in our secondhand Marc Jacobs formal dresses – we looked like we were going to the Oscars in 2005. The other women didn't even look at us; they just stared at their phones.

At the dark wood check-in desk in front of the elevator,

the supermodel-handsome host asked for their membership number.

"Don't need one. We're with Leo's party," she said, bored.

Zoe and I turned to each other. "*Membership?*"

Zoe's overly made-up face fell. I felt like an idiot for not realizing that "total nobodies" couldn't expect to just party along with Leo DiCaprio and Bruno Mars. Anxious not to humiliate ourselves further, I pulled her back to the elevator.

"Sorry, Zo," I whispered. "I had no idea!"

Even her bouncy red hair seemed to deflate at the thought of not getting in when we were this close. Then the elevator doors opened, and out stepped Eric Logan.

I had been seriously pissed when Eric stood me up, but now I couldn't help smiling at him. He looked ridiculously hot in his black Armani blazer and $1,500 Balmain jeans.

He glanced at me for a beat, and then turned away. Zoe stared after him, open-mouthed. Suddenly, he spun around.

"Kayla!" he cried out. Zoe then turned to stare, open-mouthed, at *me*.

"Hello," I said as coldly as I could manage. I pressed the elevator button for the lobby.

"You're not leaving already, are you?" he said with what seemed like real disappointment. I started to say we had another function, but Zoe cut me off.

"We can't get in!" she confided. I could have murdered her.

Logan didn't smirk, just insisted that we join him as his guests. If not for Zoe I would never have accepted, but it meant so much to her. And, well, I *did* want to see what it was all about.

Once inside the bar, Logan turned to me.

"I am *really* sorry about the other night," he said. "I can't expect you to believe this, but I absolutely could not contact you. I felt terrible. You have to let me buy you and your friend dinner – and it doesn't have to be with me. Unless . . ."

I shrugged and looked around. It was *such* a beautiful spot. Garden dining with a view of the glittering lights of West Hollywood. While Logan was at the bar ordering us Manhattans, Zoe immediately started to pump me for information about him.

"How exactly do you know the hottest non-celebrity here?" I glared at her with a "Be cool!" look. When he came back, she made up the excuse that she had to use the ladies' and vanished.

"So, please tell me," he said over his drink. "How, inside of a week and a half, did you go from paparazzi stalker to network reporter with the best get of the week?"

"'*Get*'? Is that LA speak?" I asked sarcastically.

He laughed. "Fine. 'An exclusive, difficult-to-land interview.' Isn't that in Journalism 101?"

I took a sip and tried to be casual. "I *had* to sell those photos. But I ended up making a deal with the network – a reporter gig and an advance on my salary in exchange for the pics." I smiled, a little embarrassed at my bragging.

"And the interview with this Omar Sabat? How'd you land that?"

"'To reveal a source is to lose it.' Journalism 102," I said pointedly. "But I don't know why I'm lecturing you on that . . . when you really need *Etiquette* 101."

"*Oof*, direct hit," he said.

Zoe came back and the three of us had an amazing dinner. Though he texted throughout dinner – always with an apology – Logan was very charming and made sure to ask Zoe a lot of questions, which she barely answered since she was so busy looking out for stars. Toward the end of the meal she hopped up, and a few minutes later I saw her at the bar happily chatting away at Jake Gyllenhaal who – bless his heart – was smiling at her politely.

"So, what do you have against Wayne Tennet?" Logan asked me.

"*Nothing!*" I replied, a bit sharply.

"Whoa," he said with his hands up. "No need to get defensive."

"I'm not defensive. It's a hot story and I'm interested in getting the truth out," I insisted. "What makes you think he's innocent?"

Logan just looked at me for a moment, then shook his head. "Tennet hasn't been convicted of anything, and it's my job to help him promote a positive image to the public. I take no position on his guilt or innocence."

"Even though he may have raped a minor? And *definitely* gave her a head wound?" I asked indignantly.

Just then I got a text from Zoe saying she'd gone on to a

club with Selena Gomez's personal assistant and also to "give u space." For the second time that night, I could have strangled her.

Logan was a gentleman and didn't give me a hard time at this obvious trick to make him see me home. I said I'd get an Uber ride, but he insisted on driving me.

We left the building and came out into a warm spring night; the scent of night-blooming jasmine was incredibly strong. Logan took my hand in a very natural way as we walked toward his car – a BMW M4, a car my brother would have flipped over – parked in front of a noisy nightclub. As I walked around to the passenger door, he tilted his head toward the club as if to ask if I wanted to go in.

Suddenly, a car came speeding out of nowhere. I barely had time to glance at it when the driver swerved directly toward me. I was so startled I just froze, and the front of the car – a shiny red Jaguar – clipped my arm. My purse – and my entire body – went flying into the oncoming traffic of Sunset Boulevard.

CHAPTER 10

Kayla Ross

A STAB OF PAIN brought it all back.

Every time my arm throbbed, it was as if I was there again, splayed out on Sunset Boulevard. I shook it off and looked in my rearview mirror. The bruise on my right cheek was beginning to heal. The studio had to plaster a ton of base makeup over it the first few days after the accident. My right arm still had flashes of pain, though the doctors said nothing was wrong with it. I seemed to be suffering PTSD from the whole thing.

I sighed and glanced out my car window at my destination. This school sure didn't look like any school I'd ever gone to – more like a country club, with its white columns and perfectly kept front lawn. I'd called the administration offices and pretended I was a freaked-out new housekeeper who couldn't remember what time she was supposed to pick up the niña.

At three thirty on the dot, kids starting filing out the front doors.

I got out of the car – ouch, another shot of pain in my

arm! – and joined the waiting nannies. At the end of the stream of teens I saw her. Breelyn Doyle.

She was tall and had a serious, oval-shaped face framed by blond-streaked brown hair. I would have given *anything* for hair like that when I was eighteen. She had a small bandage over her forehead. *A gift from Tennet,* I thought bitterly. She was with a girl who was probably the best friend, cute but nowhere near as pretty.

When they parted at the front gate, I came up to her with a smile.

"Breelyn? Can I talk to you?"

She looked at me without surprise, like she'd been expecting me. She was both beautiful and sort of strange-looking, like supermodels with their widely spaced eyes and empty expressions. While her face was still that of a teenager, her eyes looked adult; I guessed that came from growing up in Beverly Hills.

"I don't give interviews without my lawyer present," she said. Wow, her childhood could *not* have been more different from mine.

"I don't have a camera crew," I said. "I just wanted to talk. If you feel like it."

She narrowed her eyes at me. She seemed to be thinking it over, and just as she was about to speak, a car screeched to a halt not two feet away from us – a *shiny red Jaguar.*

I froze. For a second I again saw the glare of headlights from the awful oncoming traffic. As I shook my head to get a grip, a small but curvy auburn-haired woman jumped out of the Jag. I recognized her instantly: Valentina Doyle.

"How *dare* you!" she screeched as she got between Breelyn and me. I was so surprised by her and her *car* – and, embarrassingly, also a little starstruck – that I just stood there like a clueless idiot for a moment.

"Miss Doyle – er, Tennet," I finally stammered. "I'm Kayla Ro—"

"I know *exactly* who you are!" she seethed. "You broadcast that filthy interview with my daughter's boyfriend. I hope the ratings you got were worth the humiliation it caused my daughter."

I could feel the rage coming off her body. She seemed almost violent as she protectively grabbed Breelyn's shoulders. I took a deep breath.

"Well, that's *exactly* why I'm here," I said. "I had no idea that Omar would get so graphic. I wanted to cut it, but my producers overruled me. I'm here to apologize. I feel awful about it."

She looked at me with confusion for a beat. "*Where* are you from, girl?"

"Omaha."

She frowned for a moment, then laughed, loudly. "Oh, hell. Wichita, here. I sometimes forget that there are actually people around with manners. I've never heard of a *journalist* apologizing before!"

Now her charm scented the air like perfume. Her whole face changed and she smiled with incredible warmth. I couldn't believe someone's mood could change so quickly. Why she didn't have as many Oscars as Meryl Streep was beyond me.

She held out her hand and I shook it. The whole time, Breelyn was watching her mother, almost studying her.

"Your apology is accepted, Kayla," she said. "I guess I'm kind of a mama bear. I'll do *anything* to protect my baby here. And I have. I turned down the best role I'd ever been offered when she was only six months old. My agents wanted to fire me! But I told them I already had the best role of my life: *mother*."

It was all very Joan Crawford, and Breelyn nearly rolled her eyes; she was no Christina Crawford, that's for sure. But just then I saw Breelyn's expression change. I turned around and saw Wayne approaching. He was walking very carefully with an unsure smile on his face.

Valentina turned around, too, and – once again – her whole body went rigid. She shoved Breelyn behind her.

"Stop!" she almost screamed, all charm gone in an instant. Now it was pure hatred coming off her. "Come one step closer, Wayne, and *I will kill you*."

Tennet stopped and sighed. He started to say something, but Valentina raised her hand.

"Or *have* you killed."

CHAPTER 11

Wayne Tennet

"I AM PLEASED to report that the process worked. Justice has prevailed. My client protested his innocence from the very beginning, and now he has been vindicated."

Sydney paused dramatically – just long enough for his words to sink in but not so long to give the reporters time to start firing questions.

"Charges have been dropped and he can now return to making millions of people around the world happy through his extraordinary films. Ladies and gentleman, Mr. Wayne Tennet."

I didn't know if Sydney was expecting the reporters to clap or cheer or what, so I just sort of stared blankly into the camera lights for a moment. He'd called the press conference just half an hour before – we'd hardly had time to put together any kind of statement, and the kid, Logan, was off schmoozing clients.

Finally, a reporter shouted out: "How are you feeling, Mr. Tennet?"

I didn't know what facial expression would be appropriate. Was I supposed to smile and possibly end up looking cocky? Was I supposed to take a victory lap – and belittle whatever troubles had driven my stepdaughter to make such an outrageous claim?

"Um, I'm just relieved that this horrible nightmare is finally over," I said, and immediately realized it was the same clichéd statement that every accused person makes when they've been vindicated. But it was true. I *was* just glad it was over, and I *was* anxious to get back to my life. I wanted peace again. I hadn't had a good night's sleep since being in Australia; nearly every night I woke up certain that someone was in the house with me, certain I was being stalked. Lately I'd been going to bed with every light in the house on.

"Are you going to make a film about your experience?"

"Ah . . . I hadn't thought about it." I shrugged. "I guess I do have more insight into the legal system now. Though, to tell the truth, I'd rather have stayed in the dark!"

No one laughed and Sydney gave me a wide-eyed "don't make jokes" grimace. I knew I was sweating, and for the first time in quite a while, I wanted a drink.

"No, in all seriousness, I'm just glad to be cleared of this and I –"

"But you weren't cleared," someone – a woman – called out. "You just weren't *prosecuted* due to insufficient evidence – which is often difficult to obtain in child molestation cases."

The whole room went dead quiet for a moment – all eyes

were on me to see how I'd react. I tried Logan's method of slowly counting to three by thousands. I had to stay cool here.

"I can only repeat what I've been saying," I said, knowing my voice sounded strained. "I never touched my stepdaughter in any inappropriate way."

"And what do you expect your relationship with your stepdaughter to be going forward?" she asked.

I looked into the crowd and spotted the woman who'd started badgering me – a pretty Latina with striking black eyes. She looked to be all of twenty-three. Then I recognized her – she'd done the interview with Breelyn's scumbag boyfriend. And she was outside Breelyn's school the day I tried to talk to her. I started counting slowly again to myself but barely made it past one.

"I'm hoping we can repair the damage, obviously," I said, a little tersely, I knew. "I want to understand what's going on with her and –"

"Are you going to challenge the restraining order that your wife has filed on Breelyn's behalf?"

Why the hell is this girl going for the jugular? I wondered. It was like she had a personal vendetta against me. Sydney stepped forward, finally.

"I think you've asked enough questions," he said. "Let's hear from someone else –"

"What about the anger management course you agreed to as part of your plea bargain –"

"It wasn't a plea bargain, goddamnit!" I shouted at her, completely unable to stop myself. "It was a mutual agreement! I *want* to control my anger!"

There I was, illustrating how desperately I needed anger management. I knew what was happening, saw myself losing control in slow motion, but the thought that this dropped charge would stymie my career and my life still made me furious.

"Half of my problem is people like *you*," I said, unable to stop myself. "Why do you have to be such ball-breaking *bitches?*"

Everyone stared at me in astonished disgust, everyone except Sydney. He stared at me with something much worse – pity.

And then I knew it was over. My professional suicide was now complete.

CHAPTER 12

Wayne Tennet

MAYBE I SHOULD KILL HER.

I kept circling back to the idea, over and over.

"Let's go to the Ivy for dinner," Logan said, interrupting my train of thought. "Nothing will say that you *want* to be seen louder than being at such a high-profile spot. Just walk in like you own the place."

I was gazing out the window of Sydney's Mercedes as we drove through Beverly Hills. I could see Sydney glance over at me with a worried look.

"Doesn't have to be tonight, Wayne," he said. "Not if you aren't up for it. That press conference was rough."

"I thinks it's a great idea," I replied. "By walking into the lion's den I'll show that I truly don't give a shit what they think."

I wondered what would be the best way to do it. Shoot her? Stab her? Run her over? Make it look like a mugging? On some level I couldn't believe I was seriously thinking about doing something so horrible, but then again, she was behind this. She'd ruined my life. Anyone could see that.

"It will definitely make an impression, Wayne," Logan was saying. "I'll call and see if Fernando can get us some prime real estate right in front. He owes me a favor or two . . ."

What does it feel like to strangle a person? I wondered. She would fight and fight *hard,* so I'd not only have to squeeze her throat but also stop her from struggling. Funny, the only death scenes I'd ever shot in seven movies were by gunshot. I never realized how difficult it would really be to kill someone.

"We're in!" Logan said with his usual enthusiasm as he clicked off his phone. I'd have to play along with it – I couldn't have anyone suspect a thing.

"Awesome!" I cried out, and did a palm slap against the dashboard. The more I thought about it, the better the idea seemed. I had nothing to lose – everything had already been taken from me.

We drove up in front of the Ivy as the sun was setting. The front patio was already almost full of early-evening diners. A few photographers were hanging around, but when I put on a big phony smile for them they just blankly turned away. Looked like I was no longer news.

They put us at a table that nearly everyone entering the restaurant would have to pass. Sydney started to order a bottle of wine, then, with a worried glance at me, changed it to Perrier. He and Logan made small talk and I nodded along, though I didn't hear a word. I saw Andy Fontana approach the host stand. He'd written three of my films. As he came toward me I raised my head with a nod and a smile. He looked directly through me – like I wasn't even there. It was worse than if he'd spat on me.

I flagged the waiter down. "Bourbon on the rocks."

Sydney and Logan darted looks at each other. "Wayne, don't you think –"

"You're right." I nodded. "What was I thinking? Sorry, make it a *double*."

The double was soon doubled. I lost count of how many I had. I just got quieter and quieter, my plan festering in the back of my mind. Finally, I stood up.

"Gotta take a leak, guys," I said. "When I get back I guess we should strategize on how you two are going to resurrect me from the dead."

They looked relieved at my willingness to listen to reason. As I walked away, they huddled together over the table – obviously plotting how to deal with me. I didn't even pretend to head toward the john – I just walked across the patio and out the front. Not one person looked at me.

I hailed a cab and had him drive me around for an hour or so. I didn't want to go home right away; a persistent feeling that someone was in the house had made me jittery for weeks now. But I eventually realized I had nowhere to go, not a single person to turn to.

When I finally did have the driver take me home, there weren't any reporters out front. I almost missed them. Their presence outside had been weirdly comforting when I did my three a.m. searches around the house – flicking lights on and off, checking door locks.

The house was silent and eerily lonely as I entered. And I immediately had that feeling again – like someone had *just* been there. I walked from empty room to empty room, nothing. But then on the bar I saw something odd: a bottle of Bushmills bourbon. I knew I hadn't put it out – until tonight I hadn't had a drink in a couple of weeks, and I'd kept the stuff locked away. But then again, could I be so sure? Not in the state I was in.

I took the bottle with me outside to the pool and plopped down on a deck chair. The temperature had dropped in the last hour and a chilly breeze blew ripples across the water's surface; the pool lights sent slowly waving shadows over the dark palm trees. It looked like a movie set. Perfect atmosphere for murder.

I took a swig from the bottle and suddenly felt twice as drunk as I had moments ago. In a daze I looked around. The dim lighting here was ideal, moody, and menacing. It would highlight the terror on her face, the –

A sudden noise yanked me back to reality – as if a strip of film had been ripped in two. As I looked up and out at the shadows, a figure stepped forward. My vision blurry, I squinted to see who it was. I didn't feel fear exactly, more like perverse satisfaction that I was right – someone *was* here stalking me!

The figure stepped closer, dramatically backlit against the pool.

"Well, well," I slurred, sounding ever drunker. "What the hell are *you* doing here?"

I went to take another sip. And everything started to darken.

No! I wanted to shout but suddenly couldn't. *The fade out is happening too quickly – we're cutting away too soon!*

The screen in my mind dimmed – then went entirely black.

CHAPTER 13

Kayla Ross

"HE'S AN ACCUSED *RAPIST!* Get the hell away from there!"

I stared at Wayne Tennet's silent house as I listened to Zoe's freakout. It was hard to see the home from the street because of the wall of flowery bushes planted in front, I guessed for privacy. Then the thought of just what he might have wanted hidden from view made me feel sick.

"Kayla, I'm serious," Zoe was saying over the phone. "You need to leave *now*."

"It's broad daylight, nothing is going to happen," I insisted, though probably more to convince myself than her. "I'm just going to go to his front door and talk to him."

"Call him on the phone!" she said. "You don't have to put in a personal appearance!"

"I tried to call and it just rings. I think it's better this way, more polite or something. It almost worked with Breelyn Doyle."

I was surprised that there were no reporters out front. The news cycle had clearly moved on.

"I just feel bad about how I questioned him at that press conference," I said. "Even if he is a creep, I was too aggressive. I made it personal."

Zoe wouldn't hang up until I promised to text her every ten minutes to let her know that I was still alive and not being held in a secret dungeon. The morning felt still as I nervously approached the heavily carved front door; it must have cost a fortune, like the rest of the house. I knocked lightly and nothing happened. Then I pushed the doorbell; again, nothing but the echo of the ring from the inside.

It was strange that an expensive, empty house, in the middle of the day, could seem so spooky.

It made sense that Tennet wasn't here. He'd probably checked into a hotel or – if he was smart – left town altogether. Part of me was glad. Talking to him face-to-face would have been awkward – and a little scary. As I turned to walk away, I heard a sudden faint sound. A scream.

I froze – it had definitely come from inside the house. I listened for a moment and then heard muffled voices – a man's and a woman's. And they were arguing.

Another scream – louder this time. I instinctively grabbed the door handle and turned. Locked. I wondered if I should call 911.

Then it all went silent. Had I just imagined it?

I stepped away from the house and looked around. All the drapes were pulled so I couldn't see inside at all. A dark, expensive-looking car was in the driveway. As I approached it, I saw that the driver's window was down a bit. I hesitated for a moment, then reached in and pressed the remote attached to the sun visor. The garage door on the side of the house opened right up.

Inside the empty garage was a door leading into the house, and it was ajar. Again I heard the arguing voices. The woman's was raised in anger, though choked with sobs, too.

Was I really going to trespass like this? I hesitated but then considered that someone might really be in danger. I took a deep breath and stepped into the house.

"Hello?" I called out, my voice quivering a little. "Is everything all right?"

The place was a mess – clothes and papers everywhere, and dishes stacked in the kitchen. And it was *freezing* inside, after a chilly spring night. It seemed odd that the heat wasn't on when people were obviously in the house.

The arguing stopped for a moment, then both voices started up again, almost violently.

Then I heard the most terrified – and *terrifying* – scream yet.

It seemed to be coming from the back of the house. I was so scared I couldn't seem to move, except that my whole body was shivering. My teeth were actually chattering. I then found myself backing up against a counter and sliding to the floor in a huddle. I was paralyzed with fear – something was very wrong here. I grappled with my cell phone. I knew I had to call Zoe or the police, *anyone*.

Then the woman's scream suddenly cut off – dead silence.

I don't know how long I sat there trembling before I heard some low music – a simple piano tune. There were no more voices, just the faint music. I slowly got up and entered a dim hallway. The music seemed to be coming from behind the closed door I was standing in front of. My hand shook as I reached out to push it open. It was dark inside, though a faint light came off the far wall.

A screening room.

Eight or nine plush chairs were arranged in front of a wide screen that was showing a film – a thriller, from the sounds of the now pumped-up score. A frantic-looking woman onscreen was driving down a nighttime street. It was her – Valentina Doyle. I recognized this as the first film she'd made with Tennet.

Why is this playing to an empty room? I wondered. The scene on the screen then abruptly changed to a next-day shot of a sunny beach. Bright light flooded the room.

And that's when I saw him.

He was on the floor in front of the screen, lying on his back, nude.

An orange-colored pill bottle was lying near the top of his head. I had the weird thought that the upside-down bottle looked like a little hat on his head. I almost laughed, despite my shock.

Then light coming from the screen got even brighter. I could now see his features. I didn't feel like laughing anymore.

Wayne Tennet's eyes were wide open.

And they were staring straight up at me.

CHAPTER 14

Eric Logan

"IF TWO WOMEN *that* beautiful end up standing over my grave, I will have considered mine a life well spent," Sydney said as he looked across the cemetery.

He was staring at Valentina and Breelyn Doyle, the showily grieving widow and blank-faced stepdaughter of Wayne Tennet. Though both were dressed in tasteful, somber black, it couldn't hide their beauty. They didn't look much like each other, but from the way they stood you could tell they were related.

Tennet had a sad turnout for his send-off: only a few family members, his lawyer, his agents, and me and Sydney. It would have been an awkward group anyway, but making it worse – as Sydney kept pointing out on the way over – was the fact that we were the ones who had tried to make Breelyn Doyle look like a liar and her mother a psycho. Now Tennet's suicide seemed to confirm their claims.

As the service ended, I looked over at the entrance. There were only two photographers hanging around. The

Tennet story was officially stone-cold dead – from a PR standpoint, our jobs were finished. Probably the only thing that would revive it now was if Tennet sat up in his coffin.

"Let's scram," Sydney said with a tug on my arm. "I know it's only eleven, but I need a drink."

I looked over at Breelyn Doyle and her eyes met mine. I thought I saw something urgent in her gaze.

"Give me a sec. I'll meet you at the car," I said to Sydney as I moved over toward Breelyn. Her expression didn't change and I was certain she had something she wanted to say to me.

But just as I approached, her mother whipped around from the conversation she'd been having with Tennet's lawyer.

"Who are you?" Valentina demanded as she looked me up and down.

"Eric Logan. I work for the PR firm that represented your late husband."

"Well, well. Bet you're glad *that* job's over," she said tauntingly.

"*Mom!*" Breelyn said in a shocked voice. Valentina glanced at her, then back at me.

"He didn't deny it." She shrugged with a wry half-smile at me. "What is it you wanted, Mr. Logan?"

"Just to say how sorry I am. I only got to know Mr. Tennet recently, and even though it was under, well, difficult circumstances –"

"He didn't do it."

I don't know who was more startled – Valentina or me. Breelyn was staring straight at me.

"It's all a lie," she said. Valentina quickly took hold of her arm, and though it was meant to look reassuring, I could see it was really a warning.

"She's very upset, obviously," Valentina hissed. "This whole awful situation has been such a terrible sho—"

"He didn't kill himself," Breelyn said with tears welling up in her eyes. "He never would have done that. You have to *tell* people! They need to know."

"Bree, honey –"

"He didn't kill himself. Something else . . . happened."

A million questions went through my head. Why was she saying this now? And why to me in front of her mother?

I looked from one to the other. "Well, from what I've heard, the police investigation was pretty conclusive."

Valentina stepped forward and – reaching out – now took hold of *my* arm. She started walking me out of the cemetery with our backs to Breelyn, who mutely followed.

"Mr. Logan. *Eric*," Valentina cooed. "Please don't mind Bree. Imagine all the things she's experiencing right now. She's been put through so much already, the last thing any of us want for her is more publicity and innuendo."

She had just the right way about her – intimate and vulnerable, yet totally in charge. And she exuded sex, even now, minutes after her husband's funeral.

As we approached the black Town Car waiting to take them away, I looked back at Breelyn. She was no longer staring at me, just looking down at the ground with no expression.

"I get your concerns," I said to Valentina, carefully. "Still, if your daughter has any information or reason to bel—"

"Tell you what," Valentina interrupted. "Why don't you and I meet – let's have a drink later this week. I'm so confused about all of this myself. I have a *million* questions about Wayne and his state of mind in his last days. Maybe you can help me . . ."

She pressed her fingers into my forearm and looked up at me with wide, pleading eyes. Despite myself I was knocked over by her magnetism and felt my head nodding – way too enthusiastically.

As I helped Valentina into the car – her hand lingering in mine with a breathy "*thank you*" – I looked over at Breelyn. She was in the backseat staring ahead blank-faced. But in the corner of her mouth, there was the tiniest, almost impossible to see hint of . . . a *smile*.

CHAPTER 15

Kayla Ross

THE PIERCING SCREAM almost made my heart stop. My body instantly went rigid with fear.

The sound took me right back to Wayne Tennet's screening room where I'd heard Valentina Doyle give the same kind of cry . . . and found a dead body.

I'd been on edge ever since. Turns out that exciting experiences like being a hit-and-run victim on Sunset Boulevard and discovering corpses take their toll on a girl.

So I wasn't all that amused by the deafening shrieks of the fan girls in the spectator seats at seeing Liam Hemsworth on the red carpet at the Teen Choice Awards.

I'd snagged this assignment by show-biz cliché – the regular entertainment reporter had gotten food poisoning that morning at a champagne brunch. It also didn't hurt that I'd broken my stories during the ratings sweeps period. The station manager told me I was now "trending" higher than any of the other reporters.

So there I was – Omaha's Kayla Ross – interviewing

world-famous music, TV, and film stars as they made their way into the Shrine Auditorium. After I got all of three seconds of "Hey, howsitgoin'?" from Harry Styles as he walked past me, my director, Eddie – a Southern skinny-jeaned and goateed hipster dude with endless energy – told me to take a break. Only C-listers were in the queue for the next few minutes, so we were going to commercial.

As the makeup team refreshed my face, I looked up and saw Breelyn Doyle coming down the carpet with her arm in Omar Sabat's. Though she had the same serious expression on her face as the last time I'd seen her, he was all smiles. He waved to the crowd and posed for photos as though he was a star, not a physical trainer who happened to date a celebrity's daughter.

He caught sight of me and – after a quick glance at the cameras behind me – made a beeline in my direction.

"Hey, Kayla!" he shouted. "How's it goin'? Are we live?"

"Sorry, Omar, we're on commercial break," I said.

"S'okay, we can hang!" He grinned.

I looked at Breelyn. She had on a simple white gown – the fabric was so sheer it looked computer-generated. There was a visible scar at the top of her forehead; I wondered why she hadn't covered it with makeup.

"How are you doing, Breelyn?" I asked. "That's not a professional question – I swear the cameras are off!"

I laughed, self-consciously, and she gave me a serene smile – like nothing could ever throw her. Her gaze drifted past me and out over the crowd. She looked at the fan mob intently, almost like she was memorizing each individual face. Without a word to me, she then started to move on down the carpet, but Omar held her back.

"Yo, Kayla," he said, "our interview was off the hook! You know how many new Twitter followers I got after that? Maybe we could do a follow-up, huh?"

I glanced at Breelyn to see how she was taking such a crass attempt to cash in on her tragedy. She just reached out and calmly took hold of Omar's arm – gently, but somehow I knew it was with an iron grip – and started leading him away.

"Awright, we gotta run, but I'll check in with you!" Omar shouted to me. "Remember, I give good interviews, baby!"

He then stopped and assumed a serious expression. In a low, somber voice, he said, " 'I came over one night without calling – though I knew it wasn't cool. Bree hadn't answered her cell in, like, two hours, so I was getting worried . . .' "

He broke into a sly grin and winked. "See, I got it down, Kay-Kay!"

He waved madly as Breelyn now forcibly pulled him away. I must have been staring after him open-mouthed, because Eddie turned and gave me a curious look.

"Why the face, *Kay-Kay?*" he asked with a smirk.

The face must have been because I had a sudden strong sinking feeling that something was very, *very* wrong.

"The guy – Omar Sabat – just quoted himself from an interview he gave me. Word for word," I said. "Almost as if it had been memorized and rehearsed."

CHAPTER 16

Kayla Ross

"YOU LOOK GREAT," a deep voice said. "You must be staying out of the way of speeding sports cars."

I quickly tried to calculate which I could get to faster – in high heels – my car, or the exit from the Shrine parking garage. I was about to cut my losses and scream my head off, when a figure stepped out of the dark and into a pool of fluorescent light: Eric Logan.

More specifically, Eric Logan in a tuxedo. Even as frightened as I was, all I could think was that he should wear a tuxedo 24/7; he looked that good.

"Ohmygod, you really *scared* me!"

"Sorry! That was me trying to be funny." He apologized with his hands up. "I just wanted to tell you how beautiful you look."

"Gee, thanks," I said, trying for frosty but probably just sounding snotty. I hadn't seen him since the night I was hit by the car and he'd taken me to the emergency room. He'd been wonderful then – comforting and in charge. And he'd sat with me for over three hours. But after getting one text from him the next day asking how I was doing, I hadn't heard a word since.

Although the show had only ended twenty minutes earlier, everyone had scattered to the after-parties and the building was eerily empty. I walked on toward my car, my heels clacking noisily on the cement as Logan followed.

"I've been wanting to get in touch with you all week. Got a lot to tell you," he said. "For instance, you'll never believe who drives a red Jaguar."

"Valentina Doyle."

He stopped dead. "Damn, I can never scoop you on *anything!*"

"It's my job," I said. "Besides, there must be hundreds of red Jags in Los Angeles."

"Not that many. Seems weird to me."

I stopped at my car and turned to him with a frown.

"So you think Valentina Doyle purposefully tried to run me over? Just because she didn't like my interview with her daughter's boyfriend?" I asked mockingly.

"So, you've thought about it, too."

He had me there.

"All right," I sighed. "It *is* a strange coincidence. But that's all."

He looked thoughtfully at the ground for a moment.

"I don't know . . . Something is off on this whole thing. Have you ever thought that Tennet's death was just a little too neat? A little too convenient?"

"For whom?" I asked, wondering what he was getting at.

"Valentina Doyle, for one. You know she's inheriting a fortune from him," he said. "And his stepdaughter claims he would never have killed himself."

"You've spoken to Breelyn Doyle?"

"More or less," he said. "I think there's more to be had here."

"Actually, I really wanted to do a follow-up, especially after . . . what happened," I admitted. "But my producers say the story is as dead as –"

"As dead as Tennet," Logan finished with a sigh. "What if some new evidence came to light, something that proved . . ."

He trailed off, looking troubled.

"Proved his innocence? His *guilt?*" I asked incredulously. "You have something? Come on, you can't hold out on me now!"

He chewed his lip thoughtfully for a moment. "I might. I don't even know if it matters anymore. Tennet is gone; maybe it's best just to let things be."

I must have had a funny look on my face, because suddenly he came closer. "You think something's wrong here, too, don't you?"

"I always have," I admitted. "Like, why was Tennet wandering around his house *nude* with no heat on the night he died? I don't care how drunk or medicated he was, it was cold. And why was there an empty bottle of pills next to him but no drink, nothing to wash them down?"

"You're in the wrong profession, Kayla," Logan said appreciatively. "You should be a detective."

"You didn't see how terrified I was at that crime scene. Anyway, this is my first big story. I'm not in the position to be calling the shots at the station."

"I know. But maybe we can work together," he said excitedly. "Both of our positions could be useful in digging a little. And in some weird way, I feel like I owe it to Tennet."

"Why?" I asked incredulously. "He was a monster. He treated you horribly. And was probably a sexual abuser!"

Logan just gave me a long look, then shrugged. "Maybe I'm just using this as an excuse to see you."

"A phone call would have been a lot easier," I said, achieving frost – *finally*.

He hung his head guiltily, then slowly reached his hand out to mine. Against my better judgment I took it, and he pulled me toward him. With his other hand he cupped the side of my face.

"I have a confession to make," he said. "I'm kind of a jerk."

"I think you intentionally try to be one," I said, my heart pounding.

"Take my advice and tell me to get lost, pretty lady."

"Okay . . . get lost."

He nodded and turned his body away from me, but at the same time, he used his arm to pull me around to his front. I stiffened for a moment – it had been a *very* long time since I'd been intimate with anyone. As he kissed me deeply, I tried to let go and be in the moment.

But when I opened my eyes, I looked over his shoulder

and saw another figure standing at a distance from us in the shadows. I was about to cry out and pull away when I heard the distinct *click* of a camera. The figure then receded back into the shadows.

CHAPTER 17

Eric Logan

AS I RAN my hand down her bare body, cupping her full breast, she sighed dreamily and pressed up against me. Then she almost immediately fell back asleep. I lay rigid for a moment. I hadn't planned on this, and I needed to get out without her waking. I never liked playing the good-bye-will-you-call-me-later scene – and I especially didn't want to play it with Valentina Doyle.

"Don't mix work and play, Eric," I'd said to myself. "*Don't do it, man.*" But here I was. Deep down, I knew damned well this would turn out to be a huge mistake. But I guess I'd figured I would deal with the bill later.

I slowly inched my way out of the bed. Valentina stirred briefly but then went back under. As I pulled on my jeans, I looked down at her nightstand. It was covered with stuff usually found inside a purse: tissue, makeup, coins, and a few bottles of meds. I picked one up: clonazepam, better known as Klonopin, a tranquilizer that people use to deal with seizures or anxiety.

Huh . . . the same thing Tennet overdosed on.

I tiptoed out of the room and tried to recall which way down the dark hall led to the front of the house. We'd had more than a few drinks at the bar last night, and by the time I'd taken Valentina home, we were both pretty lit. I'd gone into the date with the intention of playing it cool and seeing what I could get on her. Instead, she'd bulldozed me with charm. The low-cut cocktail dress she'd worn had leveled whatever self-control I had.

As I passed the kitchen, the overhead light suddenly went on. I blinked and looked inside. Breelyn Doyle was standing there, her eyes wide at the sight of me.

"What are *you* doing here?" she gasped.

"*Shh!* Let me talk to you a sec," I whispered as I flicked off the light. Even when confronted at dawn by the man who'd clearly just had sex with her mother, she looked phenomenally beautiful. Everything about her was so natural; her skin was so flawless it would have looked Photoshopped were it not for the slight scar just below her hairline.

"You need to tell people he didn't kill himself!" she said, wide-eyed.

I reached out to take her arm, but in the dark my hand landed on her shoulder, almost at her neck. I meant it as a calming gesture, but I can only guess what it looked like when the lights flicked back on and Valentina stood there.

"Well, well . . . I don't seem to know my lines for this scene," she said with ice-cold fury. "Anyone care to give me a cue?"

"Hey, good morning," I babbled. "We – I just ran into your daughter on my way out. I didn't want to wake you."

"Why not?" she fumed. "Don't I deserve at least a goodbye?"

I stepped forward and tried to look nonchalant; here I was with another angry woman on my hands. I was doing something very wrong lately.

"Sorry, Valentina. You looked so peaceful, I didn't want to disturb you."

"Then things have changed since last night," she said, eyebrow raised.

It was uncomfortable to be playing this out in front of her daughter, who just stood there mutely between us. Suddenly, the front door swung open.

A muscle-bound guy with a bristly crew cut and a tanned, weathered face came in, key in hand. He looked up at the three of us, then zeroed in on me.

"Who the hell is this?" he demanded as he swung a glance at Breelyn.

"What business is it of yours?" Valentina asked as she brushed her hand lightly through her hair and, turning toward him, smiled coyly. In that single gesture her whole demeanor changed. She'd been almost shaking with anger a second ago; now she was radiating sex all over again.

"I get to know who my daughter is with at six o'clock in the morning, Val."

Ah, the first husband, Gregg Doyle. Chronically out of work photographer, according to his ex-wife. He came toward me with a mean look in his eye. At the same time, he pushed his shirt aside so that I could see the pistol hooked into his belt. It was such a cheesy macho-dude move that I almost laughed out loud.

Valentina swiftly moved in front of me. "He happens to be *my* guest, Gregg. Which makes him very much none of your business. Even if it is your visitation day."

Doyle frowned and glanced from his barely dressed wife to me to Breelyn.

"Nice example you're setting, Val."

"I try." She giggled as she reached over and ran her fingers through my hair. Then she pulled my head toward her and locked her lips on mine for a brief but intense kiss. I was beyond startled – until I saw her next move.

Without letting go of me, she gazed up at her ex-husband with a taunting smile and, reaching out, ran her fingers along the gun on his hip.

"Now, put that away," she murmured. "Before someone gets hurt . . ."

Doyle stared at her intensely, his face beet red with either anger or excitement or some trippy combination. These two clearly had an unusual dynamic. She seemed to enjoy pushing his buttons – and he seemed to love hating it. I wondered just how far she could go with him.

Valentina pushed off his chest, blew me a mock-kiss good-bye, and sauntered out of the room. Breelyn had already vanished.

Doyle turned to me. "You had your fun," he said in a perfectly calm voice. "But I see you with my ex-wife or daughter again, I'll kill you. Got that, bud?"

CHAPTER 18

Kayla Ross

"YOU KNOW I DON'T trust you, right?"

"Wise move. Never trust anyone in PR," Logan said. "Or agents. Or producers. Always assume that people in the entertainment industry want something from you; that way you'll always be a step ahead."

We were having dinner at yet another incredibly swanky, exclusive restaurant. The menu didn't even list the prices.

"Okay, so what is it you want from me?" I asked, trying to be playful but actually *really* wanting to know.

"Your trust, of course." He made a silly evil face; he was maddening.

But then he reached across the table and, taking my hand, slowly brought it to his lips and kissed it. I couldn't help it – I swooned. I'd never had a guy look at me with so much romance in his eyes.

"You weasely little shit."

Startled, we both looked up. Standing next to our table was a very glammed-out Valentina Doyle in a sparkly dress and with her hair pulled up.

"You must be Eric's 'little sister,'" she said to me in a fake cheery tone. "And you're in town on an unexpected business trip for just this *one* night. The very same night I had plans with Eric."

I shot a look at Logan. His face had gone pale, but he was trying like hell to collect himself.

"Hey, Val! Um – I think there's been a misunderstanding," he said with a nervous glance at me.

"I really don't see much of a family resemblance," she said. "In fact, your sister looks a lot like a sleazy reporter who once tried to interview my daughter."

I wished I could have said something witty back at her, but I was at a total loss as to what was happening. Logan and Valentina were *dating?* I felt like such a gullible idiot.

I stood up, almost knocking over the wine bottle on the table. I was near tears, but I wasn't going to give anyone the satisfaction of seeing them.

"Kayla, wait," Logan got up and reached out for my arm.

"Kayla *Ross*," Valentina said. "So she *isn't* your sister after all. I'm relieved, Logan. I'd hate to think that this was you with a blood relation."

She thrust her phone out at us. On her screen was a gossip website featuring a blown-up photograph of Logan kissing me, from a few nights ago in the parking garage.

And I was looking right at the camera.

Logan stared at it in astonishment, then looked at me with suspicion.

"You *knew* about this?" he said accusingly.

I looked from pissed-off Logan to smirking Valentina,

my mind whirling. Not knowing what else to do, I walked quickly to the back of the restaurant. My eyes flooded with tears, I barely found my way to the women's bathroom, where I locked myself in a stall.

I don't know how long I sat there crying. But after a while I got angry. This confirmed all my fears about opening up to a guy, a PR guy especially. And I hadn't moved halfway across the country to get involved in a lot of over-the-top Hollywood drama. I came to become a legitimate news reporter.

I was *done* with Eric Logan.

When I finally came out of the bathroom, he was waiting for me.

"You should have told me about that photographer," he said, but with no malice.

"Sorry. Stupid of me not to realize it might jeopardize your affair with Valentina Doyle!"

"Kayla, I am *not* having an affair with her," he said, trying to keep his voice low. "We talked about this. I went out with her to see what I could find out."

"She seems to have other ideas. Anyway, I really don't care, Eric," I said as he followed me to the front door. "And I figured the photographer was some kind of mistake. Why would anyone take our picture?"

He got in front of me and, taking me gently by the shoulders, looked deep into my eyes – but not romantically. This time more like a big brother.

"Kayla, please listen to me for just a minute. You're in the media now. Not only are you on television, but when you found Tennet's body *you* became part of that story," he said. "Like it or not, you're a celebrity yourself now. Privacy is a thing of the past."

"And I get no say in that?"

"No," he said. "It's part of the game, the price you pay. Look, I was going to tell you all about Valentina. I found out *plenty* – mostly that she's just as manipulative and loco as Tennet always said. But I wanted to have a nice evening with you before getting into all that. That's why I canceled on her."

I didn't know what to do or say. Why did I always end up feeling like a little girl around Logan? Everywhere else in my adult life I was doing fine, more than fine. But with him I seemed to regress ten years.

"Since Breelyn Doyle is the key to this whole situation," Logan said, "it makes sense that the only way to get to her is through Valentina. So our goal should be for you to interview one or, better yet, *both* of them."

"Are you crazy?" I cried. "Why would she *ever* agree to that? She's probably out there revving her car up to run me down again!"

"Leave it to me."

I gave him a long, lingering look. It was *not* a romantic one. "I've never met anyone so sure of themselves. You always get exactly what you want, don't you?" I said, shaking my head. "Well, here's the deal: I'll help you with this story, Logan. Because it could help me, too. But you won't get my trust. Not ever. That's the price *you* pay."

CHAPTER 19

Eric Logan

VALENTINA HAD A WICKED glint in her eye. It looked like she was trying to figure out a way to "accidentally" slip and knock the woman next to her off her StairMaster – right into the rack of weights behind them. If the fall didn't break her neck, the massive dumbbells might easily open her skull.

She and the woman – Ashton Reilly – were both breathing heavily through their workouts, but Ashton was grinning while Valentina was scowling. That's because Ashton was looking up at the cardio room's TV monitor. There she was, happily chatting away on a midday talk show. She had the female lead – supportive wife of one of the older action heroes – in a new blockbuster that had just opened. The two women were almost exactly the same age, but the difference in the state of their careers must have been brutal for Valentina.

I watched them from the back of the room until Valentina got off the machine and gave Ashton a phony kiss-and-wave good-bye. I stepped right in front her as she was wiping the sweat off her face.

"That should be you up there," I said with a nod toward the screen.

"Thanks. Your career advice means a lot," she sneered. "Considering how well you handled my husband's affairs. Not to mention your own."

She tried to brush by me but I grabbed her.

"Don't be such a drama queen," I said with an equal sneer. Something told me groveling was not the way to get to her. "Yes, I've been out a few times with Kayla Ross. But I took her to dinner last night specifically to convince her to do an interview with you."

"I find that *very* hard to believe."

"That's because you're used to idiots advising you," I said.

She was open-mouthed in shock. She wasn't accustomed to being talked to bluntly.

"Your agent is a lightweight and your publicist must be in a coma," I went on. "Your visibility should be through the roof right now, what with all that's gone on. But here you are, working out six times a week because you don't have anything else to do. When's the last time you had an audition or even took a meeting?"

It stung. I didn't know if she was going to lash out or burst into tears. I didn't give her time to decide.

"Kayla Ross is just about the hottest news anchor right now," I said, forcefully taking her over to an empty lounge area. "And she found Tennet's body! If she interviewed you as the grieving but still angry and confused widow, it would be ratings gold. You'd have offers coming in before the first commercial break."

She narrowed her eyes and looked intently at me. "And what would be in it for you?"

"I don't plan to work for Paige & Schuster forever. I want my own firm. But I need a star client."

She didn't agree then and there, but I could tell I had her. I walked her to the women's locker room and promised to rebook the dinner date I had canceled.

While I was getting dressed in the men's locker room, I saw a buffed-out, familiar-looking guy saunter in: Gregg Doyle. I was surprised, to say the least. I wondered how he could afford to go to Equinox – the most exclusive gym in town – when according to his ex-wife he hadn't had a photography gig in over a year. Apparently, he'd barely been getting by with the occasional construction job.

I turned away so he wouldn't see me. I dawdled dressing to watch him. Something shady was going on with this guy – and I had a gut feeling it involved Tennet.

As Doyle started getting undressed, he began loudly yammering with one of those retired guys who seem to spend all their time hanging around the gym just talking, never working out. Then I heard Doyle say he had to take a piss. His pal walked with him as far as the bathroom, then headed out. I glanced over at Doyle's locker. The door was open and his bag was sitting on the bench in front of it.

I didn't hesitate to move. There were only two other guys nearby and neither were facing Doyle's locker. I picked up the bag and hurriedly shifted it around to see what was in it. Dirty tennis shoes and a bag of chalk powder for his power lifts.

And, of course, his gun.

I was just putting it back down when something else slid to the side: a cell phone. Jackpot. I grabbed it and turned to race back to my locker – and almost ran right into Doyle.

Luckily, the doofus was messing around with his laces and looking down. I put his cell to my ear like I was listening to voice mail and turned my face away. He passed me without looking up.

I dressed slowly to make it look like I had all the time in the world, but I knew I needed to get out ASAP. Doyle probably wouldn't miss his phone till after his workout, so I had an hour, maybe two before he reported it. There's no better window into someone's life than a cell phone. And I had just the connection to open this sucker up.

CHAPTER 20

Eric Logan

LOOKING UP FROM HER computer, Romy raised her triple-pierced eyebrow almost to the edge of her sky-blue dyed hair. She'd definitely gone through some changes since our brief but intense college fling.

"You get that this is a criminal offense, right?" she warned. "We could both do time."

I chewed a thumbnail for a beat. I'd already committed theft; how much worse was it to read a few e-mails?

"Got it. But I think this guy might have had something to do with the death of someone I knew."

"That's what the police are for, bro."

I gave her my own raised eyebrow. Romy hadn't gone from smiley Delta Gamma sorority girl to punked-out underground computer hacker without racking up a few black marks along the way. I'd helped her out of a jam or two – and not always by strictly legal means.

"All right, all right," she sighed. "I just want to be clear about what we're doing. And by the way, this wipes out all my debts, Eric."

"Check. But I'm always here for ya, babe. For *anything*," I said with a meaningful wink. Romy had been known to give me a booty call every once in a while after a night of partying, though she always seemed to hate both herself and me the next morning.

With a roll of her eyes, she turned and went to work. She plugged Doyle's phone into her computer and started doing the magic. She leapt right over the password barrier; it wasn't even a challenge. Meanwhile, I texted Valentina a time and place for our dinner that night. And I left Kayla a message telling her that I was close to sealing the deal on the interview.

"Damn, that's weird."

I looked over at Romy, who was frowning. "What's up?"

"His e-mail is scrubbed clean. Just a few random ones about construction gigs. And all his texts beyond the last few weeks have been deleted. Every single one."

"Why would he do that?" I asked.

"Covering his tracks. Looks like he's got something to hide," she said with a shrug.

"Shit, I can't believe that Neanderthal had brains enough to do that!" I said bitterly, though if nothing else, this did confirm my suspicions that Doyle was shady. "Well, thanks anyway for trying, Ro."

She gave me a thoughtful look, then threw up her hands. "I know I should just walk away from this but . . . I might be able to recover them."

"How, if they've been deleted?"

She gave a wry shake of her head.

"Yeah, everyone thinks they 'destroy the evidence' just by deleting. But it doesn't always work that way. Especially when people use work-related computers and phones – those things are all hooked up to a main server. They're almost always traceable. Personal phones are a little trickier . . . unless, of course, you're lucky enough to have someone who knows what they're doing."

I gave the top of her head a big loud smacking kiss. She pushed me away and started in again on Doyle's phone. It took a while, but she eventually uncovered a few heavily coded text chains. Looking over her shoulder I almost leapt at her screen when I saw a conversation between Doyle and Valentina.

"Those! Open 'em up!" I shouted.

"Dude, chill out." She elbowed me out of her way.

Doyle's messages were usually limited to just a few predictably misspelled words. Valentina's were longer and alternated between suggestive teases and bullying commands. A few of hers stood out as though they were in a blood-red bolded font.

> "U say u still love me. Prove it."
>
> "He molested our daughter. Don't u care?!!"
>
> "guess I'm lucky hes at least a better lover"
>
> "Man up. Is that gun just a prop???"
>
> "Do it. Tonight. Or we're done"
>
> Romy looked up at me. "Holy shit . . ."

Yeah. I didn't know exactly what I had been hoping

to find, but this was beyond anything I could have dreamt up.

Because, as if Valentina's sentences themselves weren't incriminating enough, every single one ended with the same order, over and over:

Delete this!

CHAPTER 21

Kayla Ross

RAISING HER JAW to imply steely determination, Valentina turned directly toward the camera. "I wanted to kill him with my bare hands. Strangle him. Tear him apart. Only one thing stopped me."

I let the moment sink in. She hadn't needed much prompting so far, so I let her take her time.

"He was halfway around the world. Otherwise, I'd probably be in jail for manslaughter right now," she said proudly. "And I wouldn't have regretted it for a moment."

I caught sight of Eddie. He gave me two enthusiastic thumbs-up, then a "cut to commercial" signal. I turned to the camera and asked viewers to stay tuned for more of our exclusive interview with Valentina Doyle.

Eddie rushed over. "We're smokin', ladies. Kayla, you're doin' great, maybe just lean in a little more. And maybe take her hand at some point during the next segment, huh? You doin' okay there, Miss Doyle?"

Valentina was getting her makeup refreshed but gave Eddie a cool nod. I took a huge gulp of water from the bottle hidden behind my chair. My heart hadn't stopped fluttering since we'd gone on-air. Eddie and the network brass had decided a live interview would guarantee an explosion of tweets during the broadcast – which meant big ratings when they aired it again and again throughout the week. Considering how much pressure live interviews involved, I'd been surprised Valentina had agreed. But Logan had sold her on it, somehow. No surprise there.

Back on the air, I took a deep breath . . . and took charge.

"Now, Valentina," I said, furrowing my brow just a little, "before his death, your husband stated in a number of interviews that you often exhibit erratic behavior. Mood swings, screaming, making scenes. At home and at times in public, such as . . . in *restaurants*."

I had to do it. I had to let her know that she wasn't running this show. Her eyes widened at me ever so slightly – she was on her guard now.

"Every marriage has times of strain," she said carefully. "Especially when the marriage involves creative people. But Wayne was the one with the temper issues – as *you* and everyone else are well aware."

"Yes, but the allegations against your husband basically came down to 'he said, she said' charges and –"

"Are you questioning my daughter's integrity?" she demanded, back up.

"No, but you –"

"So you're questioning *my* integrity?"

She was angry now and had that same going-in-for-the-kill look that I'd seen outside of Breelyn's school and at the restaurant. I knew this was my moment.

"My job is to ask difficult questions, Miss Doyle," I said, amazed at how calmly I could confront her. "Mr. Tennet can no longer defend himself. And in light of his death, some of your actions are troubling."

"Such as?" she seethed.

"Your ongoing relationship with your ex-husband, Gregg Doyle, for one."

She seemed completely taken aback.

"I cannot imagine what you are talking about," she said in an icy voice. "The few times I see Gregg are when he picks up Breelyn for –"

"So, you don't converse with him regularly, almost daily, through e-mails and texts?"

She looked around the studio, then over at Eddie. "What *is* this? Am I being interviewed or prosecuted?"

I gave Eddie a nod. He in turn gave the signal to the broadcast crew to post images on the giant screen behind where Valentina and I were seated.

"Do you recognize these as texts you sent to Gregg Doyle?"

She whipped around to look at the screen behind us. The text messages scrolled up like the credits after a film:

> U say u still love me. Prove it.
>
> He molested our daughter. Don't u care?!!
>
> Do it. Tonight. Or we're done.

A range of emotions flew across her face – shock, outrage, fury. She then turned back around to face me. I've never seen such an intense look of hatred. She silently stared at me for so long I was about to cut to commercial, when she squared her shoulders and spoke.

"This is libel, invasion of privacy, and, apparently, *theft*," she said, using every ounce of self-control she had. "Since you and this station are so intent upon scoring big ratings, maybe you can televise the trial that will result from the lawsuit I will be filing."

With great poise, she unhooked her microphone and dropped it as if it were a dead bug. She then stood up and strode across the studio. All heads turned to follow her. She definitely knew how to make an exit. I gave a kind of desperate "We'll be right back!" as Eddie cut to commercial.

He ran over and gave me a spontaneous hug. "*HOLLA!* That was fantastic, *Kay-Kay!*"

"Enough with the 'Kay-Kay!'" I said, happy if a little shaken. "How serious do you think that threat was?"

"Oh, man, we can only hope she follows through." He made a silent prayer. "That'd keep this story alive all through next sweeps. Don't worry – the lawyers okayed showing the texts. It's legal, mostly. The e-mail came in through our general info tip line, so as long as we can honestly say we don't know how the texts were captured . . ."

That did *not* make me feel better about using the texts. It seemed so wrong to reveal someone's personal messaging, even if they did suggest a possible crime.

"The messages don't really prove anything, though," I

said. "Just that Valentina hated her current husband and liked provoking her ex. If I could only get an interview with Breelyn, I'd feel like I had a handle on this whole thing. But that's *never* going to happen now – her mother won't let me get within a mile of her."

Eddie stroked his massive goatee and gave me a devilish grin.

"Never say never, darlin'," he said. "Guess who's waitin' in your office."

CHAPTER 22

Eric Logan

ROMY SMACKED ME across the face, hard.

"You didn't tell me you were going to *literally* broadcast my phone hack!" she said with another half-playful whack across the face.

I frowned up at her. After the bout we'd just had, I was surprised she still had so much energy in her – or that she'd waited so long to bring up the texts appearing on television.

"You didn't ask," I said as I rolled out from under her. I was annoyed. Not with her exactly, but something about this hookup wasn't really working for me. I kept finding myself thinking about Kayla – and what she'd said.

"Dude, you are the least trustworthy person I've ever met," Romy said, as if reading my mind. "Why any woman would get involved with you is –"

"Oh, shit!" I cried out. "What time is it?"

I reached across the bed for my remote and fumbled with it until I hit the right channel. Kayla's highly promoted "explosive" interview with Breelyn had already begun.

"– but my mother didn't know anything about it," Breelyn was saying haltingly onscreen. "It's not her fault . . . I was just so afraid to say anything."

"Who's that?" Romy asked.

"*Quiet!*" I barked. "This is important."

The camera cut to Kayla's concerned face. I immediately realized that in her short time working on-air she had already taken on a more mature, thoughtful manner. She looked like a true professional. The camera cut back to an extreme close-up of Breelyn.

"And then . . . after what happened . . . after my stepfather . . . died," Breelyn continued. "That they say he killed himself because . . . because of this. I can't believe it . . . I wish I hadn't said anything. *Ever.* I feel like it's my fault, my fault that he's dead."

Breelyn was obviously having a difficult time keeping composed. Her hair was pulled back and she was dressed in a simple white sweater. She couldn't have looked more beautiful – the camera loved her.

"Pretty girl," Romy said. "So, do those texts have anything to do –"

I shot her a "*Can it!*" glare.

On the screen, Kayla reached forward and gently took Breelyn's hand. The director cut to a close-up of Kayla, and there was real emotion on her face – not the faked concern audiences were used to seeing from talk-show hosts.

I saw that Romy was staring at me staring at Kayla.

"Hmm . . . guessing this might be a *special* friend?" she

noted, dripping sarcasm. I threw a pillow at her and turned back to the TV.

"It's *not* your fault," Kayla was saying to Breelyn with feeling. "You were taken advantage of by an adult. One who was supposed to be looking out for you, not hurting you!"

"You don't understand," Breelyn wept. "He – he was good to me, too."

Kayla looked down and seemed overcome for a moment. Then she leaned in closer to Breelyn.

"I do understand, Breelyn," she said with a tremble in her voice. "Because . . . when I was a young girl . . . I was abused, too."

"*Whoa!*" Romy gasped, then covered her mouth with a "Sorry!" shrug.

The camera stayed on Breelyn, whose eyes went slightly wide with surprise. She then closed them, and her body shook with her sobs. Kayla went on.

"It was by someone who I *thought* was good to me," Kayla said, her voice trembling. "It took me a long time to realize that he wasn't, that he was harming me. And it took me even longer to realize that I had nothing to blame myself for."

Breelyn slowly reached out with her free hand and took Kayla's so that they were joined in an intimate circle. The camera held it for a moment, then quietly faded out to a commercial.

Neither Romy nor I said anything for a moment. Then

she turned to me with a sincere look, one with none of the sass that she usually gave out. "That was major. Admitting something like that on television. Do you have *any* idea how hard that must have been for her? Did you know about it?"

"No idea," I said, truthfully. I hadn't seen this coming, and felt stunned.

Romy gaped at me. "Holy shit . . . you actually care about this one."

Before I could answer, there was a jarring knock on my door. I was startled because I lived in a loft space downtown, an exclusive upscale building. Security was airtight – you'd really have to jump through some hoops to get to my door unannounced.

Romy narrowed her eyes. "If that's the feds here to bust me on a hacking charge, you are *so* going down with me."

I slowly got off the bed and pulled on my jeans. The sun was just going down, so despite the soaring two-story, floor-to-ceiling windows, the light inside the loft had gone dim. I went over to the door and hesitated. No one ever came to my door – I didn't even have a peephole. Still, although I had a bad feeling about this, my curiosity outweighed my caution.

I slowly unlocked the door and swung it open. Someone was standing a few steps back on the landing that ran along the side of the building. The sun was setting between the palm trees across the street, creating a backlight around the silhouette of a woman. She was standing very still and seemed to be staring at me.

Then, raising her arm, she shifted her position just enough to cause a break in the light that exposed her as Valentina Doyle.

She was pointing a gun at me.

And she fired.

CHAPTER 23

Eric Logan

THE DEAFENING BLAST AND the terrified scream behind me seemed to happen simultaneously.

I whipped around to see Romy falling backward onto the floor. I involuntarily started to lunge toward her but then quickly threw my weight against the door to keep Valentina out.

But she must have been charging forward as she fired, because she was past the door in a flash. Her eyes were wild and the hand holding the gun was shaking as she kept it pointed at me. She stared down at Romy curiously, as if she were an expensive rug that she wasn't quite sure she liked.

"*Val!*" I shouted, then quickly tried to calm my voice. "Put the gun down. Do *not* do this."

She just kept staring at Romy, who was lying on her side in a small pool of blood forming under her. I knelt and gently turned her over – the wound was on her left hip, just above her panties. She moaned and then suddenly gasped as she seemed to come out of a light shock. Her hand flew to the wound and she looked up at me in panic. Without any medical knowledge, I could see that the bullet had gone through only tissue and muscle, nowhere near any organs.

"You're okay, you're okay," I assured her, though my voice shook a little. "Just take a deep breath."

Bewildered and stunned, Romy stared up at Valentina.

"You always manage to dodge the consequences of your actions, don't you?" Valentina said to me in a trembling voice. "You never pay, you bastard. Everyone else does – even her, whoever she is – but not you."

"Val, I know you're upset, but I have to get her help. Put the gun –"

"*Don't tell me what to do,*" she screamed, tears overtaking her. "I listened to you and what did I get? Public humiliation. A police *investigation!* And all for the sake of your girlfriend, right? But the ratings weren't big enough, were they? Seeing me made a fool of wasn't enough. You had to go after my daughter, too."

My mind was racing. How I was going to calm her down, not get shot, and get aid for Romy was beyond me.

"Val, she's been injured. I need to call an ambu—"

"I'm all right," Romy said hoarsely. Though she was deathly white, she still tried to pull herself up. I forced her to lie back down, then reached up for a coat that was hanging on the rack near the door and put it over her.

"No ambulance. No doctors. No *police,*" she said tersely under her breath with a warning look in her eye. "Just get me to the bathroom. I can clean it."

I knew Romy's profession required her to live "off the grid" – but I hadn't realized how low a profile she actually needed to keep.

We both glanced up at Valentina, who now looked spent – and very sad.

"They've taken Breelyn from me," she said in a dead tone. "Wayne's sister filed for temporary guardianship. Because of those texts. Because of that interview. Because of *you*."

Though I was terrified of what this madwoman would do next, there was something pitiful about her now. All her glamour was gone; she just looked beaten and played out.

"They've even taken Gregg from me," she said with a bitter laugh. "Gregg's guns – his precious, precious guns – turns out they're all stolen. Yeah, I guess even this one is hot. Gregg had a prior conviction I never knew about. He can't legally *own* guns! Isn't that *hilarious?* Everybody has their little secrets."

I couldn't let Romy just sit there and bleed to death while Valentina did her monologue. I deliberately turned away from her and slowly lifted Romy up. Without looking back at Valentina, I started walking Romy toward the bathroom.

At the *click* we both froze.

I turned around to see that Valentina had the gun pressed up against her forehead.

"Maybe Wayne had the right idea," she sobbed. "Only I'll do him one better. I'll have witnesses. So there won't be any mysteries. Nothing that your Kayla can use to score big ratings."

"*Oh, my God,*" Romy gasped as she clutched me.

Still holding the gun, Valentina stared at me with intense hatred.

An eternity seemed to pass.

Then the look on her face suddenly began to change. Her sagging mouth began to lift at the corners – slowly forming a very distinct, very cruel *grin*.

She then threw her head back and let out an exaggerated cackle.

"You think you're such a player," she sneered. "How's it feel to be played for once?"

She laughed again, then shoved the gun into her coat pocket.

"You gotta admit that was good. I wish I could have had it filmed. What a great audition reel for a reality series! That's probably the first thing you thought of, huh, Logan? Capitalize on any life experience – the more tragic, the better. Too bad I couldn't give you a heads up. I wanted to surprise you with a special performance."

She gave Romy an apologetic shrug. "It was supposed to be a private show, honey. Sorry you were collateral damage."

Valentina did her signature brush-back of her hair and walked over to the door. She gave me a withering parting look.

"In a lot of ways you're a sharp guy, Logan. But I've been in this business a long time and I know a beginner from a pro," she said.

She slammed the door shut.

CHAPTER 24

Eric Logan

SUCCESS STORIES DON'T COME *much sweeter than this,* I thought as I rode the elevator up to the top floor of the gleaming new ten-story apartment building in the middle of Hollywood. This is what everybody comes here for but so few ever actually achieve.

I knocked on the door, and as soon as it opened I thrust the flowers forward – unfortunately directly into Zoe's face.

"Whoops!" she cried. "I should have let Kayla open the door. Take two!"

She slammed the door shut, so I dutifully knocked again, and after a beat Kayla opened it. I bowed and put the flowers into her arms. She gave me a wary smile, so I took a risk and leaned in and gave her a soft kiss. She tensed up as usual, so I backed off and looked around. Polished cement floors, recessed lighting, gigantic TV screen built into the wall, spectacular hillside views – the works.

"Damn!" I whistled. "If the folks in Omaha could see you now . . ."

"*Right?*" Zoe all but screamed. "And Jared Leto supposedly has the penthouse suite!"

I gave Kayla a thumbs-up. She just shrugged.

"I don't know . . ." she said. "It's just so *not* me."

"Well, *I'll* take it!" Zoe smirked as she dashed toward the door with a bouncy wave good-bye. "But for now, I will leave you guys to it."

I went over to Kayla. She looked tired; she'd had an insane week. Still, I couldn't help but think that her work pressures had *nothing* on my last encounter with Valentina.

"Of course this is you," I assured her. "Reporters who score their very own news shows are expected to live a certain lifestyle."

"I still can't believe it," she sighed. "And . . . I just don't feel like I really deserve it. Not yet, anyway. It's all happened so quickly. *Too* quickly."

I looked over at the television and saw that her interview with Breelyn Doyle was being broadcast yet again – at least the fifth time that week. Airing just three days after Valentina had stormed off the set, Kayla's talk with Breelyn became the network's highest-rated nonpolitical interview – and landed her an offer of a show of her own. I walked over to the television and turned up the sound.

"*It was by someone who I* thought *was good to me,*" Kayla was saying. "*It took me a long time to realize that he wasn't, that he was harming me. And it took me even longer to realize that I had nothing to blame myself for.*"

Kayla quickly reached over and turned the TV off. She then walked over to her enormous living room window.

"Sorry, it's . . . hard for me to watch that."

I came up behind and slowly put my arms around her. She tightened up again, but I stayed put.

"I get it. But that was a brave thing you did," I said. "It helped Breelyn a lot."

Kayla turned around. "You've spoken with her?"

"Yesterday. I had a meeting with her and her new legal guardian, her aunt Cynthia," I said. "She filed a motion after the police launched their investigation into Valentina and Doyle."

Kayla looked perplexed. "But why did you meet with her?"

"Because," I said, trying to tamp down my excitement, "you are looking at the President/CEO of Logan & Associates public relations firm. There are no associates just yet, but I do have a client: Breelyn Doyle."

"Wait – *what?*"

"Because of your interview, she's the hottest teen trending on social media. Everyone wants to sign her!" I said, beyond stoked. "And I got her a meeting with CAA this morning. She's got the potential to be a big – no, *huge* – star."

Kayla pushed me away, confused and, I thought, almost repelled.

"You don't seem very happy for me," I said.

"No, I – I just . . ." she stammered, "it just seems . . . like you're taking advantage of her awful experience. She's famous because she was abused!"

"Breelyn wants this, Kayla," I said. "I know it sounds a

little crass, but in this business you don't get too many chances to make your move. You've been lucky, it's been easy for you."

She narrowed her eyes with true anger.

"That interview *wasn't* easy for me," she said through gritted teeth. "Talking about my private pain wasn't worth having five thousand more Twitter followers."

I took hold of her again. She pushed away but then broke down and started crying.

"Will you do something for me?" I asked softly. "Will you let me take you away this weekend? Just the two of us, up the coast? Maybe Santa Barbara? No television, no deals, no pressures. Just us . . ."

She gave me a long look.

"You may as well say yes," I said. "Remember, I always get my way."

CHAPTER 25

Kayla Ross

I STARED AT THE ceiling most of the early morning. It had started raining lightly sometime during the night, and it was a comforting sound. So much had happened to me in the last few months I just couldn't take it all in. I'd landed my dream job, become sort of famous, moved into a totally chic apartment, and now . . . a *boyfriend?*

Somehow the last was the hardest to believe.

Logan stirred next to me and slowly opened his eyes. He rolled over to look at me.

"Something tells me you've been awake for a while. Wanna talk?"

I did and I didn't. I wanted to stay in that hotel bed, and I wanted to get the hell out of there. I wanted him to hold me, and I wanted him to leave me alone.

He must have sensed how confused I was because he just ran his hand lightly, back and forth, over my arm.

"You know how you once told me you were a jerk and that I should tell you to get lost?" I asked him. "Well, I'm kind of . . . messed up. You might want to tell *me* to get lost."

"Now she tells me," he sighed mockingly, then pulled me into an embrace. "You aren't any more messed up than anyone else, Kayla. We've all got issues."

"But . . . you probably already guessed this . . . I haven't been with anyone this way. *Romantically*, I mean," I said. "I've avoided it. I put all my focus into becoming successful."

Logan nodded. "It worked."

"Yeah, I guess it did."

"I've made some sacrifices to get where I am, too," he said, kind of reluctantly. "I'm still finding out if they were worth it. Were yours?"

I didn't know how to answer, so I just kissed him. I was thinking that, as terrifying as it was, to fully live I would have to start trusting people again sooner or later.

As Logan took a shower in the suite's ridiculously ornate bathroom, I started thinking about the week ahead. I hadn't even signed my new contract yet and I was already facing endless meetings about my show – the name, how it was going to be structured, time slot, on and on. I'd promised myself not to check my messages until we headed back that afternoon, but I couldn't help it. I picked up my phone and found that it was dead. I'd been so nervous and uptight the night before, I'd forgotten to charge it.

I plugged it into a bedside charger and saw that Logan's laptop was open, so I went over and logged in to my Gmail account. There were at least thirty messages, a daunting number to go through now. With the rain, our drive back to LA was going to take forever; I'd have plenty of time to go through them.

As I closed the browser window, I noticed how neatly Logan's desktop icons were arranged. There were a zillion folders and they were stacked in perfect rows and all clearly labeled. It made me smile. It was so *him* to have to have everything in place and under control. As I glanced away, one folder name jumped out at me: "bdoyle_pool."

I'm not a snoop. I like to think I have strong values, and that I respect others' privacy. But some impulse practically forced me to move the cursor over the folder.

I clicked before I could stop myself. The folder contained a long row of jpeg images. I didn't know why, but my heart was beating madly.

I was suddenly terrified of what I was about to see.

CHAPTER 26

Eric Logan

"KAYLA! YOU'RE NOT GOING to believe this!" I yelled from the bathroom.

I'd gotten the text I was banking on. I was so excited I ran out of the bathroom still wet, with just a towel around my waist.

Kayla was furiously packing her clothes.

"What's going on?" I asked.

She turned around. Her face was drained of blood and she was trembling. I tried to approach her, but she backed away.

"*Don't touch me!*" she screamed.

"What's the matter? What happened?"

She pointed at my laptop. One of Breelyn's nude photos was displayed. It wasn't one I'd have shown Kayla if given the choice.

"Oh, shit." What else could I say?

"You – you *took* those?" Kayla gasped.

"No," I said. "I did not. I took them off Tennet's computer."

Kayla's eyes grew even bigger. "You hid evidence to help your client? And why didn't you just delete it? Why'd you put it on your own computer?"

I sighed and sat on the edge of the bed. Kayla moved over to the door and stood there rigidly with her hand on the knob.

"Just calm down and listen to me," I said. "Tennet didn't take those photos. He never even knew they existed, let alone that they were on his computer."

She stared at me in total confusion.

"Then who put them there?" she demanded.

I hesitated for a moment. The rain outside picked up and started whipping against the windows.

"Breelyn, of course."

Neither of us said anything for a while. We just stared at each other as the rain came down in a steady beat. I'm sure she was running back through the events of the past few months. She had a lot to go over.

"It was a good thing I found them before Tennet or anyone else noticed them," I said. "Breelyn almost ruined everything by planting them. She had that dumbass Omar take the photos. After all the precise plans I'd made, she could have blown it all apart."

Kayla was dumbstruck. "I don't understand."

"You were never meant to," I said. "I just needed you to help keep the story alive in the press. From the moment I first met Breelyn, I saw what that idiot stepfather of hers couldn't see: that she had *major* star potential. He wouldn't cast her in his films, though – he was worried that she was too young and that acting would make her go Hollywood. So I had to find a way to get her into the media spotlight."

Kayla slumped against the door and slowly slid to the floor.

"Sorry you had to find out this way," I said. "I'd rather not have told you, but, well, you did snoop. If you're going to do that, you have to be prepared to find something you might not like. Or might not want to know. Let's call that Journalism 103."

She stared bullets at me. "You killed Tennet."

"Mmm, I may have nudged him in one of the directions his depression was leading him. But mostly I just staged the scene. Can't believe I forgot to put his drink next to his body."

Kayla put her hands up over her ears. I wanted to go to her, but it seemed best to let her digest for a while.

"*Why?*"

"The story was starting to die." I shrugged. "Tennet hadn't been prosecuted, which wasn't surprising, since he'd never laid a hand on Breelyn. But he'd become too much of the story – I needed the focus back on Breelyn, my future client."

I held up my phone. "And it all paid off this morning. Breelyn has just signed for the lead in a huge new sci-fi franchise at Warner Brothers. She's going to be every bit as big as I told her she'd be! And my new firm is going to be the go-to PR destination for every rising young star."

Kayla was just staring at the floor. I knew it was a lot for her to take in, but at some point she'd begin to see the big picture – how my success was great for her, too.

She finally looked up at me. "Why are you telling me all of this? I'm going straight to the police."

"With what?" I asked. "You have no proof that I had anything to do with Tennet's death – officially a suicide. No thanks to Breelyn. Even though we'd agreed to have no contact with each other, she kept trying to find ways to tell me to suggest a murder angle in the media. But for obvious reasons I didn't really want the police on that track – until I found Valentina and Doyle's texts! That was a gift from above."

She slowly got up.

"I doubt they were serious about killing Tennet," I said. "From what I know of them, it was some kind of kinky game. They'll probably be cleared. By then the DA won't want to go publicly chasing her tail on another potential dead end. Think about this, Kayla," I said. "You don't want your own involvement made public. You were smart to track down Omar Sabat. That interview started everything for you. But guess who fed him his lines?"

If possible, she grew even paler.

"Omar said what I told him to tell the press – and he'll keep doing that. He gets that taking photos of an underage girl – even if she's his girlfriend, even if she's eighteen now – could land him some serious jail time. That's why I keep those photos. They also keep Breelyn in line. She knows that if these ever went public it could make her look a bit too complicit in her stepfather's deeds. So she'll deny their existence forever."

Her whole body jolted as though she were hit with an invisible blow.

"Look, I know I owe you some apologies, Kayla. The Jag was supposed to just scare you, not actually hit you. I'm sorry, but I wanted you to have some suspicions about Valentina. You'll come to see that it was all worth it."

Kayla shook her head and opened the door.

"Oh, and the illegally obtained texts," I said casually, turning over my final card. "You didn't ask how I got them – you didn't seem to want to know. You just saw a great 'get,' didn't you? And, maybe, a chance to get back at Valentina while you were at it?"

As she walked into the hallway, I took her arm.

"Your whole success rides on this story, Kayla. Dreams – they're my ace in the hole."

CHAPTER 27

Kayla Ross

"THE WHOLE STORY was a lie. Not a word of it was true."

Seated across from me, Breelyn somehow looked younger and more vulnerable than ever. I couldn't tell if it was due to her minimal makeup or the cute juniors-department jacket she was wearing.

I glanced off-camera at Eddie, who looked very worried. I'd thrown this at him late in the afternoon – only an hour before my regular segment was to run. I felt guilty that I had counted on his trust in me to go on-air live without a game plan.

"My stepfather, Wayne Tennet, never, *ever* touched me in any inappropriate way," Breelyn said softly to me, then turned directly to the camera. "He was always wonderful to me, and I'll never forgive myself for saying what I did about him."

"Then why did you?" I asked a little tersely, considering I still didn't know if I wanted to hug her or slap her.

"My boyfriend – or the guy I *thought* was my boyfriend – made me," she said softly. "He threatened me – all the time. He – he sort of brainwashed me into doing anything he said. I was so afraid of him. But I didn't know who I could tell about it. My stepfather was so far away in Australia and my mother . . . well . . ."

"But why make such a horrible charge if it wasn't true?" I pressed.

"It was part of his plan to get me away from my parents," she said with a small sob. "He wanted to control everything about my life."

"And who are you talking about, Breelyn?" I asked. "Omar Sabat?"

"No," she replied, now full-on crying. "His name is Eric Logan. I met him last fall at an awards dinner honoring my stepfather. He kept telling me that I should be an actress and that my stepfather should put me in his movies."

"Is that what you wanted?"

"Not really." She shook her head. "I just wanted to get asked to prom and keep my GPA high enough to go to USC. But – but after he . . . raped me . . . I didn't even care about anything anymore. I was just so ashamed."

Was that true? Was she telling the real story now or was she acting, improvising a new plot line? I couldn't tell. I wondered if *she* even knew at this point.

I turned to address the camera.

"I can't corroborate Breelyn's story," I said. "But I can and must state that I have had dealings with Eric Logan related to this story. In fact, it was Mr. Logan who supplied this station with the incriminating text messages between Valentina and Gregg Doyle."

Eddie's eyes were bugging out of his head. I wasn't sure if he was going to keep the cameras going or cut to a commercial. Breelyn was looking down, weeping. My hands were shaking and I could feel my own tears just below the surface. But I was determined to keep it together.

"I used the texts without questioning how they had been obtained, and for that I would like to offer my apologies to my employer and to my viewers," I said, choking back any hint of emotion. This was the hardest thing I had ever done.

"Furthermore, I have reason to believe that Mr. Logan coached the statements given by Omar Sabat in my interview with him in February. For these reasons and . . . because I developed a personal relationship with Mr. Logan that now makes me question everything I have reported about this story" – I took a deep breath – "I am resigning from this station. This will be my last appearance. Good night and good-bye."

CHAPTER 28

Kayla Ross

THE TEARS COULDN'T BE held back anymore. I jumped down from the platform without even making sure that Eddie had cut to commercial. As I staggered off the set, everyone was whispering in confusion. Breelyn started to say something to me, but I went right past her. Whatever she had to say – even if it was just "See ya!" – I wouldn't believe a word of it.

I all but ran across the sound stage and out one of the side doors into an alley. I fell apart. All the stress, excitement, tension, and confusion of the last few months came pouring out. It took a long time to pull myself together. And then I had to come to terms with the fact that I'd actually done it – thrown away everything I'd worked for. The job, the fame, the dreams. I was trembling and crying and devastated and yet . . . on some level I felt immeasurable relief.

Taking a deep breath, I finally walked around the side of the building to the front entrance.

And there he was.

He was giving me a strange look. I couldn't tell if it was anger or admiration. Maybe both.

"Why? *Why* did you do that to yourself? To me, to *us*?" he asked, sounding more exasperated than anything else. "Do you have any idea how big I could have made you?"

I stopped in front of him and looked into his eyes. I had no idea what I was looking at.

"That's the point, Eric," I said. "This whole time, the bigger I got, the smaller I felt. I've decided I like the normal-sized Kayla Ross best."

"So what – you're going back to Omaha to cover mall openings and city council meetings?" he asked incredulously.

I paused and nodded. "Yeah, actually, that sounds pretty good right about now. If they'll have me, that is."

I started to walk away, but he grabbed my arm. Too late, I remembered Wayne Tennet's body, splayed out and still.

"Okay, that's fine for you," he said. "But how did you get Breelyn to agree to this – to throw away *her* own career just as it's beginning?"

He seemed genuinely puzzled. Maybe he wasn't quite the smartest guy in the room after all.

"You really don't get it, do you, Eric?" I said. "You've underestimated your own creation. Breelyn doesn't *ever* want the story to end. So tonight was just the latest episode of her hit show. You were an important supporting character. But now . . . you've been written out."

As I turned away, a police car pulled up. An officer and a man in a suit – a detective? – got out and quickly approached Logan, who backed away with his hands innocently up. I turned away. I didn't know whether to feel sorry for him or glad or angry or what. But it didn't matter. It was no longer my concern.

A few feet away from the cop car sat a beat-up 1998 Honda Civic, the trunk and backseat filled with boxes and suitcases.

"You look awful," Zoe said as I got in the passenger side. "Guess I'd better drive the first hundred miles, huh?"

"That would be great, best friend," I said, as I let my head fall onto her shoulder. "I'm going to take a nap. I have some dream adjustments to get to."

THE NEW DETECTIVE MICHAEL BENNETT THRILLER

Ambush

James Patterson
& James O. Born

Detective Michael Bennett's enemies know where to find him.

An anonymous tip about a crime in Upper Manhattan proves to be a set-up. An officer is taken down – but despite the attackers' efforts, it's not Michael Bennett.

New York's top cop is not the only one at risk.

One of Bennett's children is attacked. And a series of murders follows, each with a distinct signature, alerting Bennett to the presence of a professional killer.

Bennett can't tell what's driving the assassin.

But he can tell it's personal.

arrow books

THREE MISSING WOMEN. TWO IMPOSSIBLE CASES. ONE DETERMINED DETECTIVE.

Don't miss the next thrilling instalment in the Women's Murder Club series.

Available now in hardback

‘CLINTON’S INSIDER SECRETS AND PATTERSON’S STORYTELLING GENIUS MAKE THIS THE POLITICAL THRILLER OF THE DECADE’

LEE CHILD

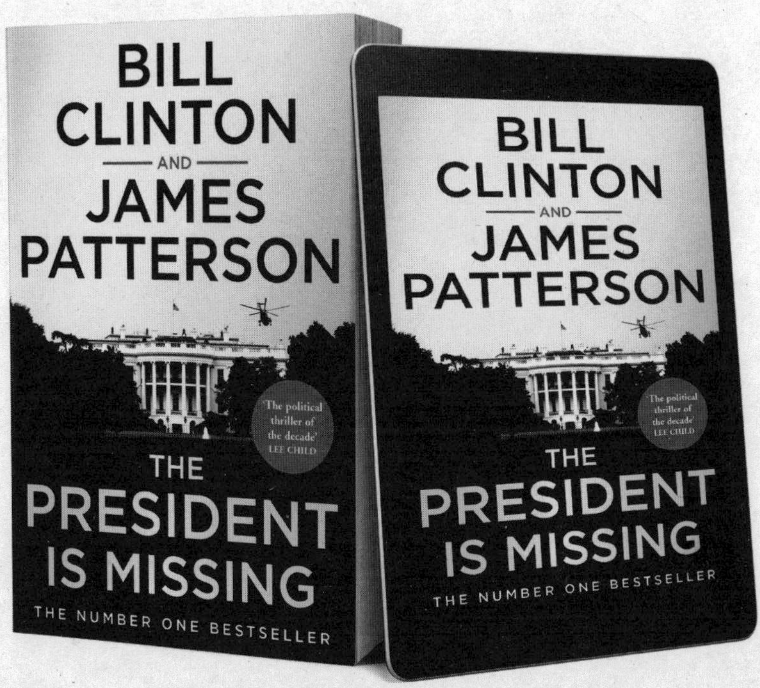

‘Difficult to put down’
Daily Express

‘Satisfying and surprising’
Guardian

‘A quick, slick, gripping read’
The Times

‘A high-octane collaboration . . . addictive’
Daily Telegraph

Also by James Patterson

COLLECTIONS

Triple Threat (*with Max DiLallo and Andrew Bourelle*) • Kill or Be Killed (*with Maxine Paetro, Rees Jones, Shan Serafin and Emily Raymond*) • The Moores are Missing (*with Loren D. Estleman, Sam Hawken and Ed Chatterton*) • The Family Lawyer (*with Robert Rotstein, Christopher Charles and Rachel Howzell Hall*) • Murder in Paradise (*with Doug Allyn, Connor Hyde and Duane Swierczynski*) • The House Next Door (*with Susan DiLallo, Max DiLallo and Brendan DuBois*)

ALEX CROSS NOVELS

Along Came a Spider • Kiss the Girls • Jack and Jill • Cat and Mouse • Pop Goes the Weasel • Roses are Red • Violets are Blue • Four Blind Mice • The Big Bad Wolf • London Bridges • Mary, Mary • Cross • Double Cross • Cross Country • Alex Cross's Trial (*with Richard DiLallo*) • I, Alex Cross • Cross Fire • Kill Alex Cross • Merry Christmas, Alex Cross • Alex Cross, Run • Cross My Heart • Hope to Die • Cross Justice • Cross the Line • The People vs. Alex Cross • Target: Alex Cross

THE WOMEN'S MURDER CLUB SERIES

1st to Die • 2nd Chance (*with Andrew Gross*) • 3rd Degree (*with Andrew Gross*) • 4th of July (*with Maxine Paetro*) • The 5th Horseman (*with Maxine Paetro*) • The 6th Target (*with Maxine Paetro*) • 7th Heaven (*with Maxine Paetro*) • 8th Confession (*with Maxine Paetro*) • 9th Judgement (*with Maxine Paetro*) • 10th Anniversary (*with Maxine Paetro*) • 11th Hour (*with Maxine Paetro*) • 12th of Never (*with Maxine Paetro*) • Unlucky 13 (*with Maxine Paetro*) • 14th Deadly Sin (*with Maxine Paetro*) • 15th Affair (*with Maxine Paetro*) • 16th Seduction (*with Maxine Paetro*) • 17th Suspect (*with Maxine Paetro*) • 18th Abduction (*with Maxine Paetro*)

STAND-ALONE THRILLERS

The Thomas Berryman Number • Hide and Seek • Black Market • The Midnight Club • Sail (*with Howard Roughan*) • Swimsuit (*with Maxine Paetro*) • Don't Blink (*with Howard Roughan*) • Postcard Killers (*with Liza Marklund*) • Toys (*with Neil McMahon*) • Now You See Her (*with Michael Ledwidge*) • Kill Me If You Can (*with Marshall Karp*) • Guilty Wives (*with David Ellis*) • Zoo (*with Michael Ledwidge*) • Second Honeymoon (*with Howard Roughan*) • Mistress (*with David Ellis*) • Invisible (*with David Ellis*) • Truth or Die (*with Howard Roughan*) • Murder House (*with David Ellis*) • Woman of God (*with Maxine Paetro*) • Humans, Bow Down (*with Emily Raymond*) • The Black Book (*with David Ellis*) • Murder Games (*with Howard Roughan*) • The Store (*with Richard DiLallo*) • The President is Missing (*with Bill Clinton*) • Revenge (*with Andrew Holmes*) • Juror No. 3 (*with Nancy Allen*) • The First Lady (*with Brendan DuBois*) • The Chef (*with Max DiLallo*) • Out of Sight (*with Brendan DuBois*)

DETECTIVE MICHAEL BENNETT SERIES

Step on a Crack (*with Michael Ledwidge*) • Run for Your Life (*with Michael Ledwidge*) • Worst Case (*with Michael Ledwidge*) • Tick Tock (*with Michael Ledwidge*) • I, Michael Bennett (*with Michael Ledwidge*) • Gone (*with Michael Ledwidge*) • Burn (*with Michael Ledwidge*) • Alert (*with Michael Ledwidge*) • Bullseye (*with Michael Ledwidge*) • Haunted (*with James O. Born*) • Ambush (*with James O. Born*)

PRIVATE NOVELS

Private (*with Maxine Paetro*) • Private London (*with Mark Pearson*) • Private Games (*with Mark Sullivan*) • Private: No. 1 Suspect (*with Maxine Paetro*) • Private Berlin (*with Mark Sullivan*) • Private Down Under (*with Michael White*) • Private L.A. (*with Mark Sullivan*) • Private India (*with Ashwin Sanghi*) • Private Vegas (*with Maxine Paetro*) • Private Sydney (*with Kathryn Fox*) • Private Paris (*with Mark Sullivan*) • The Games (*with Mark Sullivan*) • Private Delhi (*with Ashwin Sanghi*) • Private Princess (*with Rees Jones*)

NYPD RED SERIES

NYPD Red (*with Marshall Karp*) • NYPD Red 2 (*with Marshall Karp*) • NYPD Red 3 (*with Marshall Karp*) • NYPD Red 4 (*with Marshall Karp*) • NYPD Red 5 (*with Marshall Karp*)

DETECTIVE HARRIET BLUE SERIES

Never Never (*with Candice Fox*) • Fifty Fifty (*with Candice Fox*) • Liar Liar (*with Candice Fox*) • Hush Hush (*with Candice Fox*)

NON-FICTION

Torn Apart (*with Hal and Cory Friedman*) • The Murder of King Tut (*with Martin Dugard*) • All-American Murder (*with Alex Abramovich and Mike Harvkey*)

MURDER IS FOREVER TRUE CRIME

Murder, Interrupted (*with Alex Abramovich and Christopher Charles*) • Home Sweet Murder (*with Andrew Bourelle and Scott Slaven*) • Murder Beyond the Grave (*with Andrew Bourelle and Christopher Charles*)

For more information about James Patterson's novels, visit www.jamespatterson.co.uk